# The Worthy Ones

# The Worthy Ones

A NOVEL

by
**Charlie L. Russell**

Illustrated by
**Marvin McMillian**

Copyright ©2002 by Charlie L. Russell

A Jukebox Press First Edition

All rights reserved. No part of this book may be reproduced, stored in a retrieval system, or transmitted in any form, by any means, including mechanical, electric, photocopy, recording or otherwise, without the prior written permission of the author.

Published by Jukebox Press
P.O. Box 2069
Berkeley, CA 94702-0069

ISBN: 0-932693-11-3

Design and production by Archetype Typography, Berkeley, CA
Cover design by Scott Perry
Photos by Ted Pontiflet
Jukebox logo designed by Hillary King

To order copies contact BookMasters, Inc.
30 Amberwood Parkway
Ashland, OH 44805
800.247.6553
Price: $15.95

## Acknowledgments

I would like to thank some of the many people whose help was invaluable: Sandra Johnson, Cyma Rubin, Tom Feelings, Tanya Russell, Sam Rutland, Georgia Macon, Teddy Pontiflet, Naomi Johnson, Richard Barclift, Nicole Bennett, Jim Lacey, Katheryn K. Russell, Gloria Gideon, Doris Johnson, Cecil Berkley, Kim McMillon, Diane Saul, Mona Scott, Lauretta Robinson, Harold Wilson, Myrtle Phillips, Denise Maunder, Joe Milosch, Deborah Johnson, Charles Kelly, Susie Butler, Allan Lincoln, Saundra Darrington, Robert Johnson, Ruth Beckford, Reggie Lockett, Gail Hawkins, C. P. Weaver, Charlie L. Russell, Sr.

Charlie L. Russell
Spring, 2002

# The In-Migrants

# A Partial Listing of the Characters

Mattie Fae Johnson

Renauld "Sugarbear" and
Coreen Johnson
/ / / /
Lynn  Beatrice  Mattie  Bootsy

Sodonia and
Aaron Pettaway
/ /
Gabriel  James

*Friends of Mattie*
Emma Pace  Odilia Toy

*Friends of Gabriel and James*
Bertrand "Punchy"  Oscar "Noah"  Mordecai
Haskins  St. Elmo  Leaks

*Participants in the love triangles*
Oreville Hunter  Thelma Jenkins

*The Mount Calvary Baptist Church Board of Elders*

C.C. Carridine   Reba Hightower   Deacon Meldrick
Merryweather
Bradford Sykes  Thaddeus Stier

*Societal rivals*
Essex Dawson  Dr. Edgar Hill

# The Return of an Exiled

**Louisiana, Summer, 1928.**

LIKE MOST AFRICAN AMERICANS in the town, the Johnson family lived in a community called the Quarters: a hodgepodge of houses in an assortment of architectures and styles, ranging from fine, well-built houses with brick chimneys to straight and narrow shotgun houses. A network of trails, like webs of rumors and gossip, wound and unwound. Every once in a while, a well-kept house, painted in purity white, trimmed in envy green, squash yellow or sunkissed orange, might be seen. But for the most part, the houses in the Quarters wore their colors of brown, blue and gray in a sober manner, without gloom or distinction.

On some of the front porches swings dangled on chains suspended from the ceiling. Many hosted tables, plants and flowers. Others were as bleak and bare as Dracula's soul.

The backyards revealed the inner identities of the dwellers: swings made from discarded automobile tires; unkempt tall grass that climbed inelegantly toward the indifferent sky; graveyards for dead automobiles, dead furniture and just plain junk; barbecue pits made from odd-shaped stones; trees with their own personalities and attitudes; scarecrows; clothes on lines flopping in the wind; well-kept garden vegetables that flourished in munificent growth.

Music—religious, rhythm & blues, jazz and the blues—played on Jew's harps, banjoes, radios, harmonicas, Victrolas, pianos and guitars; sung and hummed, solo or in trios, quartets and bands; on the docks, in churches, speakeasies, barges and the fields. Music—joyous, sad and triumphant, rising up like vapors on the wings of invisible smoke—bonded the members of the community, helped them to maintain another night and manage another day.

The Johnsons lived in a gray house with a swing hanging from the ceiling of the front porch. English ivy, curling and climbing, ran in graceful curves along the ceiling and above the door. A giant tree, its gnarled roots burrowing into the rich earth, dominated the front yard. Beyond the front yard, a road wove its way around a bend.

Everyone in the Johnson household was unhappy. Lynn, eighteen, had been seething ever since Beatrice unexpectedly announced her wedding plans. Lynn was a year older than Beatrice. Though she didn't even have a boyfriend, Lynn had convinced herself that her sister's getting married before her was an insult. Beatrice was unhappy because financial considerations were denying her the big church wedding that she'd dreamed of, like the ones in the movies where the bride climbed a spiral staircase and tossed her bridal bouquet to the eager hands of her girlfriends.

Beatrice had dreamed two nights in succession that her exiled father, Sugarbear, would make a dramatic appearance before the wedding with bags of gold coins. In reality, she held no hope for miracles; she considered herself the most unfortunate bride in the entire world.

Bootsy, the baby of the family, considered the wedding a nuisance and a distraction. She felt miserable because the wedding preparations kept the family's attention away from her. The third daughter, Little Mattie, also felt miserable: Beatrice's wedding jeopardized her chance to be the first family member to graduate from high school. She was the unhappiest of them all.

Like her daughters, Coreen's discontent was also connected to the wedding. But her concern was more visceral: *It's a question of the fragility of my nerves,* she reminded herself, knowing that she must deal with her mother-in-law after she got the news about Little Mattie. *I don't want to have to deal with that woman. At least not before my nerves are collected.*

The early morning sun was not visible on the horizon but you felt its warmth.

Little Mattie, pulling a wagon filled with clean laundry, rounded the house. She wore a white blouse and a pair of loose-fitting blue jeans. Fourteen, she had a positive sense of herself; wise beyond her years, she was what the old folks called an old spirit. She had smooth, honey-brown skin, even-shaped teeth and hazel-brown eyes. She loved to rip and run, climb trees and play sports.

Bootsy, twelve, ran to catch up. She was dressed in a checkered, black and white dress. She wore her cornrowed hair in a style that emphasized her dark eyes and attractive features. When she was old enough, she wanted to sing in the church choir like her sister Lynn.

Coreen stood on the front porch, hands on her hips. A hefty, full-bosomed woman of forty-seven, she had dark eyes and straight black hair, legacies from her Seminole mother.

"Little Mattie, remember what I said about Mother Johnson," she referred to her mother-in-law, Mattie Fae Johnson. "I don't want her dipping in my business about your schooling. Don't even dare to think about going anywhere near her house whilst y'all out delivering that laundry. You hear me?"

"Yes, Mother."

Coreen went into her workroom and started ironing a red dress. Early in their marriage, Sugarbear had established his pattern of absenteeism for extended periods of time and she'd started doing laundry for the survival of her family. Over the years, by hardwork, luck and an uncanny ability to keep customers once she'd acquired them, her reputation grew and she counted among her clients some of the most prominent European American families in the town.

She took a bottle of gin from its hiding place and took a nip.

In the backyard, Lynn and Beatrice, heads down over their tin washboards, washed clothes in wooden tubs. Beatrice wore a red bandanna. A real cutey pie, she had an attractive figure and a nice personality. Lynn, who sported Sugarbear's Stetson hat, was big-boned and beefy. Behind them, clothes boiled and bubbled in a black cauldron. Further back in the yard, dresses, pants and shirts clinging to the clotheslines, swayed sensually.

Coreen tiptoed to the backdoor and studied her daughters.

Beatrice adjusted her bandanna, wiped sweat from her brow and took a white shirt to the clothesline. Lynn stopped washing to scratch her buttocks, constantly looking around expectantly as if at any moment, she anticipated the arrival of some dusky Lochinvar on a white horse.

"Lynn, git a move on your buffalo butt," Coreen yelled. "And stir up them clothes in that pot." She returned to her workroom, cranked up her Victrola and played Bessie Smith's *Empty Bed Blues*.

*It ain't just the money,* her mind wandered. *It's his always being away so much that's what creates bad feelings in the house. Nobody can ever just relax and be comfortable . . . Sugarbear was restless before I met him but fool me, I thought it was something that I could make go away . . . It's that damn Sanite DiDi's fault. Her and her voodoo. Telling him about some spirit. Filling his head with stories about gold coins and jewelry. When she got him under her spell, it was like throwing buckets of gasoline on a burning barn . . . Why are our people like that? When he and his friends finally found them gold coins, why did some niggah have to run and tell Sheriff Winchester? . . . God, I miss him so . . . Married eighteen years and I was true except for that one time and then it was only because I wanted somebody to hold me.*

# 2

Little Mattie and Bootsy approached a white mansion with sculptured shrubbery and bright-colored flowers. Magnolia trees guarded the manicured lawn. They took the path to the rear. Bootsy knocked on the door.

Linda Edgewater, dressed in a pretty pink dress with a thin white belt, appeared.

"Hi, girls," Linda was in her early forties. She had blue eyes, a lard-white, angular face and bountiful natural blond hair. "How are you doing today?"

"Just fine, Miz Edgewater," Little Mattie and Bootsy chimed. They gave Linda her laundry.

Linda's four blossoming daughters, who ranged in age from ten to sixteen, arrived. They carried jars of preserves that they wordlessly handed to Little Mattie and Bootsy.

"Tell Coreen I'll be by tomorrow morning to pick up my red dress," Linda handed Little Mattie a neatly folded dollar bill. "Here's something for you." She gave Little Mattie several magazines. "Here's an extra penny for each of you to keep for yourself."

"Thank you, Miz Edgewater," Little Mattie and Bootsy chorused.

The sun was a naked glare in the sky.

Little Mattie pulled the wagon. Bootsy walked at her side. In the meadow below them, cows, squatting and standing, lounged under a cluster of trees.

"Bootsy, it's your turn to pull the wagon now," Little Mattie said. "I've been pulling it ever since we left Miz Price's house."

"Li'l Mat, take it a little further. Be a dear heart, please."

"O. K. But you have to take it past the big pine tree."

"Naw, naw," Bootsy said. "That's too far out the way. You just want to go that way so you can go by Grandmother's, to tell her what Momma said about you taking Beatrice's place."

"You going to tell Momma if I do?"

"Maybe. Maybe not."

"I'll take it past the big pine tree."

"My arms are still tired. Couldn't you pull it a little farther than that?"

"I'll make a deal with you," Little Mattie said. "I'll pull the wagon all the way to Grandmother's if you promise not to tell Momma that we went there. You promise not to tell?"

"Yes, I promise."

Invisible birds tweetered and twittered in the thickets.

A sand-colored rabbit with white trimmings hopped down the path. Discovering the sisters' presence, the rabbit stopped abruptly. Then, bright eyes popping with fright, it made a quick U-turn and dashed into the thickets.

"Did you see that?" Bootsy squealed.

"That li'l scamp was surely a running fool," Mattie replied. "For a minute, the poor thing, I thought his little eyes was gonna pop right out."

"I wasn't looking at his eyes. I was looking at his thighs. Why couldn't he have just taken a few bunny hops and jumped in the wagon with them jars? Then Momma could cook an even more scrumptious supper for Mr. Curtis Jollivette."

# 3

Cato A. Johnson, who'd studied architecture in the army, had collected a group of his friends to build the grayish-white house from his own design. Fashioned from fine pine and solid oak. Dominated by a squatty chimney made from mortar, pieces of glass and colorful rocks. Bird-shaped weather vane attached to the dust-colored roof. A sundial in the front yard. Tall, odd-shaped hedges on one side of the house.

On the other side of the house, Cato's widow, Mattie Fae Johnson, hoed in her garden. A solid woman of seventy, she was her family's last living link to slavery. She had an oval face and seal-brown skin slightly wrinkled around the edges. Dark circles encased her brown eyes, which still held embers from the flame that once lit up her entire being.

Mattie Fae put down her hoe. She trudged around the persimmon tree, past the cackling chickens in their coop and the oinking pigs in their sty, to the well. She drew some water in an oak bucket. Using the pear-shaped gourd, she drank deeply and felt a joyous surge as the water replenished and pacified her body.

A breeze flavored with nature scents caressed Mattie Fae's face as she chopped weeds from a row of watermelons. Suddenly, she commenced coughing. She felt the onslaught of a debilitating fatigue. Fearing that she would faint, she went to the kitchen and took her jar of herbal tea from the icebox. She poured herself a cupful that she emptied with three long swigs. She went into the living room, plopped down into her rocking chair and started rocking, relaxing into a rhythmic flow as her body gradually amended and rectified itself.

As was her unconscious custom, she viewed the portrait of Cato hanging above the fireplace. The portrait depicted Cato in his Ninth Cavalry dress uniform, sitting astride a palomino; his left hand held the reins; his right hand rested on his saber. He was wearing the uniform when the Ku Klux Klan murdered him in the massacre of 1885. Cato never saw their son, Sugarbear, born later that same year. Since his death she'd never involved herself physically or emotionally with another man.

Viewing Cato's portrait rekindled sweet memories—his laughter, vibrant voice, the comfort and pleasure of his strong body, his boyish passion for life—sweet memories that accompanied her always and formed an integral part of her day-to-day existence.

Little Mattie outran Bootsy to the front door.
"Grandmother," she knocked.
The doorknob wiggled; the door opened.
"My, why what a pleasant surprise. Come in," Mattie Fae led the way to the living room. "Any word from your father?"
"No ma'am, not since his last letter," Little Mattie replied.
"He'll be home soon," Bootsy chimed in. "Momma said she can feel it in her bones."
"How would you girls like some lemonade?" Mattie Fae asked.
"That would be just so swell, Grandma," said Bootsy.
"Good. Fetch some water from the well. Little Mattie and I will squeeze the lemons."
Bootsy rushed off.
Little Mattie started boohooing.
"What's the matter, baby?"
"Oh, Grandmother," Little Mattie burrowed her face in Mattie Fae's breasts.
"What is it, honey? Tell Grandmother."
"Momma's making me quit school. She said since Beatrice is getting married, I must take her place washing laundry." Mattie only had a vague notion about what she wanted to be in life but she knew she wanted to accomplish something big: so that her picture would hang on school walls with the other famous Negroes. "Grandmother, I promised you I'd be the first one in the family to graduate from high school. I *can't* quit now. I'm the best in my grade in mathematics. I can read better than any other student in the school, except for one boy. And he's graduating next year."
"There, there. Grandmother will think of something. Come, let's go in the kitchen and get started with the lemonade."

Puffy white clouds edged away from the sun.

Mattie Fae sat on the front steps between Little Mattie and Bootsy. Little Mattie issued a deep sigh and nestled her head on her grandmother's lap. Mattie Fae, feeling Little Mattie's pain, comforted her with a soothing circular motion of her hand on her shoulders and nape. Bootsy told Mattie Fae about the rabbit who hopped away and poured herself a second glass of lemonade.

"Grandmother, tell us again about how you first learned to read," Little Mattie urged.

"Well, all right. Remember, it was during Reconstruction. Of course, I was only a child myself. No bigger than a minute. Our people were passionate about things in those days. The biggest passion was reading and writing. Everybody wanted to learn. Old. Young. It didn't matter. Many were the days when the whole family went straight from the field to the Freedmen's Bureau's school. After supper, everybody gathered around the kitchen table and studied by candlelight 'til deep into the night. Girls, one day I'll be gone to Glory. If you don't remember anything else I said to you, remember this: without an education we will always be treated like savages."

"I remember something else you told us, Grandmother," said Little Mattie. "You said: *'An education is the most wonderful gift that you can give to yourself.'*"

"Why, thank you, baby."

Bootsy poured herself another glass of lemonade.

"How would you girls like a watermelon to take home?"

"That'll be swell," Bootsy said. "You the very best grandmother in the whole, entire world."

Little Mattie, remembering Coreen's warning about visiting her grandmother, managed a half smile. "I'll go get the wagon," she hurried off. When she returned, Mattie Fae put a plump watermelon into the wagon.

Hugging and kissing, they made warm goodbyes.

"Mattie, I'll speak to Coreen about your schooling Sunday at church," Mattie Fae went back inside. Although it was only Friday, she started shining the metal eyelets on her black, high-top shoes in preparation for the services on Sunday. She worried about her other great love: Sugarbear. Her only child, she'd spoiled him. In return, he broke her heart. At the age of fifteen, he left home and stayed away three days. Thereafter, he remained on the go, searching for something nameless and inexplicable. Something felt but impossible for him to articulate. Then he met the voodooist who gave his wanderlust a purpose: for the past fifteen years he'd spent most of his time on the move, searching and digging for buried treasures.

Mattie Fae finished her shoes and brushed her wig. Except for church, she rarely went out in public anymore. However, even at her age she still retained the vanity of a beautiful woman, so when she did make a public appearance, she took special care.

Her mind feasted on the past:

*The Sunday afternoon church social. Seventeen. All spiffy in a white dress with a red belt and a white hat with a silky red band. Standing near the punch bowl when, feeling his aura, she turned and faced him.*

*Elegant, cocoa-brown and handsome. Rows of medals arrayed on his Ninth Cavalry dress tunic. Honest, hazel-brown eyes.*

"Hello, Miss Davenport. I just came over to let you know that I've decided to marry you."

"Marry me! Why, I don't even know your name."

"A mere oversight and one easily rectified. Cato Armstrong Johnson, at your service."

# 4

Coreen, standing on the front porch, peered down the road.

*I wonder what's taking them so long?*

Some mill hands, singing the *Old Black Bottom Dance,* came her way. Dressed in flour-smeared overalls, goggles hanging from their necks, they beat out a pulsating rhythm on their lunch pails with their hands.

"*Now listen, folks, open your ears.*"

A chubby man with bright eyes broke into a dance, twirling and whirling.

"*Old Black Bottom will make you shake your feet. Believe me, it's a wow.*"

Coreen returned to the kitchen and tasted the black-eyed peas. Satisfied with the consistency but not the flavor, she added a sprinkle of pepper and a splash of vinegar.

"Something sure smells good in here," Beatrice wore a pink housecoat. She carried a towel and a box of bubble bath powder. "What you got cooking in the oven, Momma?"

"A surprise. Don't worry, I'm fixing a scrumptious supper for you and Curtis."

"You need any help?"

"No, go on and take your bath."

The sun continued its rendezvous with twilight.

In the backyard, Beatrice sprinkled the sweet-scented powder into a tin tub. She removed her housecoat, revealing her sleek, brown body.

Little Mattie and Bootsy approached the house.

"What took y'all so long?" Coreen came out of the front door.

Little Mattie and Bootsy exchanged glances.

"Miz Price wasn't home when we got there, so we had to wait until she came back," Little Mattie answered. On the way home she'd invented a fib to explain the origin of the watermelon. "It took her forever to come. And she gave us the watermelon, too."

"It's a big one, see?" Bootsy said. "Miz Edgewater gave us the jars of preserves."

"Come on," Coreen took the watermelon. "Y'all bring in them jars." She led them into the kitchen. "Little Mattie, did Miz Price give you that watermelon instead of paying for her laundry?"

"No," Little Mattie dug into her pocket. "Here's all the money."

"Y'all go get ready for supper," Coreen took the bowl of banana pudding from the oven. *In all the years I been knowing Miz Price, she never gave me nothing. Hmph, that stingy heifer wouldn't give a sick sparrow a crumb if she owned a bakery shop. Why would she all of a sudden just up and send me a watermelon?*

Coreen spent her early years in an orphanage where she learned how to count and write her name. Beyond that, she was limited. However, she possessed an abundance of mother's wisdom and a native intelligence that more than compensated for her lack of a formal education. Plus, she was the suspicious type and her daughters' explanation about the origin of the watermelon made her wary.

She went to the doorway and called Bootsy.

Momentarily, Bootsy appeared.

"You want me, Mommy?"

"Yes, baby. Mother dear knows you must be near about famished by now. Here, take this wing to tide you over 'til supper."

"My favorite piece of the chicken! You the best Mommy in the whole, entire world."

"How about helping me set the table?"

"Oh, goodie!"

"You fetch the plates. I'll get the silverware."

"The good plates, Momma?"

"Yes, baby. But first, go get yourself another piece of chicken. Oh, by the way, how was your grandmother doing today? I hear she's been feeling poorly."

"Oh, no. Grandma was feeling just fine."

"That's good. Did she mention whether or not she heard anything from your father?"

"No. Momma, you know what Grandmother did? She made a big pitcher of lemonade and I drunk me three whole glasses."

"So, y'all did go over there? After I told you not to, didn't you?"

Bootsy, finally recognizing her blunder, started crying.

"Your grandmother gave y'all that watermelon, didn't she?"

"Yes, Momma."

"I ain't got time to whip y'all right now. Go tell Little Mattie I want to see you both in my room after the company leaves."

The fact that they were having a male guest for supper created a sensation amongst the ladies. It provided them with a delightful distraction and gave them the opportunity to forget about their unhappiness. That the guest was Beatrice's fiancé, Curtis Jollivette, only served to electrify the occasion and charge the atmosphere with bright anticipation. Ten minutes before the guest arrived, each of the ladies had attended to her toilette and put on her special dress.

Curtis Jollivette sat at the head of the dining room table like visiting royalty. A light-skinned, good-looking man of twenty-three, he wore light-colored slacks and a double-breasted blue blazer with white buttons. He chauffeured for a successful banker and he viewed himself as a success as well.

"Now you take the kingfish, Huey Long. He's one outta sight politician," Curtis buttered his cornbread. "He's my kind of governor."

Beatrice, seated on Curtis' left, laughed all through the meal. It seemed that she was always either looking at him or touching him.

"My God. The way the kingfish talks about them rich white folks! He's for the common man for sure, you can bet your bottom dollar on that. He's promising to build a lot of new roads. God knows we need them. When I drove my boss to

New Orleans, it took three days. In some places there wasn't any road at all, just cow trails."

"I was in New Orleans a few times," Coreen said.

"New Orleans is one old, hot town, I'm telling you. The fun capital of the Western Hemisphere. It has the finest theatres, the classiest speakeasies and the greatest dancers. Not to mention all that hot jazz music down on Rampart Street."

"So y'all going out dancing tonight, huh, Curtis?" Lynn asked.

"Yep. We're going to do some serious skipping."

"Surprise!" Coreen entered with the bowl of banana pudding. She served Curtis first.

"Mmmm-mmm," Curtis smacked his lips. He leaned over and whispered in Beatrice's ear.

"Well, I like that," Beatrice pinched Curtis' arm playfully. "Momma, you know what he just said? He said good as your banana pudding is, he might be marrying the wrong woman."

Coreen purred.

Little Mattie and Bootsy laughed and giggled.

After supper, Coreen and Curtis retired to the living room. Coreen cranked up her Victrola and played Fletcher Henderson's *Sugar Foot Stomp*. Apropos of nothing, she reminded Curtis that Lynn was the featured soloist at her church, where she herself served on the usher board.

Beatrice came in.

"I'm ready," she wore her white tam at a flirty angle. She had applied a coat of lipstick and penciled in a thin line of magenta around her eyes. "How do I look, hon?"

"You look swell, Bee," Curtis stared at Beatrice like there was a recess in heaven and she was some angel magically down on earth making a guest appearance.

"Don't keep my daughter out too late now, Curtis."

"Don't worry. She's in the loving care of Curtis the Joy. Miz Jollivette's brassy baby boy."

"Boy, git on out of here," Coreen smiled as she closed the door. A scowl appeared on her face. Her body became rigid. She went into the kitchen. With a nod, she beckoned Bootsy into her bedroom. She took a leather belt from the closet.

Bootsy entered, crying.

"Close that door," Coreen loved to lecture while whipping. "Why? Why would you do something that I made a point of telling you not to do?" She applied a series of lashes. "'Cause you think you grown, don't you?"

"No, Mommy, I don't think I'm grown! I'm good, Mommy! I'm good, Mommy! I'm good!" Bootsy scooted about the room. "Oh, Mommy, I love you! You the sweetest Mommy in the whole, entire world! Ouch! Oh! Oh!"

"All right," Coreen said at last. "The next time I tell you something, you better mind me. Understand? Go tell your sister to git her butt in here."

Seconds later, Little Mattie entered and closed the door behind her. As with Bootsy, Coreen lectured between lashes. But Little Mattie, unlike Bootsy, accepted her whipping in silence, which infuriated Coreen.

"I'll teach you who runs this house! Your grandmother don't run this house! I pay the rent! Feed you! Clothe you! Me! Me! Me!"

"Mother, that's enough," Little Mattie ran from the bedroom.

"Girl, git your butt back here."

Little Mattie ran out the front door and disappeared into the darkness.

"Girl, you better git back here," Coreen called. "You hear me? I said you git back here."

The next morning, Coreen's Victrola played Blind Willie Johnson's *I Know His Blood Can Make Me Whole*.

Deacon Meldrick Merryweather's black Plymouth stopped in the driveway. Meldrick, an energetic man of forty, hopped out. A salesman for the North Carolina Mutual Insurance Company, he boasted that when he was on top of his game, he could sell a blind man a flashlight, an Eskimo a refrigerator and give a highway patrolman a speeding ticket.

"Morning, Deacon. Come on in," Coreen led the deacon into the living room.

"A top of the morning, Coreen. How are things?"

"Oh, fair to middling. You know how things can go."

"Mother Johnson asked me to come over and get some of Little Mattie's clothes."

"Just a minute, I'll be right back," Coreen detested her mother-in-law for putting her in such an awkward position. She took some of Little Mattie's clothes from her closet, including something for her to wear to church. She returned to the living room and followed Meldrick outside.

"Coreen, you heard anything from my buddy, Sugarbear?" Meldrick put Little Mattie's clothes in the rear seat and got into his car.

"No, not lately. But he'll be home soon. I can feel it in my bones."

"Well, see you tomorrow at church," Meldrick drove off.

Linda Edgewater arrived in her new black Cadillac with fat whitewalls.

Coreen went inside and returned with a red dress.

"Here you are, Miz Edgewater. Thanks for the jars of preserves."

"It was nothing, believe me. Have you heard anything from Sugarbear?"

"Not since his last letter from Mexico. But now that his time is up, we expect him any day."

"Coreen, I know I keep saying it. But it's awful that the sheriff took his gold coins and made him leave town. The way you've held your family together these past three years is nothing short of remarkable."

"Thank you, Miz Linda."

"Well, I'm off to pick up my daughters from their violin lessons."

## 5

The smell of barbecue curled and climbed into the Southern night where the moon hung in the sky like a giant sweet potato pie. Gabriel and James Pettaway approached the Savoy. Handsome, slender six-footers with smooth, dark skin, they looked alike, walked alike and made the same gestures with their hands when they talked.

"James, remember what I said now. No gawking," Gabriel wore a brown suit and a tan cap. He was nineteen. Only the thin scar running in a jagged line along his right cheek marred his handsome face. "No need letting folks know we still new in town."

"Don't blow your wig, cat," James wore a blue suit and a white cap. "You might be a year and a half older than me but that don't add up to my being a square."

Gabriel led the way inside.

"HUSH! KEEP STILL! AND USE MUM!" the sign above the bar proclaimed.

The joint was jim-jam-jumping. A gutbucket band played *Everybody Loves My Baby*.

A dark-skinned man wearing a white, cupcake-shaped chef's hat came in through the backdoor. He carried a slab of beef that had been cooking on the barbecue pit outside. He unlatched the door of the oven and placed the slab of beef inside. Using a long, wooden fork, he fiddled around with the other pieces of meat already smoking.

On the dance floor, couples whirled and twirled, bouncing and rocking to the beat.

"What's that step they doing?" James asked.

"The Lindy Hop, the dance that's so hot up in Harlem," Gabriel answered. "Hey, I spotted us some seats. See that chick sitting by herself in the booth, in the white dress? Come on. Let me do the talking. I'm gonna use my second best line."

Gabriel slid into the booth and sat down opposite the lady in white. She looked up at him expectantly, a puzzled expression on her cute face.

"Sorry I'm late, honey bunch," Gabriel said, like they were more than just friends. "That fool chauffeur of mine got us lost twice on the way over here."

"You here now, sweets," cooed the lady in white, amused by Gabriel's fresh approach. A twenty-nine-year-old hairdresser, she had dark eyes and blue lips. "That's all that matters."

"Sit down, man. This is my brother, James. I'm Gabriel. What's your name?"

"Inez. Inez Chambers."

"So, you look like you're in the know, Inez," Gabriel said. "Tell me. Do you think Babe Ruth is going to hit sixty home runs again this season?"

"I can't say that I really care," Inez revealed a will-o'-the-wisp smile. "You see, I mainly go for bedroom sports myself."

"Tell the truth, snaggletooth," Gabriel rolled his eyes suggestively.

James studied the dancers.

A waitress in a brown and white checkered dress appeared.

"Give the lady what she's drinking," Gabriel said. "A double gin for me and a sarsaparilla for my brother."

"Inez, you know how to do the Lindy Hop?" James asked.

"I'm a regular whiz at it."

"Come on," James led Inez to the dance floor. "I'm gonna do some Lindy Hopping."

# 6

The next morning the Pettaway family encircled the kitchen table, righteously feasting on grits, eggs, golden-brown biscuits, buttermilk, blackberry jam and bacon fried to a brownish-gold crisp. After years of barely eking out a living as a drayman, Aaron Pettaway got the notion that his luck might change for the better if they left their rural hometown. They'd arrived in the town about a month ago. Dressed in their Sunday best, they were off to visit their third church, still searching for a congregation that they felt comfortable enough to join in fellowship.

"You two sure must have had yourselves a grand old time last night," Sodonia Pettaway loved being the woman of the house. From the time her feet hit the floor in the morning until her head touched her pillow at night, she stayed on the move—cooking, washing, cleaning, preserving, darning, ironing and stuff. Since their elopement, she and Aaron had never spent a night apart. "I heard y'all when you came in. After one o'clock in the morning."

"I just don't see the sense in it," Aaron Pettaway still retained his own boyish good looks. Tall like his sons but more powerfully built, he was principled, patient and spiritual. "Out prowling around in the middle of the night."

"Where were you, anyway?" Sodonia asked.

"Out dancing," James poured himself another glass of milk. "The music was so good it made you want to quit this world altogether! You should have seen me, Momma. I learned a dance called the Lindy Hop."

"Yeah, he picked it up pretty fast," Gabriel spread some jam on his biscuit.

"Momma, let me show you how it goes," James rose to demonstrate.

"Boy, sit down," Sodonia stopped James before he completed the first step. "You know in this house we keep the Sabbath holy."

Aaron finished bridling his mule, Kate. He removed the "For Hire" sign from his brown wagon with the yellow spokes.

"My, you look so handsome in your suit and tie," Sodonia, firm in her blue dress, carried a camera. "Hold that smile." She snapped Aaron's picture.

Gabriel and James joined their parents.

"Take my picture, Momma," James mugged.

Passing the camera back and forth, the Pettaway family, assuming various poses and combinations, froze their images in time.

## 7

Mount Calvary Baptist Church sat on a hill overlooking a filigree of trails that curled and wound their way to its doorsteps. Founded in the 1880's and established to improve the social and moral conditions of its members, the church involved itself in a multitude of community activities. The church's hierarchy, the Board of Elders, came from the *petite bourgeoisie* but the majority of the congregation derived from the working class. Two unique elements bonded the classes: the *music* of the church's gifted choir and the *word*, delivered by its minister, C.C. Carridine, renowned for his oratorical skills.

A steady stream of worshipers, in wagons, carriages and automobiles, on foot, horseback and bicycles, flowed to the church.

Coreen Johnson, wearing her white usher's uniform, stood near the entrance of the auditorium. Although she wore her happy face, she fumed inside. Earlier that morning she'd bumped into Mattie Fae and discovered that Little Mattie was not at church. She confronted her mother-in-law on the spot. The two exchanged angry words before agreeing to meet in the church office after the service.

"Good morning, folks," Coreen recognized the Pettaways as first-time visitors. "Welcome to Mount Cavalry Baptist Church." She guided them into the auditorium.

Meldrick Merryweather and six other deacons sat in the pulpit. Ladies in pink dresses distributed paper fans. Lynn Johnson, shaking a tambourine, led the purple-robed choir down the center aisle to their place behind the piano. The deacons stood up as Minister C.C. Carridine joined them. Fortyish and suave, he had an inelegant face with a doorknob for a nose. He acknowledged the deacons with a nod.

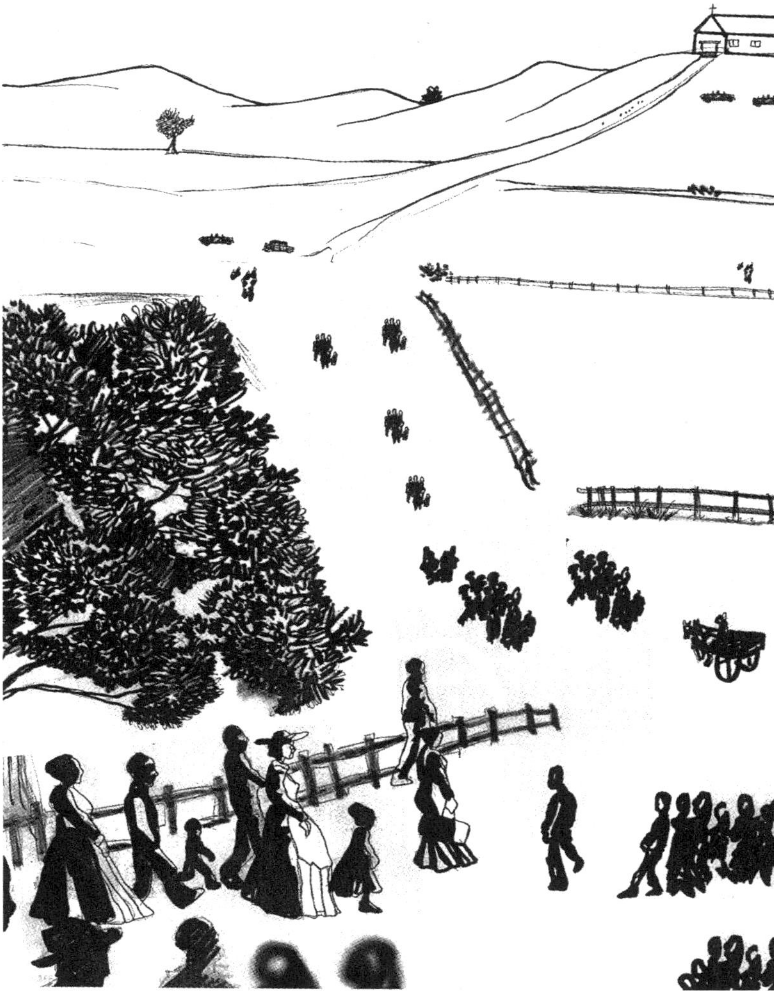

Lynn Johnson possessed a marvelous voice. When she finished singing *His Eye Is on the Sparrow,* several people, including Sodonia, were crying.

Reba Hightower adjusted her glasses and read the announcements. Mount Calvary gave financial aid to the old folks' home and the orphanage. It also involved itself in a variety of self-help programs, hosted a series of social affairs and held weekly Bible classes. Reba did her best to mention every meeting and activity. High yellow and forty, she articulated each word in the precise, prim and proper manner of a high school principal, which in fact she was.

The choir sang *God's Going to Set the World on Fire.*

"Amen. Let the church say, amen," Minister Carridine undid his coat button, revealing the gold chain of his pocket watch. "My text is taken from the second chapter of Isaiah," he opened the Bible. "The twelfth verse: '*For the day of the Lord of hosts shall be upon everyone that is proud and lofty and upon everyone that is lifted up and he shall be brought low . . .*'"

". . . Heed what I say, my beloved brothers and sisters," Minister Carridine's voice trembled. "Heed what I say. For I have heard the whistle of the condemnation train that's running down the Tracks of Time, carrying the wicked and the unjust! Running down the Tracks of Time at breakneck speed on the way to Hell with a cargo of condemned souls."

A woman wearing a black veil, possessed by the Holy Ghost, spoke in tongues.

"Get off that condemnation train, brothers and sisters. For tomorrow, tomorrow we shall all be delegates at that Judgment Day convention. Hallelujah! When the twin shores of Eternal Contradiction meet at the crossroads of Infinity. Hallelujah!"

Four ushers carried the woman in the black veil from the auditorium, still speaking in tongues, her body wiggling.

"On that Judgment Day. Where He shall take the faithful

unto His kingdom. Hallelujah! Where there will be no more suffering, injustice, burning, beating and lynching! When the righteous shall be gathered unto Him to live for all Eternity. He shall place in their hands the Scriptures of Universal Wisdom. And they shall stand beneath a panoply of stars, singing His praises for evermore, amen."

The choir chirped *My Lord, What a Morning*.

# 8

An oppressive heat stifled the office. Mattie Fae paced back and forth. *Calm down. Calm down,* she urged herself. Yes, she must be calm if she was to convince Coreen to accept her plan for Little Mattie. She must not let her feelings show. It would be difficult. Over the years, she'd prayed and prayed. But even after appealing to the good Lord for guidance, she still disliked her daughter-in-law.

"I thought for sure that my daughter would be at church today," Coreen entered and slammed the door behind her.

"I didn't bring her because I didn't want anyone to see the welts you left on her."

"Yeah, I beat her ass. I'll beat it again, too, if she defies me. You shoulda sent her back. I told you that the last time. I can't properly run my house if she gonna run to you every time I do something she don't like."

"Is it true that you are making her quit school?"

"Beatrice is gitting married. Now Little Mattie has got to help with the laundry. Ain't no mystery to that."

"That's the trouble with your generation. You have forgotten that not too long ago, it was against the law for colored folks to know anything about reading and . . ."

"The whole thing is, you don't respect me. It goes way back, too. When you told Sugarbear that I got myself pregnant with Beatrice so he'd have to marry me, you said I wasn't good enough for him. Don't deny it."

"There's nothing to deny," the rich vein of truth in Coreen's statement angered Mattie Fae. "I felt that Renauld could have made a better marriage. I simply voiced my feelings. After all, you did have a reputation for being, well . . . wild."

"Yeah, I was wild. That didn't stop him. The fact that I didn't want him at first didn't stop him, neither. Coming to where I worked, night after night. With his sweet words."

"Coreen. Really," Mattie Fae started coughing. Several moments passed before her coughing subsided. "I have no interest in such matters."

"I'll tell you something else, too. Ain't a woman born, outside of Mary, who got pregnant all by herself."

"No. I suppose not. Except in the case of you and Bootsy. Oh, excuse me. You never claimed that was a miracle."

(Coreen had conceived Bootsy during one of Sugarbear's absences. The exact nature of the circumstances never saw the light.)

"Don't you dare! That child doesn't know. Sugarbear forgave me a long time ago. He treats her better than all the others. It's not fair for you to bring up something that's been long forgotten."

"Coreen, I shouldn't have said that. I'm sorry. I really didn't mean for things to turn out like this. You see, I have a plan. Why don't you let Little Mattie come live with me? I'll buy her books and clothes, too. What do you say to that?"

"And another thing," Coreen's eyes watered. "You've never given me any credit for trying, you never have. Not even after I repented and joined church. If you want to hold my past against me for the rest of my life, that's between you and God . . ."

"Daddy's here," Bootsy rushed in. "See out the window." She pointed.

Sugarbear, wearing a sombrero and a serape, was surrounded by a group of smiling, backslapping well-wishers. A tad over six feet, he had wide sideburns and a clean-shaven face with a plump under-chin. He weighed a solid two hundred and seventy-five pounds. Handsome face glistening, ringed fingers sparkling, he flicked an ash from his cigarillo.

## 9

Coreen was twenty-seven when they met. Sugarbear was twenty-three. The first time he hit on her at the dancehall where she worked as a singer/waitress, she advised him to go home to his mother. That night, as they lay down beside each other, she recalled that he was the only person who had ever told her that he loved her.

Not counting his mother, Coreen was the only woman Sugarbear ever loved.

"Hunnn."

"What is it?"

"I was thinking about the first time I saw you," Sugarbear took Coreen in his arms. "You're still the sweetest thing I've ever laid my eyes on."

Sugarbear felt Coreen's tears on his chest.

"It's all right," he caressed her head. "It's all right."

"I'm fine now. You're here."

They kissed.

## 10

Mattie Fae, with Sugarbear's assistance, convinced Coreen to let Little Mattie live with her. Little Mattie, at the high point of her young life, stayed with Mattie Fae for the remainder of the summer and returned to school that fall.

Beatrice and Curtis spent their honeymoon in New Orleans.

Death claimed Mattie Fae before the year's end. In one of the largest funerals ever held at Mount Calvary, members of the community praised and eulogized her spirit.

As the mourners walked away from the grave, Coreen tapped Mattie on her shoulder.

"You can forget going to school."

"But Daddy said I could still go."

"Sugarbear still ain't found a job, so he don't have nothing to say on the matter."

# *Juneteenth*

**Spring, 1931.**

IT WAS A TIME OF ECONOMIC HARDSHIPS and social unrest, of bread lines and a dozen apples for a nickel, when the Great Depression spread through the Western World. The age of dictators: Hitler in Germany, Mussolini in Italy, Franco in Spain and Stalin in Russia. The days of the fascist Vichy in France. Sir Oswald Mosley menaced England. A Japanese sun ascended in the East. Asia and Africa, plagued by mutually destructive squabbles, were embroiled in a losing proposition with the Western colonial powers.

Disenchanted radicals and zealots from both ends of the political spectrum—oblivious to President Herbert Hoover's pronouncement that posterity was just around the corner—dominated the political scene, often appealing to the frightened passions, insecurities and baser instincts of the white masses.

This appeal was adroitly and successfully exploited in the South, where it was the era of the white supremacist demagogues. These demagogues blatantly baited the disenfranchised blacks in the name of poor whites and through corruption, revivalism and salesmanship claimed political power: Benjamin Tillman, Cole Blease and Olin D. Johnson of South Carolina; James Vardaman and Theodore Bilbo, Mississippi; Bibb Graves,

Alabama; Ruby Lafoon, Kentucky; Eugene Talmadge in Georgia—Huey Long in Louisiana.

In 1928, the people of Louisiana had elected Huey Long to be the governor for a four-year term. During his tenure he initiated a highly-publicized highway improvement project and one of the jobs that accrued from that program was construction laborer. The job consisted of a ten-hour, five-and-a-half-day weekly schedule. Whites called it "nigger work." Blacks called it "H" work: hot, hard and heavy.

But for James Pettaway, who worked as a laborer on a highway construction crew, it was the season of love. He'd seen Mattie Johnson at different church affairs and at the dances given by the Colored Knights of Pythias. He hadn't noticed her until about three months ago when they'd participated in a men-against-women softball game sponsored by the church. Her fine, brown frame caught his attention first. Next he observed the spirited manner in which she ran and played. Then he saw her hazel-brown eyes and the beauty of her face. Both had performed well in the game. Thereafter, they spoke whenever they saw each other and he heard the melody of her voice. When she let him walk her home after church—even though her sister, Bootsy, had to tag along—he'd felt her aura and sensed her smell.

That particular Saturday morning, James worked behind the grizbo, a tar-dispensing mechanism pulled by a team of six mules. Sweat darkened the band on his brown felt hat. His muscular arms rippled and glistened in the blistering sun. As he leveled the tar with a wooden spatula, Mattie Johnson weighed mightily on his mind.

"Gee! Gee! I say, gee!" the spidery muleskinner barked to the wide-eyed mules as the grizbo emptied itself.

Break time.

James lit a cigarette and joined several of his coworkers. They stood at the rear of the orange company truck, drinking water from a water bag and talking trash. Saturday was payday and they got off at noon.

Big Sam, the squatty straw boss, rolled their way. An old thirty-five, he stood five-feet-eight and weighed two hundred and sixty pounds. He had thick shoulders, hammy hands and a clean-shaven, beefy face.

"Y'all taking a break, or a vacation?" he pulled the brim of his hat down to his black eyes. "Pettaway, you working overtime today."

"Ah, come on, I already worked three Saturdays in a row."

"I ain't asking, I'm telling."

"But Big Sam, I mentioned it to you before. My brother and me are trying out for the Knights' baseball team today. Remember?"

"Maybe I'll git somebody else," Big Sam gave James a sour scrutinous stare. "Then again, maybe I won't." He rolled on.

James returned to work. Fleeting images of Mattie excited his heart. The way her eyes sparkled, the sway and switch of her skirt when she walked, her all-or-nothing charm. He and Big Sam did not speak for the remainder of the morning. Around noon, his coworkers started cleaning and putting away their tools. James, hoping for the best, did likewise.

"Here comes the money man," the muleskinner pointed toward the beige coupe speeding their way. "The eagle is flying."

The foreman, a porky man with hundreds of freckles on his parchment-white skin, pulled his car to an abrupt stop.

"Morning captain, sir," Big Sam bared his teeth. "Where you want these niggahs?"

"Over there, I guess," the foreman indicated a shady spot beneath a tree.

"Ah right, boys. Line up," Big Sam demanded. "Be quick about it."

Several men made comical faces behind Big Sam's back as they formed a line along the side of the car.

A coworker, extending a hand, pulled James onto the back of the company truck.

"Pettaway, where the hell you think you going?" Big Sam called. "Git your skinny ass off that truck!"

"Come on, Big Sam. You know I asked you before. This is the first day of practice."

Several of James' coworkers pleaded with Big Sam to give him a break.

"Ah right, then," Big Sam said. "You can go this time but don't make a habit out of it."

# 2

Morning glories climbed from the ground to the eaves of the veranda. Four o'clocks bordered the front window of the sturdy, gray house. Shirts, drawers and pants, clinging to the clotheslines, flapped in the wind. Aaron Pettaway's perfectly-furrowed garden blossomed with bright-colored vegetables.

The giant magnolia tree presided over the front yard where Gabriel Pettaway polished his early-model black Ford, Lizzie. Gabriel, who drove a six-wheeler for an oil company, had recently purchased the car. He kept it immaculately tuned and impeccably clean.

A light-colored car pulled up. James hopped out. He'd taken a shower and changed clothes.

"See y'all Monday," he called as the car sped away. "Big brother, I need some advice."

"Not now, cat. We don't want to be late for practice. Let's talk on the way. Go get your shoes and glove. Hurry up. We gotta stop by the cleaners to pick up Mordecai Leaks."

"James, what did you need some advice on?" Gabriel guided Lizzie down the highway.

"Mattie Johnson."

"Oh, no. Not her again," Gabriel chuckled.

"It might make you laugh but it's not funny to me. I asked her to the Juneteenth dance. She said she wasn't going with *anybody*."

"Did she say why?"

"She said so many guys asked her to go, she couldn't make up her mind. I gotta figure out a way to get her to change her mind and come to the dance with me."

"I've never had eyes for a chick who's stuck on herself."

"Mattie's not like that. She's just choosy. Give me some advice, big brother."

"First of all, you gotta slow-walk a chick like Mattie. The worst thing in the world you can do is to chase her. You got to lay in the cut. You know, make her curious."

"Solid. But how?"

"Ignore her. That'll make her wonder. Then she'll run after you."

"You must take me for a silly-dilly fool. I'm not following any wacky advice like that."

"Suit yourself, baby brother."

# 3

Mordecai Leaks, moving with precision, maneuvered a trouser leg onto the presser; simultaneously, the machine hissed moist white steam. Twenty-five, pudgy and dimpled, he had dark mischievous eyes and a cleft palate that he despised. He'd started working at the Ebony cleaners as a teenager. By avocation, he was a collector and creator of African American folklore.

"Mordecai, you heard the latest?" a coworker asked. "Louis Armstrong is going to play for the Juneteenth dance."

"Oh, boy. That means that the auditorium's going to be jammed wall to wall," Mordecai went to the window. Lizzie pulled up. "On time she came. Here are my partners now." He retrieved the black satchel in which he kept his catcher's equipment.

"See you later, alligator," his coworker called.
"After a while, chocolate child," Mordecai went out.

Mordecai jumped in the back seat and Lizzie eased off.
"What's the good word, buddy?" James asked.
"Save your dough," Mordecai laughed. "Gabriel, you hear the latest?"
"No, what's that?"
"Louis Armstrong is going to play for the Juneteenth dance."
"Oh, my. Satchmo can really toot his horn," James rapped.
"Say, Mordecai, how about doing *The Signifying Monkey?*" said Gabriel.
"All right," Mordecai took a breath and began: "Said the monkey to the lion one hot summer day: 'I just met that big burly elephant down the way. He sure scandalized your name today.

'He vilified your sisters, your brothers and your daddy, too. And he talked about your momma so *bad* that it made *me* mad.'

The lion roamed the jungle like a swish of the breeze, knocking coconuts off the trees.

Finally, he spied his man lying under a tree. The lion said, 'Elephant, I heard that you been talking about me and my family in a sinful way.'

The elephant said, 'Cat, you'd best continue on your way. I'm taking my nap and I don't have no time for play.'

The lion struck lightning-fast. But the elephant sidestepped and grabbed a piece of his ass.

They rustled and tussled all that day.

I don't see how in the world the lion managed to get away.

When he drug himself home, more dead than alive, the monkey climbed a tree and started talking his signifying jive:

'Mr. Lion! Mr. Lion! You don't look so well. Looks like you been catching some pure D hell! Got more scratches in your

face than a dog with the seven-year itch. Calling yourself the king of the jungle. Now ain't that a bitch!
  Don't say you didn't get beat. I saw the whole thing from a ringside seat.'
  The monkey, high on the limb, was laughing and jumping up and down.
  'Til one foot slipped and he fell to the ground.
  Like the spontaneous combustion of hot summer heat, the lion was on the monkey with all four feet.
  And the monkey's last words as he lay dying were: 'Mr. Lion. Mr. Lion, you finally stopped me from signifying.'"

## 4

Baseball sounds—the zing of fastballs, bat smacks, infielders' chirpy chatter—wafted in the breeze. The manager, Bradford Sykes, stood before the dugout. Forty-two and solid-looking, he had coffee-bean-brown skin and twinkling brown eyes. He owned the community's preferred mortuary. He also served as the treasurer for the most progressive lodge in the community, the Colored Knights of Pythias.

  "All right! All right! Everybody gather around," Bradford Sykes strolled to the pitcher's mound. "For the benefit of you new players, I'm going to bring you up to date. We're playing our main rivals, the Odd Fellows, at the annual Juneteenth baseball game. They've beaten us three years in a row, so we must win this one. Any questions? Good, let's get cracking. St. Elmo, you pitch. All right, you Pettaway brothers, show me what kind of bat you swing."

  Oscar St. Elmo (A.K.A. Noah) assumed the pitcher's mound and warmed up. Tall, deaconesque and twenty-three, he worked as a filler for a bottling company. He hadn't gone beyond the eighth grade but he read a lot. His opinions were highly regarded and sought after by his peers.

"Come on, Noah. Hum that pea," Mordecai pounded his catcher's mitt.

Gabriel stepped into the batter's box. St. Elmo threw a fastball that he hit solidly into left field. He also hit several other balls very well.

"Wonderful. Wonderful," Bradford called. "You're next, young Pettaway."

St. Elmo's first two pitches completely fooled James and he missed widely. He fouled off the next three balls but on his last attempt he stroked a solid liner over the left-field fence.

After practice, Bradford Sykes poured beer from a keg.

"You ran like a deer out there in center field, young Pettaway," he filled James' mug.

"Thank you, sir," James went to the bleachers. His teammates discussed the recent lynching of a black man accused of raping and killing a young white girl.

"How did the mob know it was him?" Gabriel asked.

"The newspaper said they acted on an anonymous tip," St. Elmo replied. "Can you imagine that? You go to a man's house by torchlight. Hang him in his front yard, before the eyes of his wife and three little children. On a tip?"

"That was a mean one all right," Bradford commented. "Sheriff Winchester left his body hanging for weeks. Even after the girl's stepfather confessed to the crime."

"If white people don't want us in America, why'd they bring us here in the first place?" James asked. "We were in Africa, minding our own business. They came over, put us in chains and shipped us across the ocean like sardines. When we got here, they bought and sold us like animals. But somehow, we get the blame. Why do white people hate us so much?"

"Our only sin is the color of our skin," St. Elmo answered. "White people fear dark skin. It's a European disease, buried deep in the craw of their culture."

St. Elmo's explanation gave them an immediate surge of assurance. But an underlying sense of uneasiness remained unabated. His explanation had exposed an unreasonable truth: the color of their skin condemned them to an intractable, Promethean struggle for survival in their native land.

The conversation, which served their need for a collective confirmation of their sense of reality, continued. They discussed the best way to deal with white aggression. Though they did not use these exact words, the consensus was that in dealing with white people they had three choices: flow, flee or fight. They were a captive people with no defense against the power of the State, the violence of the Ku Klux Klan, or the hostile nature of the average white person. The majority argued for flight, to avoid whites whenever possible.

"Rare is the white boy who'll fight you man to man. Whites are group fighters," the first baseman spoke for the minority who would fight. His name was Bertrand Haskins—however, his friends called him Punchy. A twenty-year-old cotton mill worker, he had a likeable face, a barrel chest and powerful arms. "They only fight when they got you outnumbered. By himself, the average white man ain't doodly-squat."

"As for me, I'll play the head-scratching Uncle Tom in a minute," Mordecai announced. "While they thinking I'm stupid, I'm laughing at them to beat the band." He was the only one who advocated flow. As far as he was concerned, whites were slow-witted and easily outfoxed. "All you got to do is use your brains and play games. When it comes to dealing with ofays, I reach way deep into my bag of tricks." To make his point, he divulged one of his favorite tricks: *If you catch a sucker, bump his head.*" The trick involved convincing an unsuspecting white person that he was under the protection of a powerful white man. "It's guaranteed to work on country bumpkins."

The trick's originality appealed to James' imagination and he committed it to memory.

"It's almost time for Amos and Andy," Bradford remarked. "I must go."

"Yeah, me too."

"Right."

"Yeah, it's time to split."

"We all must go. But, before we do . . ." Mordecai sprinkled beer on the ground. "A moment of silence for the many, many, many generations who survived the Middle Passage. And the many, many, many generations in this land who've been here, suffered and gone: the worthy ones."

No one moved. They looked at Mordecai with anticipation, awaiting his specialty, a feat that allowed him to particularize each event he attended. Mordecai cleared his throat and chanted:

"As I looked out of the window of the Ebony Cleaners, the brothers Pettaway I spied, having dropped by to give your boy a ride.

Whilst we trucked along in Lizzie, the Ford machine, I revealed that Satchmo, the trumpet king, is going to play for the dance on Juneteen.

At James' request, I related the tale of how *The Signifying Monkey* met his final rest.

During practice Mr. Sykes was cool and serene, as he watched us Knights prancing on the diamond green.

Noah was too, too profound on the pitcher's mound.

Punchy, the way you patrolled first base, you acted like you owned the place.

Gabriel, you hit some solid liners, too. And James, you might have swung and missed a few

But you finally hit one a mile or two into the sky so blue.

So now, here we are, sitting in these bleachers brown.

Talking that talk and guzzling our beers down.

On that note, that's all she wrote."

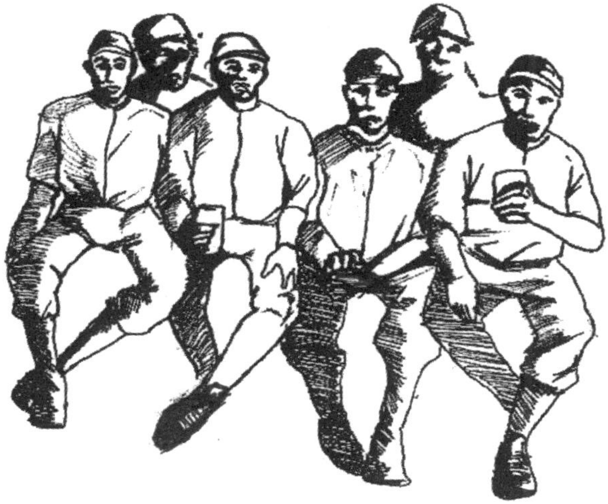

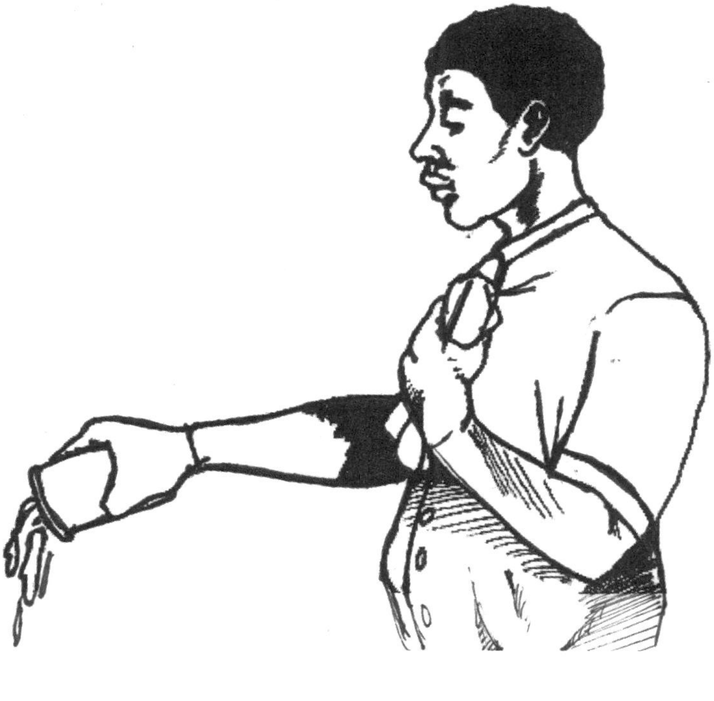

# 5

Lizzie, headlights slicing the darkness, glided across the highway like a black swan.

James sat in front, next to Gabriel. In the rear, St. Elmo passed a fifth of corn liquor to Mordecai, who lifted the bottle and gobbled. They arrived at the Knights' palatial mansion. Gabriel parked near the entrance. The lyrical trembling of horns and the provocative sounds of tom drums vibrated from deep within the mansion.

"There goes Punchy and his gal," Mordecai pointed his finger at the Knights' first baseman and his companion, who walked toward the entrance. "Just look at Emma Pace. Walking like she's got an oil well between her thighs."

James' mind wandered. Despite his initial rejection of Gabriel's advice, during the past month he had followed it. So far, sad to say, Mattie never noticed his not noticing her. That morning, Gabriel had suggested a new strategy. *No. Not this time*, he promised himself. *I followed his advice before but not this time. No! No! No!*

"Let's go inside and do some funning," Mordecai bounced out of the car and led the way.

Photographs checkered the walls: Marcus Garvey. Florence Mills. Booker T. Washington. Zora Neale Hurston. Langston Hughes. Bill "Bojangles" Robinson. Fletcher Henderson. Jack Johnson. Jelly Roll Martin. W.C. Handy. Paul Robeson. W.E.B. Dubois.

In the lounge, snuggling couples, seated on black leather divans before the crackling fireplace, crooned *Blue Turning Grey Over You.*

Gabriel, St. Elmo, James and Mordecai walked to the table where Bradford Sykes and another man sat collecting admissions.

"Howdy, gents," Bradford said. "That'll be two bits apiece.

Before you check your hats, let me introduce you to another lodge member, Mr. Thaddeus Stier. He's also a high official in A. Philip Randolph's Brotherhood of Sleeping Car Porters Union. Thaddeus, these are four of my best players." He introduced them individually.

"Nice meeting you, gentlemen," Thaddeus Stier was a self-assured, outgoing man of forty-two. "Be diligent in your endeavors against the Odd Fellows. And the good Lord willing, the Knights will savor the luscious taste of victory next Saturday."

As they walked to the checkroom, James pulled Gabriel aside.

"Big brother, the new strategy you suggested this morning, are you sure it will work?"

"That's not the question, baby brother. The question is, what do you have to lose?"

"But if I take Thelma Jenkins to the Juneteenth dance to make Mattie jealous, she might stop speaking to me."

"Mattie's been speaking to you and what good has it done?" Gabriel adjusted James' tie. "Take my advice, O.K.? Thelma Jenkins is a swell looker, too. Besides, she's let the whole world know she's sweet on you."

Mordecai and James stood in the doorway of the ballroom. A red-suited band hurled hot music from the bandstand. Stylish couples partied at candlelit tables. On the dance floor, frisky feet off-timed to the drummer's beat.

"Ain't nothing out here tonight but cows and scarecrows," Mordecai commented.

Punchy and Emma Pace came their way. Emma was eighteen and foxy. Her white scarf coiled stylishly around her slender, brown neck.

"You looking mighty fetching this evening, Emma," Mordecai bowed super-courteously.

Emma, a real snob, pretended she didn't hear or see Mordecai.

James sensed a presence behind him. He turned and gazed into the brazen, brown eyes of Thelma Jenkins, a seventeen-year-old dairy worker. Charming face all aglow, her feline figure purred with a delightful sensuousness. Fleshy lips slightly parted, she conveyed the expression of a young woman blessed with an unquenchable *joie de vivre*.

"What's the matter, James? You don't know nobody now," Thelma spoke in a singsong, countrified accent. Her red dress barely covered her knees, which was daringly high for that particular set. "I waved at you when you first came in."

"Oh, yeah? I didn't see you," replied James.

"Hi, Thelma," Mordecai chirped. "You look sweet enough to sop with a biscuit."

Emma and Thelma, who traveled in different social sets, studiously ignored each other.

"Come on, I need some air," Emma tugged Punchy away.

A fine pretty in a tight-fitting orange dress whispered Mordecai's name as she flowed by.

"Later, James. Nature calls," Mordecai pursued the fine pretty.

"Well, guess I'll mosey on," Thelma turned to go.

"Wait. You want to dance?" James asked.

Thelma's heart flip-flopped. Smiling deliciously, she took his hand.

# 6

Lizzie owned the night. Punchy and Emma sat up front with Gabriel. Mordecai, James and St. Elmo sat in the back.

"Noah, you taking anybody to the Juneteenth dance?" Gabriel asked.

"Naw, I'm flying solo," Oscar St. Elmo answered. "Who you taking?"

"My favorite dish of course, Inez Chambers," said Gabriel.

"Mordecai, who you coming with?" Punchy inquired.

"Me, myself and I," Mordecai replied. "No sense in bringing ham hocks and black-eyed peas to a banquet."

Fortunately for Mordecai, he didn't see the killer look Emma shot his way. Otherwise, he might have died on the spot, *tout de suite*.

Gabriel parked in front of a darkened house. Punchy escorted Emma to her door.

Lizzie zipped through the night. The quintet harmonized *Ain't Misbehavin'*, à la their hero, Fats Waller.

"James, you didn't say who you taking to the Juneteenth dance," Punchy remarked.

"He's like me and Noah," Mordecai teased. "Taking his own sweet self."

"A heap see. Only a few know," James signified.

"Well, I'll say," Mordecai cocked his head. "Who you taking?"

"Thelma Jenkins."

"All right, then!" Gabriel congratulated James. "Now, on to the Say When!"

# 7

The Say When was not the type of establishment that you could just luck up and find. There were no signs to identify the dirt road that intersected the highway, or the series of crosses and turns as the road curved and wound its way past thickets and trails around a bend before it unraveled and you saw the single string of orange, red, white and yellow light bulbs strung across the front of the club. Frequented by proud-scented loggers, construction workers, mill hands, dockhands and sweet men; frequented by long-legged levee women, ginger-talking domestics and sweet-smelling coochie mommas, the Say When was raucous, raunchy and rowdy—one of those rough, tough and ready bucket-of-blood type joints where looking at a man, his woman or even his drink in the wrong way could be an invitation to a knife fight.

Lizzie's headlights exposed the men and women milling about the entrance. Wisps of the blues floated from within. They entered and maneuvered through the crowd. A trio of musicians—piano, guitar and harmonica—played a blues with a complicated ostinato. On the dirt dance floor, gyrating couples twirled in sublime harmony.

"The jungle at its very best," Mordecai commented.

"*My woman's got a heart like railroad steel,*" the piano player crooned in a falsetto voice.

A man with a razor-slashed face bumped James aside.

"Say you," James made a move.

"Easy, young blood," Mordecai grabbed James' arm, restraining him. "He's a fool. You don't want to mess with him. He's had a few drinks and now he's ready to kick Tarzan's ass."

The man with the razor-slashed face cut in on a brother who, cigarette dangling from his lips, danced with a woman in a yellow dress. The brother shook his head and walked away.

Gabriel led the way through the swinging doors and into a dimly-lit room where groups of men shot dice, played pittypat and Georgia Skin.

St. Elmo danced with a sister in a red dress, completely absorbed in the pulsating rhythms.

Across the way, the man with the razor-slashed face stumbled onto the dance floor, swayed and righted himself. Again, he cut in on the brother who, cigarette dangling from his lips, danced with the woman in the yellow dress. The brother glared and stalked off.

James joined Mordecai at the crap table. The *croupier* wore a bodacious white hat and a black shirt with pearly buttons. Powerfully built, he projected a haughty attitude that announced his total command of his table.

Mordecai threw three sevens in succession.

"Shoot all that money! I can't lose with the stuff I use," he sang. "These bones are hotter than ten old maids at a revival meeting in the summertime." He threw the dice. "Humph!"

"Seven's the winner," the *croupier* proclaimed.

"That's it for me, gents," Mordecai collected his winnings. "I've got a couple of corners to turn."

The quintet exited the Say When.

"Let's go to Mary Jack the Bear's," Mordecai, exuding the giddy excitement of a winner, waved his money. "I'm *buying some* for everybody."

The woman wearing the yellow dress ran from the club.

"They fighting over me and ain't neither one my man," she vanished into the darkness.

Eager to see, the quintet rushed back inside. But only St. Elmo, on his tiptoes, managed to get a bird's-eye view.

"It's that fool and some guy he's been messing with all night. Oh! Oh! The guy knocked the fool down. I can't see anymore. They're on the floor now."

"I got a hunch," Mordecai said. "Let's leave before somebody starts shooting."

Heeding Mordecai's intuition, they left the club.

Gunshots rang out. A screaming and yelling crowd stampeded from the Say When. The quintet sprinted to the car.

Gabriel guided Lizzie down the highway. The quintet warbled *Black and Blue.*

"Oh-oh! This might be trouble," Gabriel looked in the rearview mirror.

"What is it, Gabe?" James asked.

"A car is coming fast."

"You better slow down," Mordecai cautioned. "It might be the highway patrol."

Gabriel slowed down.

A light-colored sedan pulled up beside Lizzie and hovered, exposing four sullen-faced white men whose icy stares made them feel the terrifying sense of fear.

The sedan sped past them. The quintet relaxed. Up ahead, the sedan slowed.

"What that guy doing?" Gabriel asked.

"Pass the fools," Punchy urged.

When Gabriel attempted to pass, the sedan swerved and blocked his way. He tried to pass three more times but on each attempt, the sedan prevented Lizzie's safe passage.

"I know a trick," Gabriel muttered. "There's a steep curve coming up ahead." The sedan approached the curve. Gabriel angled Lizzie for a pass on the left. When the sedan entered the curve, he veered Lizzie to the right and zoomed past it. The sedan careened, almost jumped the curve and righted itself. Gabriel stomped the accelerator. Lizzie gulped down long stretches of highway. In the rearview mirror, the sedan's headlights faded into darkness.

# 8

The evening breeze eased through the open window into the kitchen where Mattie Johnson pressed her sister Lynn's hair with a hot straightening comb. Her grandmother's death had plunged Mattie into a period of emotional darkness. For over two years she had experienced states of depression, anger and frustration. She lived endless days of *déjà vu*. Where nothing mattered but everything mattered at the same time and her heart was always crying. She'd not only lost her best friend but when Coreen forced her to quit school, she took away her dream of accomplishing something big in life. Through studying the Bible and prayer, she was able to forgive Coreen. She achieved inner peace by promising herself that *her* children would have the chance to have their pictures hanging on school walls. Now Mattie was out of her darkness. She felt good about herself and looked forward to a brighter life.

"I'm almost finished," moving with a subtle sensuousness, Mattie stepped back and inspected her handiwork. "Just one more minute."

"You should be through by now," Lynn, who was in love, emitted an earthy fragrance. "You know Shelby will be here soon to pick us up."

"See if you like it," Mattie handed Lynn a mirror.

"I guess it'll do," Lynn studied her reflection.

"Lynn, your beau just drove up," Bootsy came in. She wore her hair pulled back into a chignon, which gave her otherwise pretty face a severe expression. Bootsy called herself a soldier of the Lord. She did not chew gum or wear makeup and she preferred loose-fitting black dresses. "Mattie, you coming to the Juneteenth rehearsal at the church with us? This is the last one before our performance tomorrow night."

"No. I still have Odilia and Emma to do."

"I'm so glad I'm leaving," Bootsy declared. She started a monologue about how glad she was that she wouldn't be around to hear Mattie and her friends gossip about boys. "Boys talk bad and they are nasty." She held her nose.

Much to Mattie's relief, Coreen entered.

"Mattie, don't forget to wake up your father for work," Coreen said. She had stopped drinking after Sugarbear returned. A healthy sheen covered her face. "Lynn, Bootsy, come on. Let's don't keep Shelby waiting."

"See you all," Mattie called. "Have a good rehearsal."

Several minutes later, Odilia Toy entered. Nineteen, short but comely. She had a sweet and gentle disposition. Indeed, there was something fetching about her, something elusive and endearing. Odilia, Mattie and their mutual friend, Emma Pace, were natives of the town. Their friendship went back to their jacks, pick-up-sticks and double-Dutch days.

"Hi, Mattie. What have you been up to?"

"I picked up my things from the layaway," Mattie combed Odilia's hair. "Wait until I show you the dress I bought for the Knights' baseball game. It's a real killer-diller."

"I can't wait to see it," Odilia said. "I heard that the new schoolteacher walked you home after church. Did he?"

"Yes, Mr. Hunter walked me home."

"Well, what happened? What did y'all talk about?"

"A whole lot. He knows more about everything than I do about anything. He's the smartest man I ever met in my life. He knows all about Negro history."

"Is that all you talked about?"

"If you must know, he did ask me to the Juneteenth dance. But since I've already said I'm not going with *anybody*, I had to turn him down."

"Mattie, sometimes I don't know about you," Odilia protested. "Oreville Hunter would be such a great catch."

"Excuse me a minute, I must go wake up my father," Mattie rushed off.

Emma Pace swooped in. Her personality ran perpendicular to Odilia's. She had a saucy tongue and a spicy attitude. She knew the intimate details about a lot of other people's business and she loved to gossip.

"Hi, Odilia," she plopped down in a chair. "These feet are killing me. That white woman tried to work my can off today. "

"Thank you, daughter," Sugarbear closed the door behind Mattie and started dressing. He had ballooned up to a cool three hundred pounds. He led a clean life and neither smoked nor drank. The taut skin on his face issued a healthy glow. But he was not the characteristic jovial fat man. On the contrary, he often felt depressed. Financial considerations forced him to sell his rings and take a night watchman job at a sawmill. Plus, he had not received a word from the *spirit* since his return. Not one prospect for buried treasure had come his way.

By his own admission, he'd fallen upon evil times. Which convinced him that some unidentifiable conjuror had hexed him. He'd sought the wisdom of the voodooist, Sanite DiDi. An associate, one Zack Greystone, was to deliver her message to him at the Juneteenth picnic.

"How do you like it?" Mattie passed Odilia the mirror.
"It looks just swell," Odilia gave herself a wink.
"Mattie, guess who showed up last Saturday night at the Knights' dance? Thelma Jenkins," Emma snickered. "That Jenkins bunch ain't been out of the cotton field a year. And they're already known all over town for their drinking and hellraising. You should have seen Thelma. Dressed like some floozy."
"That country heifer," Odilia sneered.
"I can't stand that scrawny thing," Mattie scowled.
"Evening, young ladies," Sugarbear cruised in like a prized yacht. He glided to the icebox and brought out his lunch pail. "Well, I'm off to work." He navigated his way across the kitchen and eased through the door.
"See you in the morning, Poppa," Mattie called.
"Before I forget," Emma snapped her finger. "Mattie, guess who is playing for the Knights' baseball team? Another one of your rejects, James Pettaway."
Mattie perked up. Like her friends, she rooted for the Knights. She hadn't known that James played for her team.
"James sure can dance. He does a step that goes like this," Emma demonstrated.

# 9

The following evening, rain clouds darkened the sky. The air felt crisp and smelled clean.
Gabriel eased Lizzie to a stop behind the church. Other cars were already parked there, as well as buggies whose horses were

hitched to posts. James got out. Extending a hand, he helped Sodonia out of the car. Sodonia looked nifty in her pink dress. Aaron, like his sons, wore a light-colored suit. James and Gabriel sported derbies. They walked in a single file on the gritty path. Behind them a horse issued a melancholy neigh. They rounded the church and veered toward the entrance. Gabriel and James tipped their derbies to a red-dressed acquaintance as they followed their parents into the church.

Mordecai, Punchy and St. Elmo arrived fifteen minutes before the hour. They also wore derbies. Their well-conditioned bodies exuded confidence and youthful arrogance. The auditorium, already three-quarters filled, hummed with energy. An usher guided Minister C.C. Carridine, Reba Hightower, Thaddeus Stier, Bradford Sykes, Meldrick Merryweather, Dr. Edgar Hill and Essex Dawson to their seats.

Lynn Johnson swept down the aisle with her beau, Shelby Staggs, a dark-skinned, clear-eyed chap of twenty-seven. Lynn stopped when she reached the row in which her family sat. Coreen nudged Sugarbear and they made room for Shelby.

At seven o'clock, a handsome, light-brown-skinned man of twenty-five came out and faced the audience: "Ladies and gentlemen, my name is Oreville Hunter. This evening, I'll be serving as your master of ceremonies."

A group traveling on C.P. Time rambled in. The latecomers included Odilia, Emma and Mattie. Finding it impossible to get seats together, they scattered. In one of those million-to-one chances, Mattie found a space in the row behind the Pettaways. As she took her seat, James looked back and caught her eye. The beginnings of a smile formed on her face but James turned his head away before she completed it.

"It is my pleasure to introduce the third-grade boys who will lead us in the Pledge of Allegiance," Oreville looked offstage and made a beckoning gesture with his finger.

Three jolly boys of eight tumbled onto the stage and placed their hands over their hearts. In a haphazard, halting manner, they led the audience into the pledge. They grew increasingly confident. By the end of the pledge they were in sync, articulating each word boldly. When they finished, they looked back and forth at each other, obviously confused.

"Bow and come off!" demanded a woman's shrill whisper from offstage.

The jolly third graders regained their composure and bowed. Amidst the jovial laughter of the audience, they marched off, heads held high.

"I'm sure that some of you, especially you young people, don't know the history of Juneteenth," Oreville said. "Juneteenth originated because—Mr. Lincoln's 1863 Emancipation Proclamation not withstanding—not all of our ancestors received their freedom at the same time. Slaves in Arkansas, Louisiana, Maryland and Missouri were not freed until 1864. Slaves in the other rebel states were not emancipated until the South surrendered in 1865. Some brothers and sisters in Galveston, Texas, started the first Juneteenth celebration in 1866.

"And now, Miss Lynn Johnson will sing the Negro National Anthem, *Lift Every Voice and Sing,* written by the Johnson brothers, J. Rosamond and James Weldon, in 1900."

Lynn sang the first verse. Upon her request, the audience joined her on the second verse.

The program was spirited and had a tendency to ramble. This created a vacuum that the audience filled audaciously, becoming spirited participants, egging on the performers with humorous comments and asides.

A lad of twelve with large, white eyes recited Paul Laurence Dunbar's "Ode to Ethiopia" in a self-possessed manner. Lynn sang a superb rendition of *No More Pinch of Salt For Me.* A teenage boy boldly recited Claude McKay's "If We Must Die." The audience received each presentation excitedly but long after the event had passed, everyone agreed that the highlight of the first half of the program was Bootsy's spirited and flawless recitation of Phyllis Wheatley's "Liberty and Peace."

During the intermission, some members from the audience lined up at the refreshment table to buy slices of cakes and pies, mincemeat patties, cookies, nuts, punch and tea. The Pettaways emerged from the auditorium into the vestibule. Mordecai, Punchy and St. Elmo stood at the end of the refreshment line. James and Gabriel joined them.

Sodonia and Aaron found themselves walking beside Coreen and Sugarbear.

"How're you doing, girl?" Coreen asked in a warm manner.

"Fair to middling," Sodonia smiled. "You must be so proud of Lynn and Bootsy."

"Oh, I am."

Coreen and Sodonia paired off and continued their conversation.

Aaron and Sugarbear were deeply religious and you'd have thought that they would have become friends like their wives. For some reason they never hit it off. Perhaps Sugarbear's mysticism and worldliness contrasted too starkly with Aaron's practical, centered personality. After exchanging lackluster hellos, they turned their heads the other way from one another.

Other members from the audience spilled from the church. The light from hanging lanterns created weird, moving silhouettes that wove back and forth in unstated rhythms.

Minister C.C. Carridine, Thaddeus Stier, Bradford Sykes and several other men, including Dr. Edgar Hill and Essex Dawson discussed Huey Long's "Complete the Work" election campaign. Although they could not vote, they followed the campaign with a keen interest.

"It's still like Mr. Washington said: '*The essential issue is economics*,'" Minister Carridine blew into his cup of tea. "The kingfish speaks of creating jobs. That is definitely in the best interest of the Negro."

"Huey Long's no different from all of them other politicians as far as the Negro is concerned," Thaddeus Stier said. "None of them are going to do right by us."

The conversation shifted to the issue of Negro disenfranchisement. Dr. Hill, a self-proclaimed pragmatist, argued that Negroes would not be able to vote in his lifetime.

"It's true that the 14th Amendment gave us the right to vote but the white politicians stop us with their obstructions. They can stop us from voting," Dr. Hill declared. "But they can't stop us from being enterprising and entrepreneurial. I also agree with Mr. Washington. *Economics* is the real issue. We must concede on the issue of voting."

"As a businessman, I can not deny the importance of economics," Essex Dawson spoke up. "However, a Negro can have all of the money in the world but that won't save him from being discriminated against, or lynched. That brings us to politics. I stand with Mr. Dubois on this. The poll tax must be eliminated. We must be able to vote so we can elect people who will legislate anti-discrimination and anti-lynching laws. Without the vote the Negro will remain a second-class citizen. I'm not conceding anything."

James, Gabriel, Punchy, St. Elmo and Mordecai, hands laden with food and drink, came out of the church and bivouacked near the entrance.

Thunder rumbled in the distance. A streak of lightning cracked the sky.

As Mattie, Odilia and Emma walked down the steps, Emma saw Punchy and his friends.

"Odilia, look over there," Emma pointed. "See the tall guy standing next to Punchy? He's the one I was telling you about. His name is Oscar St. Elmo but everybody calls him Noah. Let's go over so I can introduce you." She led the way.

"Hi, Punchy," Emma said sweetly. "Where are your manners? Introduce us to your friend."

James stood rigid. *What should I do? Should I continue to ignore Mattie, or what?*

Mattie thought of something pleasant to say to James.

Punchy introduced St. Elmo to Odilia. Odilia extended her hand for a handshake and flashed a coy smile.

"Mattie, Noah. Noah, Mattie," Punchy said.

"Nice meeting you, Noah."

"It's nice meeting you, too, Mattie."

"Mattie, you and James already know each other," Punchy laughed.

"James, I didn't know that you played for the . . ."

"Hey, Gabe. I'm gonna go get me some punch," James stalked off.

Thunder roared. Lightning flashed. Rain sprinkled. Amidst squeals and howls everyone dashed back inside the church.

## 10

Mattie stopped washing the breakfast dishes and stared out of the window. Mother Nature, with her whimsical ways, had sent down glorious bursts of sunshine that blotted out all memories of the previous night's rain. But nothing blotted out the memory of James' rudeness from Mattie's mind. Angered by James' behavior, she'd slept fretfully. Now she was experiencing a different feeling. The feeling surprised and puzzled her: she felt hurt by James' behavior.

"Why you looking out the window like you a Zombie?" Bootsy entered with a picnic basket. "It's like Momma's always saying. The way you be daydreaming, one of these days your mind is gonna wander off and get lost."

"Oh, yeah. Don't let me have to maul your hair, either," Mattie spoke with more heat than she'd intended to.

"I was only playing," Bootsy took some food from the icebox and put it in the basket.

"Well, sometimes you play too much," Mattie snapped with uncharacteristic bitterness.

Mattie stood on the front porch as Shelby Staggs put the picnic basket in the trunk of his early-model Dodge. Shelby worked as a bellhop. He wore a straw hat, white shirt and white pants with red suspenders. Lynn, holding the hem of her flowery dress, hoisted herself into the front seat. Coreen sported Sugarbear's Panama hat. She and Bootsy sat in the rear. Shelby backed the car down the driveway.

"Mattie, don't forgit," Coreen stuck her head out the window. "Before you leave for the baseball game, wake up your father. Deacon Merryweather is bringing him to the picnic."

The car sputtered off.

Odilia Toy and Emma Pace crossed the road and waved as they came Mattie's way.

Emma and Odilia, seated on the couch, itched with curiosity.

"Mattie, have you been able to figure out what was wrong with James last night?" Emma asked. "What's going on between you and him?"

"Emma," Odilia said. "Bet you dollars to donuts that James acted the fool because Mattie refused to go to the dance with him."

"Naw, it's got to be more than that. Let's try to figure this out," Emma rubbed her chin. "Mattie, before last night, when was the last time you talked to James?"

"Not in some time. It's been at least a month," Mattie answered. "Now that I think about it, I haven't spoken to him since I told him I wasn't going to the dance with anybody."

"See," Odilia snapped her fingers. "Didn't I just say that's what it was all about?"

"You know something else? Last night, when I sat behind him in the church, he looked back and turned his head away like he didn't see me," Mattie paced the floor, her anger newly inflamed. Anger, like the dog that bites the hand that feeds it, knows no master. Anger commends confusion and rebukes reason. Anger caused Mattie to take a course of action that, although understandable, was uncalled for: "There's no way in the world I can root for the Knights with James Pettaway playing on the team. I'm going to the picnic with my father."

"If you going to the picnic, I'm going with you," Odilia announced. "In fact, I don't believe any of us should go to the baseball game."

"Whoa, whoa. Hold on a minute," Emma protested. "Punchy is expecting me to be there to see him play. I can't let him down. Besides, we need to know what's happening in the enemy camp. After the game, I'll bring back all of the behind-the-scene particulars."

## 11

Hundreds of community members—creating a yellow, pink, white, green, red and black rainbow—picnicked on the horseshoe-shaped meadow. At the open end of the horseshoe, a silvery lake, blending in with the horizon, melted into the sun.

Meldrick Merryweather parked his car in the wooded area that surrounded the round end of the horseshoe. Sugarbear, carrying a brown paper bag, rolled out of the car. His untucked red shirt hung over his stomach like an umbrella.

Mattie and Odilia joined him.

"How you young ladies doing?" Sugarbear stretched his arms.

"Everything's copasetic, Mr. Johnson," Odilia replied.

"I like your new shirt, Poppa," Mattie said with a daughter's sweetness. "You look sharper than a tack."

Shrieking boys with toy pistols played cowboys and Indians. Two elderly dudes, egged on by a group of onlookers, tossed horseshoes. Willow-legged girls jumped double-Dutch rope.

Zack Greystone, Sugarbear's associate, basted a slab of ribs over a grave-shaped pit. Subject to a whim, he looked over his shoulder: his "Barbecue for Sale" had fallen on the ground. He raised his snub nose, sniffed the wind and retrieved the sign. It occurred to him that the fallen sign might be an ill omen. He put his hand into his pocket and caressed his good luck charm.

Sugarbear and company arrived.

"I saw y'all coming before you got out the car," Zack said.

"Here, Meldrick. Take my dominoes and y'all go on," Sugarbear gave Meldrick the brown paper bag. "Mattie, be sure to tell Coreen I'll be there directly."

Sugarbear and Zack waited until Mattie, Odilia and Meldrick walked out of earshot.

"Well, Zachariahs?" Sugarbear whispered.

"Sanite DiDi said you've been hexed by a demon," Zack whispered. "Three things must be done. First, you must memorize the seventh Psalm in the *Seventh Book of Moses*, backwards."

"Ah, the *black man's* Bible. What's the second thing?"

"She'll make you a tobi. Like this," Zack pulled his good luck charm from his pocket.

"Thirdly?"

"Sanite DiDi must perform a special ceremony for you."

Deacon Merryweather, Odilia and Mattie were surrounded by the strains of guitar music that soared above the festive hum. They zigzagged through groups of men, women and children who played, fed their faces and lounged in the sun. Mattie and Odilia stopped at a concession stand. Merryweather continued on his way.

"What can I do for you ladies?"

"A strawberry ice cone for me."

"I'll have a pineapple one."

Some fifty Mount Calvary Baptist Church members picnicked near the lake. Coreen Johnson, moving from table to table, piled a plate with an assortment of meats, vegetables and sweets. Bootsy got up from the multicolored quilt she'd shared with Lynn and Shelby Staggs and hurried off. Two shivering teenage girls in baggy bathing suits, eyes reddish, streaked past.

"Lynn, where's Bootsy off to?" Coreen joined Lynn and Shelby.

"To find out when the sack race is going to start," Lynn answered.

Oreville Hunter approached. He wore a black swimming suit and carried a towel.

"Hi, Mr. Hunter," Lynn said.

"Hi, Lynn. Hello, everybody," Oreville replied. "Say, doesn't that water look great?"

"That water's not bothering me and I'm not going to bother it," Shelby chuckled.

"Yeah, Mr. Hunter. That lake look mighty cold," Lynn said.

"It just looks cold. But you quickly become accustomed to it."

Meldrick Merryweather arrived.

"Deacon, didn't Sugarbear come with you?" Coreen asked.

"Oh, yes. He just stopped to chat with Zack."

"Once them two start talking, there's no telling when he'll git here," Coreen declared.

"He'll be along soon," Meldrick said. "He gave me his dominoes and he specifically told Mattie to tell you he'd be here directly."

"Is Mattie here also, Deacon?" Oreville asked.

"Sure as shooting. Her and Odilia Toy."

Oreville's heart pounded.

"Well, I'm off for my swim," he said. "See you all."

Near the lake, a man with a white handkerchief tied around his forehead fried catfish in a huge black caldron. His two young daughters, eyes bright, held on to his apron. Further away, a dimpled youth in a red cap pulled the string of a kite whose tail, wiggling like an eel, jerked toward the sky.

Oreville, who'd captained his swimming and boxing teams in college, was in excellent condition. He swam to the middle of the lake and floated. Body swaying with the water's gentle rhythm, feeling sunbeams on his closed eyelids, he daydreamed of Mattie Johnson.

Sugarbear, head propped up on his elbow, contemplated the

dominoes in his hands. Shelby, seated on Sugarbear's right, was Lynn's partner; hat tilted back, he pondered his bones. Meldrick, Sugarbear's partner, eyed Lynn.

Coreen used the Panama to shoo flies from Sugarbear. Mattie and Odilia kibitzed.

"It's still your play, Lynn," Meldrick commented. "Studying is not going to change your hand. You don't have but one play. I told you when you took that last count, all money is not good money." He was the type of player who, after two plays, could tell who was holding what particular domino. "Play your five trey, so my partner can count twenty."

Oreville walked up.

"Hi, Mr. Hunter."

"Hi, Odilia. How are you, Mattie?"

"Just swell, thank you, Mr. Hunter."

"Lynn, Shelby, come on," Bootsy trotted their way. "The sack race is starting soon."

"Let's go, too, Odilia," Mattie said. "Remember, I nearly took first place last year."

"Why don't you come with us, Mr. Hunter?" Odilia suggested.

"I don't know..."

Odilia nudged Mattie.

"Yes, why don't you, Mr. Hunter?" Mattie asked. "It'll be a ton of fun."

"Swell. But I must go get my clothes."

"That's all right," Odilia said. "We'll wait for you."

"Excellent," Oreville dashed off.

"See you, Mattie," Odilia turned to go.

"But—But—Where are you going?" Mattie asked.

"To catch up with Bootsy and them. So you and Mr. Hunter can have some privacy."

As they walked, the fresh wind blew freely across their faces.

"Mr. Hunter, when you walked me home from church, you

mentioned something I wanted to hear more about. I didn't say anything at the time. I didn't want you to know how dumb I am."

"Mattie, you're not dumb. There are just some things you haven't been exposed to as yet. But you're smart and what's even more important, you have a curiosity about life. You might not realize it yourself but you are an unpolished original."

"Mr. Hunter, I told you before that I had to quit school after my grandmother died. You don't have to flatter me."

"But I'm not flattering you. You *are* an original. And stop calling me Mr. Hunter, please. I'm Oreville, O.K.? What was it you wanted to know more about?"

"To be truthful, you said lots of things I wanted to know more about. But you can start with the Mason Dixie line."

"You mean the Mason-Dixon line. It's a line that runs east and west across America. And if I recall my history correctly, it's named after the two English astronomers who surveyed it. During slavery it was the dividing line between the slave and the non-slave states. Now when you cross it, it means the end of segregation on interstate transportation. St. Louis, Missouri, is the first major train station north of it—the connection point to Detroit, Chicago and California. My father's a Pullman porter and he says crossing the Mason-Dixon is still a symbol of freedom for our people. He said grown men drop to their knees and pray when they reach the station in St. Louis."

In the distance, two men wielded a violin and a banjo in front of a circle of dancers who, twirling rhythmically, kicked up a cloud of dust.

"How did you happen to come down here from Chicago? To teach, I mean?"

"To cut a story of some length, it was my father's doing. He and Thaddeus Stier are good friends. Mr. Stier told my father they needed a teacher down here. Before you could say Yankee-Doodle Dandy, my father and mother were seeing me off at the train station. My father said he wants me to sample the real world. That's what he calls the South. But that's not the real reason he sent me down here. He hopes that the experience will get the theater out of my blood. He wants me to become an attorney."

"We're almost there. Come on, let's race," Mattie dashed off.

"Hey, no fair," Oreville gave chase.

## 12

"Hush! Hush up and be quiet a minute," the bearded man said good-naturedly. "I know y'all anxious to git the sack race started. But first I want to introduce Mistah and Missus Essex Dawson. Mistah Dawson owns the Dawson mattress factory. He's donating two pairs of tickets to the Juneteenth dance to the first woman and the first man to cross the finish line. So, how about a big hand for Mistah Dawson and his beautiful wife, Betty!"

The couple wore matching brown and white cowboy outfits and pearl-colored cowboy hats.

"Howdy, everybody," Essex waved his hand like a politician at a rally. "It's a pleasure seeing all of you good people. I won't bore you with any lengthy remarks. Let the race begin!"

"And may the best man and woman win!" Betty's brown eyes sparkled.

"Everybody to the starting line," the bearded man ordered. "Remember, if you fall on your butt, just jump right back on up. On your mark! Ready. . . . Set. . . . Git!"

The race was fun for Lynn and Shelby; hopping and bumping into each other, they kept falling down. Odilia, who was not athletically inclined, quit at the halfway point. Bootsy, who jumped to an early lead, tired in the home stretch and finished in sixth place. Oreville, viewing the race as a challenge and an opportunity, skipped flawlessly. Mattie simply tried too hard and finished out of the running.

"I won. I won," Oreville greeted Mattie as she crossed the finish line. "Now you have to accompany me to the dance."

"But I said I wasn't going to the dance with *anybody*."

"Mattie, you don't want me to waste the extra ticket, do you? Come on, be a sport."

"Well, all right. I guess."

## 13

The vanilla-, taffy-, chocolate- and licorice-colored audience who attended the Juneteenth dance that evening represented all social strata of the community. They lined up for drinks in the congested lobby of the auditorium, occupied all available tables and jammed the smoky balcony. The men wore black and white. Most of the women, by some intuitive means of communication, had decided to wear pink, yellow or red, which imbued the spring rite with a regal glow.

Louis Armstrong's penguin-suited band, minus its leader, played *Rockin' Chair*.

Bradford Sykes sat at the center of the Knights' table. His blue-eyed wife, Nancy, sat next to him. Her pink gown emphasized her yellowish-white shoulders. Gabriel Pettaway and Inez Chambers returned to the Knights' table and sat next to Mordecai. Thelma Jenkins, whose low-necked, apple-candy-red dress exposed the crevices of her bosom, sat next to James. In a heightened state of bliss, James puffed on his cigar.

"You ready for another cigar, Gabriel?" Bradford asked.

"Don't mind if I do."

"Get one for me, James," Thelma urged.

"Would you like one, young lady?" Bradford offered Thelma a cigar.

"I'm ever so much obliged, thank you. My brothers smoke them but I never tried one before," Thelma lit the cigar and took a deep draw. She commenced to cough so hard that James had to pat her on the back.

Emma Pace, seated between Punchy and St. Elmo, enjoyed Thelma's discomfort.

"That's what she gets," she whispered.

Out on the dance floor, Oreville Hunter tried to overcome his lack of rhythm with sheer energy. His partner, Mattie, adorned in a ruby-red gown with its bodice shaped by the sly suggestion of her bosom, flowed with an elegant ease.

The penguin-suited band ended the song.

"I'll dance better after I warm up," Oreville guided Mattie to their table where they joined Sugarbear, Coreen, Lynn, Shelby Staggs, Curtis and Beatrice Jollivette and Odilia Toy.

Dr. Edgar Hill and his wife, Helen, took a hearty leave from a table of African American Creoles and made their way through the crowd.

"Helen, over here," Betty Dawson called. She and Essex shared a table with Thaddeus Stier and his flirtatious young wife.

"Helen, your gown is so lovely," Betty said.

"Edgar, what do you have to say now?" Essex Dawson chuckled. "My boy, James Pettaway, hit that ball higher than the new Empire State Building they just opened in New York City. *I* predicted that we'd beat you Odd Fellows."

"*True*. But *you* neglected to back up your prediction with a wager," Edgar responded.

"My mind's eye told me to bet you, too."

"I'm certain that a rematch can be arranged on my end. However, I'll understand if you Knights are afraid to try your luck on the field again."

"Luck. Are you kidding? You Odd Fellows got yourself a rematch," Essex said. "This time, we're going to do some *serious* betting."

"Punchy, did you speak to Noah about what I asked you to?" Emma asked.

"No. But I was going to get around to it. Man, Emma has a girlfriend whose got big eyes for you and . . ."

"That's *not* what you suppose to say," Emma protested.

"That's the gist of what you told me," Punchy laughed.

"I'll tell him myself," Emma said. "Noah, I have a friend, Odilia Toy. You met her that night at the church. Punchy said you'd like to travel one day. Odilia would, too. She's also serious-minded like you. We thought it might be a good idea to visit her table during intermission. To see what else you two have in common, so to speak."

Thaddeus Stier dropped by for a visit.

"Hey, Mordecai," Bradford Sykes puffed on his cigar. "How about letting Mr. Stier hear your account of the bottom of the ninth of our game today?"

"Ah right, then. I'll do it again," Mordecai flashed a smile. "Like you said, it was the last inning, our last chance at bat. The Odd Fellows were leading nine to seven.

I came up first and finagled a walk. Punchy sent me to third with a double just inside the third base chalk.

But their pitcher struck out the next two Knights with the white blurs that he threw.

Our loyal fans wailed and prayed in the stands. Their fears grew and grew.

But us Knights were cool as mountain dew.

For James Pettaway was wiggling his bat in the pew.

'Strike one!' the umpire yelled. 'Ball one! Ball two!' 'Strike two!'

'Ball three!' the umpire filled the count.

Then, the pitcher reared back and a haze of smoke he threw.

James waited until the last second or two and swung his bat graceful and true.

Away, high over the center fielder's head the white dot flew. And even as I speak, it's probably still spinning and climbing into the blue."

"Wonderful, wonderful," Thaddeus clapped his hands.
"How about a toast, men?" Bradford called. "To the Knights. True champions!"
"To the Knights. True champions!"

Louis Armstrong, trumpet tucked under his arm, walked down the hallway and stood behind the backstage curtain. He buttoned his tuxedo and signaled the pianist. The band established a lively rhythm. White handkerchief dangling from his trumpet, Louis walked onto the stage playing *Struttin' with Some Barbecue*.

The audience issued waves of ecstatic thrills and scrambled to the dance floor. Gabriel led Inez on a fluid stroll. Sugarbear, who was good at what he did, guided Mattie with ease. Emma and Punchy got down and dirty. Lynn and Shelby bounced about. Odilia tried but failed to follow Oreville's awkward steps. Essex and Betty did their thing with style. Edgar and Helen made smooth moves. Mordecai coolly off-timed with a yellow-coated cutie. The white-suited James, twirling gracefully, spun Thelma in a series of elegant whirls.

A beautiful barrage of lyrical notes flew from Louis' trumpet. From the belly of the dance floor, a group of dancers started moaning and groaning. Another group moaned and groaned. And another. And another. And another. Louis, sensing that the audience was too hot for him not to cool down, signaled his band. Swinging lively, they played softer and softer. Softer and softer. Softer and softer:

Until you could hear the rustling of skirts and the pitter-patter of feisty feet.

"James, I saw Mattie dancing with her father," Mordecai said as they returned to the Knights' table. "What's with you and her, anyway? Somebody said you clowned her that night at the church because she turned you down when you asked her to this dance."

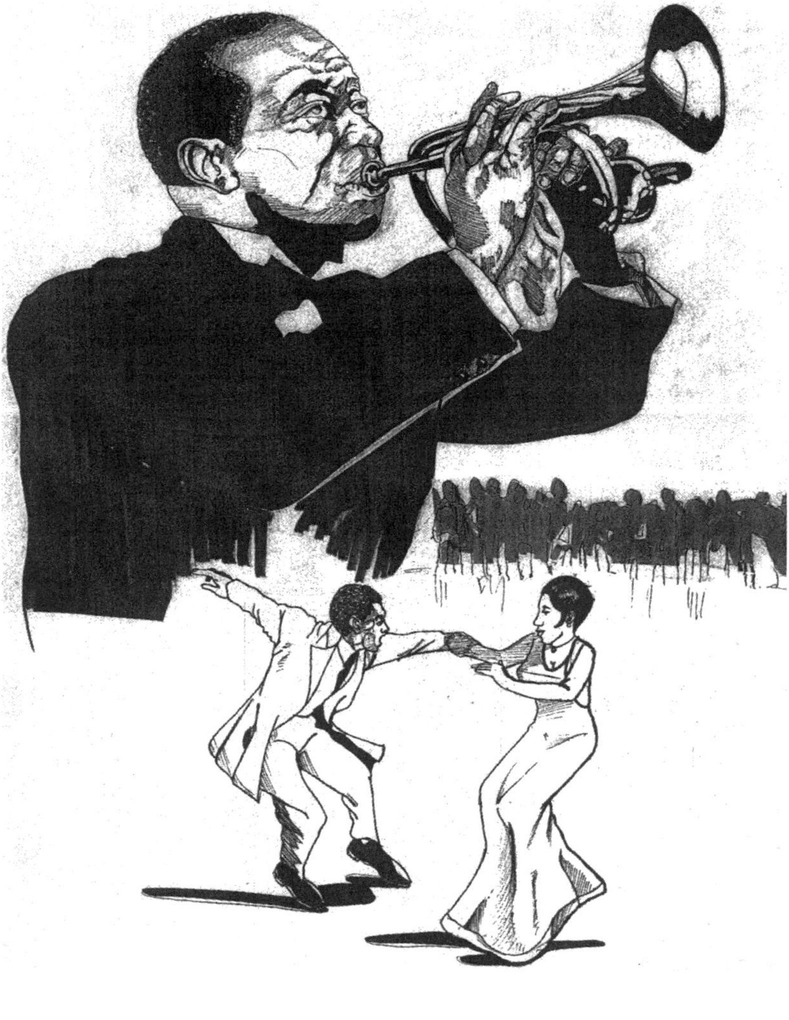

"Mattie said she wasn't coming with anybody. She didn't exactly turn me down."

"*It's* a thin line."

"It's a *line,* nevertheless. I'm still gonna make her my girl some day."

After Louis Armstrong played *West End Blues,* he announced the intermission.

"Now for the task at hand. Come on," Emma led Punchy and St. Elmo away from the table.

"James, I'll meet y'all in the parking lot," Mordecai giggled. "Right now, I must go witness a lamb being led to the slaughter, willingly."

Odilia and St. Elmo sat at the table. Emma, Punchy and Mordecai, standing a respectful distance away, watched and gossiped.

"If your name is Oscar," Odilia crossed her legs. "Why do your friends call you Noah?"

"You see, I read a lot of different books, magazines and newspapers. By my always being informed, the fellows started seeking my knowledge. Mordecai began calling me Noah Webster, after the guy who wrote the dictionary. Before long, it was just plain Noah."

"Emma said you wanted to travel some day," Odilia uncrossed her legs. "Where would you like to go first?"

"Gosh, I'd like to visit so many places. Especially Harlem. The sight of so many black folks at one time must be something wonderful to see," St. Elmo paused.

Odilia's eager eyes implored him to continue.

# 14

Stars, winking and blinking, dazzled the constellation. Dozens of celebrants caroused in and out of the rows of cars that circled the auditorium. Some cars idled with their headlights on, which created an air of mystery and intimacy. Lizzie's doors were flung open wantonly. Inez, who sat in the front with Gabriel, lit a cigarette. A long-legged Knight and his red-packaged date partied in the rear seat. James, seated on the front fender, passed a bottle of gin to Thelma, who was wedged between his legs.

"Ooooh-wheee! This stuff is strong," Thelma wiped her mouth with the back of her hands. "All it don't kill, it'll surely fatten."

"It looks like the intermission's about over," Gabriel hopped from the car. "People are going back inside."

Mordecai and Punchy arrived.

"James, didn't you say Mattie wasn't coming to the dance with anybody?" Mordecai asked.

"Yeah."

"Emma told Punchy and me that the schoolteacher brought Mattie to the dance tonight. Didn't she, Punchy?"

"She sure did."

"Hell, James is with *me*," Thelma returned the bottle to James. "He don't care who she came with. Do you, honey?"

"*Dang tooting.* I don't care who she's with."

"Let's go back in," Gabriel led the way.

James hesitated.

"What's the matter, honey? Ain't you coming?" Thelma asked.

"Not right now. Go on back inside with the others."

"But, honey."

"No, go on. I'll be there in a minute."

"Well, all right," Thelma departed.

James felt a strong urge to cry but he forced it back. An empty silence prevailed. Within the silence, he heard the shrill, chirping sounds of crickets, the staccato strains from Louis' trumpet and his own heartbeat. He raised the bottle and drank.

*Why did she have to come to the dance with somebody when she said she wasn't coming with anybody? Now I'm out here whilst my heart is back at the dance with her.*

Mind muddled, he easily convinced himself that Mattie had

lied to him. His feelings dissolved into anger. He decided that he'd been unjustly separated from something essential to his existence, something rightfully his. Feeling an acute sense of loss and betrayal, he drained the bottle and flung it high into the night.

## 15

Emma, Punchy, St. Elmo, Odilia, Oreville and Mattie stood near the Knights' table.

James appeared and brushed Oreville aside.

"Hey buddy, watch it," Oreville growled.

James, ignoring Oreville, got in Mattie's face.

"Why, Mattie?" he demanded. "Why did you lie to me?"

"What are you talking about?" Mattie asked.

"Buddy, what's your problem?" Oreville snapped.

"Stay out of this, you," James barked.

"The lady obviously doesn't know what you're talking about," Oreville snarled. "Move on like a good sport."

"I said stay out of this," James pushed Oreville in the chest.

Caught by surprise, Oreville spilled over a chair. Gabriel bear-hugged James. Oreville sprang to his feet. St. Elmo and Punchy jumped between the two rivals.

"Yeah, I pushed you," James boasted. "You going to do something about it, or do you have sugar in your tank?"

"Buddy, I don't know what your problem is but it's obvious that you need a spanking," Oreville took off his coat. "Let's carry this matter outside so I can accommodate you."

"You ain't said nothing," James also took off his coat.

## 16

A crowd followed James and Oreville along the path that paralleled the auditorium.

Gabriel started Lizzie.

"So the battery won't go dead," he explained as he flicked on the headlights.

James and Oreville stepped into the glaring headlights. Skillfully parrying Oreville's roundhouse right, James stung his forehead with a stiff jab. Oreville countered with a right hand that landed just below James' left ribcage with a thud. In one motion, James ducked Oreville's overhand right and countered with a neat left hook that snapped Oreville's head back.

They circled each other.

James faked a punch.

Oreville threw a thunderous right cross. The blow, which surprised James, caught him smack dab in the middle of his chin. He crumbled awkwardly to the ground, face up, lights out.

The scene scintillated; next, it sizzled; then it got nasty. Thelma and Mattie exchanged wicked blows. It took Gabriel, St. Elmo and three other Knights to keep Mordecai away from Oreville. Emma and Punchy attempted to separate Mattie and Thelma and all four tumbled to the ground. Odilia, on the verge of tears, ran back and forth reminding everyone that they were Christians.

Only James, who, lights back on, sat on the ground watching and the purring Lizzie maintained their composure.

# 17

When the Mount Calvary Board of Elders heard about the scuffle at the Juneteenth dance, it embarrassed and angered them. They summoned those church members involved to appear before them in the auditorium after the service. Minister C.C. Carridine, Thaddeus Stier, Meldrick Merryweather, Bradford Sykes and Reba Hightower occupied the pulpit. James, Gabriel, Punchy, Oreville, Odilia, Emma and Mattie sat in the front row.

"These young people have already admitted their guilt," Minister C.C. Carridine said. "Perhaps this would be a good time to retire to my chambers and consider their just punishment."

"A common brawl at the social event of the year," Reba adjusted her glasses. "What is this younger generation coming to?"

"Oh, I don't know," Thaddeus Stier said. "The majority of them are fine young men."

"Yes, and as to the young ladies," Bradford Sykes added. "They come from good stock."

"I'll be forty-six years old on my next birthday, if I live and don't anything happen," Meldrick Merryweather leaned forward in his seat. "Not to excuse any devilish acts but I remember my youth as a time of playful shenanigans. And more than a few foolish judgments along the way, I'm not proud to say. But I learned from my youthful errors. They made me a better man."

"In my opinion, we should expel every single one of them, lickety-split," Reba hissed.

"Come, let us discuss their punishment in my chamber," C.C. Carridine led the way.

Reba Hightower's remark about expulsion stunned the young people. To be expelled from church was like being driven from the Garden of Eden.

James, Gabriel and Punchy sat rigid. Oreville, face distraught, slouched. Emma cupped her sorrowful face with her hands. Odilia noisily sniffled into her handkerchief.

Mattie felt a rush of self-loathing. Hands clammy, she stared at the floor. She blamed herself for everything.

The elders returned.

"We have reached a decision," C.C. Carridine announced. "Emma. Punchy. Odilia. Mattie. I know you and your families well. Your conduct was inexcusable. We are not going to tolerate it."

Each one of the minister's words hemmed Mattie into a smaller and smaller emotional space. Breathing in short, powerful bursts, she couldn't stop panting.

"Mr. Hunter, Mr. Stier tells me that you come from an excellent family. Why a fine schoolteacher like you would act the hooligan is beyond my comprehension. As for you Pettaway brothers, I can't rightly say I know you. But your parents speak highly of you. Brother Sykes also spoke well of you. Be that as it may, you have all admitted your guilt. Therefore, it is our judgment that you shall . . ."

"Reverend Carridine, excuse me for interrupting you, please," an emotional implosion hurled Mattie to her feet. "It's all my fault. I said I wasn't going to the dance with anybody. I wound up going with Oreville. I'm so ashamed. If I had kept my word, the whole thing wouldn't have happened. Reverend Carridine, I just can't sit here and watch my friends' lives be destroyed because of me."

"There, there, daughter. No one's life is going to be destroyed. Brother Merryweather spoke well when he reminded us of the ways of youth. Youth can be such a devilish taskmaster. Still, be that as it may, it is our judgment that each of you be placed under a month of silence. You may continue to attend church but there will be no communications between you and other church members during that period. Is that understood?"

## 18

Early evening stars winked and blinked.

Mattie approached the Edgewater mansion. Over the years, she had established herself as an even-tempered individual, not one to easily display her emotions. Her outburst at the meeting with the Board of Elders surprised her friends. Her subsequent behavior amazed them. After all, who'd have thought that after the way James made such a fool of his self at the Juneteenth dance that she would end up falling for him? But such was the case. That James *actually* fought over her flattered her. Thus aroused, a new raging sensation inflamed her.

Linda Edgewater, seated at her desk, winked at her image in the mirror. Her blue gown exposed her plump white shoulders. She coated her fleshy lips with lipstick.

"You ready to tie this for me, my love?" Forrest Edgewater

offered his tie. The owner of a successful bag factory, he had ash-white skin and golden-brown hair graying at his temple. "Oh, before I forget." He put a sparkling necklace around Linda's neck.

"Forrest, it's so expensive. You shouldn't have."

"You do it more than justice."

Mattie knocked on the door.

"Come in," Linda called.

"I came to let you know that I'm here, Miz Edgewater."

"Good. Did Coreen tell you why I needed you tonight?"

"Yes ma'am. She said you wanted me to help serve dinner."

"Mr. Edgewater and I are celebrating our twentieth wedding anniversary. We've invited three other couples to join us. Come, let's get you a uniform."

Mattie served hors d'oeuvres. Melody Clemmons, Miriam Dobson and Amy Scottsdale praised and appraised Linda's necklace.

"Tell me, John," Forrest Edgewater swallowed an oyster, savoring the aftertaste. "What do you make of that nasty dispute between Ford and his Detroit workers?"

"It's directly related to the nation's chronic economic crisis, I'm afraid," John Clemmons answered. "Though it grieves me to admit it, some of my fellow bankers are exploiting the situation. They are foreclosing farm mortgages with the zeal with which our forefathers once collected Indian scalps."

"All is not lost. We have a Republican, Herbert Hoover, in the White House," Wilson Scottsdale, the town's leading stockman, chuckled. "Even though he continues to try to hoodwink us into believing that there is a chicken and a Ford around the corner for everybody."

"On the other hand," Dr. Malcolm Dobson pinched his jaunty, brick-red mustache. "You have two Democrat governors, Huey Long and Franklin D. Roosevelt, engaged in a debate about whether proper etiquette requires you to crumble corn pone into your potlikker or dunk it."

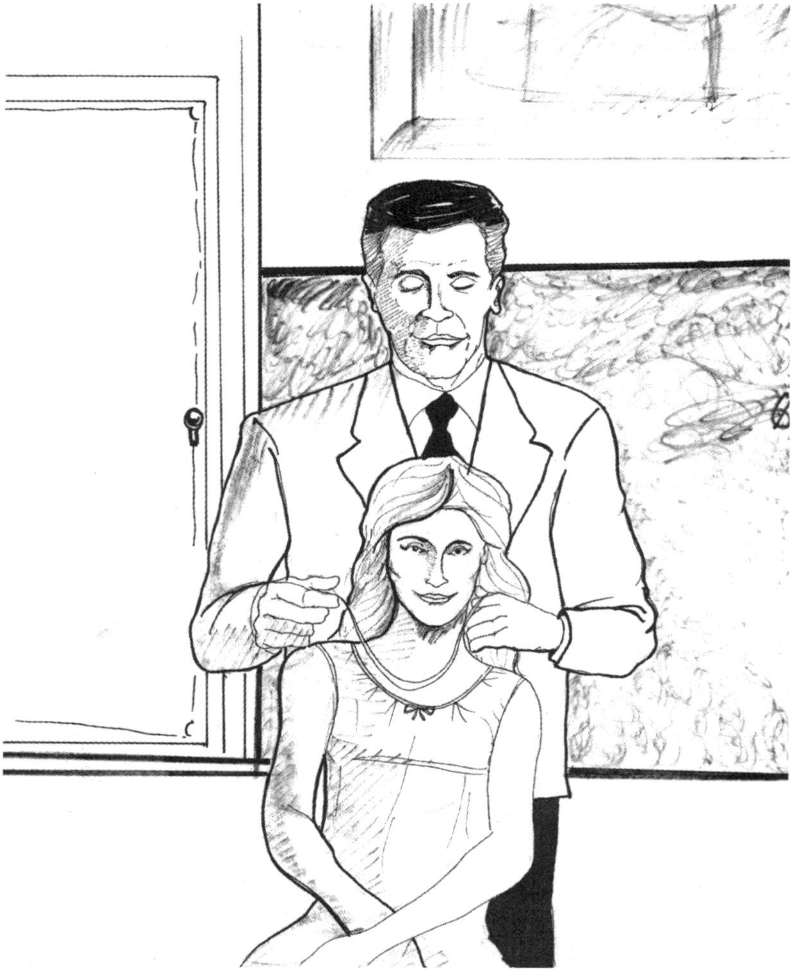

The glittering assembly, seated around the silver-bedecked table, dined festively.

"Wilson, what do you make of the latest poll that shows that Huey Long's 'Complete the Works' ticket is trailing by fifteen points?" Malcolm asked.

"Polls this early in the campaign are meaningless," Wilson Scottsdale replied. "You can't count the kingfish out at this juncture. Not by a long shot."

"If Long's ticket wins, we all face a great danger," Dr. Dobson said. "He's already been elected to the United States Senate. If his handpicked bunch of cronies win, there'll be no end to the mischief he'll be able to create."

"Give the man some credit," Wilson replied. "He gave us free schoolbooks, new bridges and thousands of miles of paved roads."

"But at what a great cost," Forrest laughed. "Admit it, Wilson. Huey Long has developed graft into a goddamn craft."

The men retired to the drawing room for their after-dinner cigars.

"Wilson, I heard a joke about your boy the other day," Forrest said. "Huey Long made a bet with a nigger and a Jew to see who could stay the longest in a room with a polecat. The Jew went in and stayed five minutes. The nigger stayed ten minutes. Huey went in and thirty seconds later the polecat ran out."

They were still laughing when Mattie entered and announced that their presence was requested in the living room. They took a few hasty puffs and doused their cigars.

"Now for a special treat. Our daughters will play their violins for you," Linda gave way to her four lovely daughters, who performed a naïve but spirited rendition of Mozart's *Jupiter*.

# 19

"Wake up! Wake up!" Aaron Pettaway shook James.

"Huh?" James sat up.

"Git up, boy. Your ride is gonna be here in a minute."

"I'm not going to work. Our rematch with the Odd Fellows is today."

"With the white folks having a Depression and most of our people struggling to put food in their bellies, how dare you miss work for some daggone baseball game. Don't you know it's lucky you even got a job? You penny slick and dollar thick."

Later that morning, Gabriel and James polished Lizzie.

"James, what happened between you and Poppa this morning? Momma said he got on you for not going to work."

"*You penny slick and dollar thick*,'" James mimicked Aaron.

"You only work a half day on Saturdays. You could've made it to the game on time."

"No, no. Big Sam might have made me work overtime," James replied. "I couldn't take any chances. I told the guy I ride with to tell him I'm sick."

"You changed your mind about not coming to the dance tonight?"

"Nope."

"I can't believe you still avoiding Mattie. What's the matter, you scared of her?"

"Mattie don't scare nobody. I'm going skipping with Thelma Jenkins tonight."

## 20

That afternoon, Mattie dressed for the baseball game. Knowing that she would be seeing James, she surrendered to the cozy smile spreading itself within her.

## 21

Bradford Sykes conferred with the Knights' pitcher. It was the bottom of the sixth inning. There was one out. The pitcher had just given up a hit that tied the score and loaded the bases.

"You've done your best but it's time to give that arm a rest,"

Bradford said. "Let's go with another pitcher." He beckoned St. Elmo from the bull pen.

Mattie, Emma, Odilia and Inez, having already died and lived several times during the course of the game, sat behind the Knights' dugout.

"Here you go, Noah," Bradford gave St. Elmo the ball. "Don't give the batter anything to hit but a lot of air." He trotted back to the dugout.

St. Elmo retired the next Odd Fellow batter with three straight pitches.

Out in center field, James, who was aware of Mattie's presence, found it difficult to concentrate on the game.

The Odd Fellows' powerful first baseman, swinging two bats, pranced to the plate.

"Come on, Noah. Chunk some smoke," Mordecai sang.

St. Elmo kicked up his leg and threw a fastball that the first baseman hit to center field.

James awkwardly drifted under the ball and transformed a routine fly into a difficult catch.

Mattie clasped her hands over her eyes like she was at the Colosseum and she couldn't bear to witness the lions mangling the Christians anymore.

The inning was over. The game gave way to the conventional seventh-inning stretch.

"That's the way to go, Knights!" Mattie was in a heightened state of ecstasy. "Now let's score some runs."

Essex Dawson and his wife, Betty, sat next to Dr. Edgar and Helen Hill. Surrounded by their colorfully-dressed entourage, they illuminated the grandstand behind home plate.

"My, Essex, that was certainly bold," Dr. Edgar Hill adjusted his ascot. "Betting that my boys wouldn't score against your new pitcher. With the bases loaded, mind you."

"Essex, we're going to the concession stand," Betty Dawson wore white-rimmed dark glasses. "Shall I bring you anything?"

"Yes, doll. A Coke," Essex Dawson replied.

"What about you, Edgar?" Helen styled a silvery-white blouse whose open collar exposed her flawless, copper-brown neck. "Do you want something?"

"A Coke will suffice for me, also, my love."

"Helen, the treat is on your husband," Essex laughed. "Edgar, give my wife the twenty dollars you *owe* me."

James, seated in the dugout, wiped his face with a towel.

"What happened on that ball?" Gabriel asked. "I thought you was going to drop it for sure."

"I just got a bad jump on it, that's all."

"Man, you'd better wake up. You act like you sleepwalking out there."

"I'm all right, don't worry," James said. In the aftermath of his Juneteenth fiasco, he acted like he'd erased all traces of Mattie from his memory. But the truth rested at the opposite end of the spectrum. Mattie lived inside him, along with the organs, thoughts and feelings that composed his life.

It was the bottom of the ninth. The scoreboard read: "Odd Fellows 18, Knights 19." Two outs. The Odd Fellows had men on second and third. Their first baseman, who had already hit two home runs, stood in the batter's box.

"Come on, Noah," Mordecai chirped. "Hum that pea! He can't hit what his eyes don't see!"

The first baseman smacked St. Elmo's first pitch high and deep into center field.

James heard the gasps from the fans. He saw vividly how clear the sky was. Catching sight of the whispering white ball, he gave chase. Leaping, he extended his glove; simultaneously, he felt a thud and found himself in a brilliant but friendly darkness.

Mattie, seeing James crash into the wall, put her hands over her eyes again and gasped.

"Mattie, he'll be all right, don't worry," Odilia tried to sound optimistic.

"Yeah, he's going to be all right, girl," Inez promised.

"Look," Emma exclaimed. "Two men carrying a stretcher are running to get him."

## 22

That evening, a stylish crowd was already getting down seriously when Gabriel, Inez and James entered the Knights' mansion.

"Gabriel, you and Inez go on," James advised. "I'm going to sit in the lounge."

"James, you want some company?"

"No thanks, Inez. I'll be all right," James went into the lounge and sat on a divan. A fire blazed in the fireplace. He still felt a distant wooziness but the vibrant pink-white sounds inside his brain had finally ceased resounding.

Mordecai sat down beside him.

"Man, that was one hell of a catch you made to win the game for us. They had to pry the ball from your glove. You badder than Peter Weater-Straw, the devil's son-in-law. By the way, Inez told Mattie you was out here in the lounge."

"So?"

"What's your story? You afraid to come inside?"

"Nope. As a matter of fact, I was just getting ready to come in."

"What did you decide to do about your other woman? Man, don't look at me like I'm crazy. Wasn't you supposed to go dancing with Thelma Jenkins tonight?"

"Goll dang," James slapped his own forehead.

The band jumped the blues. Mattie sat alone at the table, oblivious to the stylishly-dressed dancers stomping and romping about the dance floor. Having decided that things between her and James couldn't continue as they were, she was determined to apply some clarity and sanity to the situation. She'd thought about what to say to him but now, knowing that he was in the lounge, she felt herself wavering.

The music stopped. Gabriel, Inez, Punchy, Emma, St. Elmo and Odilia returned to the table. Mattie, feeling embarrassed and conspicuous, tried to imagine what they were thinking, if they were feeling sorry for her.

"Excuse me," Mattie said to no one in particular and left the table. She met James and Mordecai in the hallway. Mordecai excused himself.

"James, do you feel all right?"

"I'm fine."

"Golly, James. We go to the same church. At least we can be friends."

"I don't want to be your friend."

"Can I ask you why?"

"I just don't."

"Let's go on the veranda," Mattie took James' hand. "Come on, it'll be nice outside."

The glow from the moon tinted the veranda with a romantic hue. A playful breeze spread autumn smells.

"Tell me," Mattie playfully poked James' stomach.

"Tell you what?"

"Why you won't be my friend."

"Because," James searched for the right words. "My heart is set on us going together."

"Couldn't we go together and be friends, too?"

"I don't know. I never had a girlfriend before."

"Me neither. I mean, I never had a boyfriend before. I'm willing to try, if you are. O.K.?"

"If it means I get to kiss you."

Mattie's eyes sparkled. Her emotions swelled. She gave him her lips.

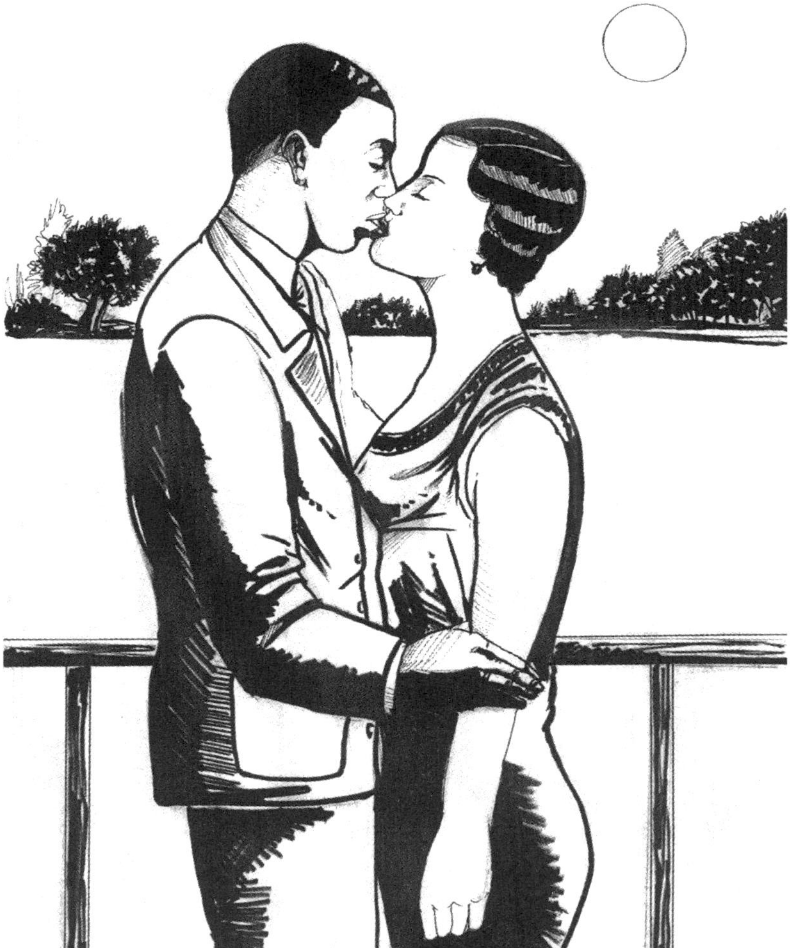

# Of Duos and Triangles

ABOUT A MONTH LATER, THE WORD about James' dramatic catch at the baseball game reached Big Sam's ears. At lunchtime, seated beneath a tree, he smiled anticipatorily.

"Pettaway, bring your lunch bucket over here," he beckoned.

James saw no danger in the request. This was not the first time that Big Sam had singled him out to talk to. He left the crap game and joined the squatty straw boss.

"How you feeling today, James?"

"Just great. Like I could go the distance with the heavyweight champ, Max Schmeling."

"That's how it is when you young. When I was your age, I didn't know what tired meant. I'd work all day and raise Cain all night. In them days we niggahs did anything us could to git by, toting, digging, lifting. My first job was carrying sacks of garbage on my back for ten cents a day. I made it to where I am today because I learned how to git along with white folks with this," Big Sam touched his own forehead.

"I learned how to git along with niggahs with this," he demonstrated a massive fist. "I see a lot of myself in you. You got a lot of mother wit. That's why I done took such interest in you. If you ever learn to control your brassiness, one day you might get to be a boss like me."

James squeezed his eyes with his palm to conceal his disdain.
"I heard about that catch you made at that baseball game, on the very day you sent word you was sick. Hush! Don't even try to fix your mouth to tell a lie. I got you by your nuts now, young niggah. So, no more complaining from here on in about working overtime. Ever. You can bottle that mess. From this day forward, you gonna be working under my total command. I'm gonna work you 'til *I* sweat."

# 2

Emma Pace, standing at the window, searched the darkness.

St. Elmo and Odilia sat on the sofa.

"Hmmm," St. Elmo read a newspaper article. "Satchel Paige and some all-stars from the Negro League are playing baseball in Cuba this winter. '*Cannonball Redding, Home Run Johnson, Showboat Thomas, Cool Papa Bell, Schoolboy Griffin, Turkey Stearnes and Josh Gibson.*'"

Odilia nodded her head as if St. Elmo had just recited a passage from the Gospel.

Mattie entered and served tea to her friends from a black-lacquered tray.

"Mattie, is James bringing Punchy with him when he comes to pick us up?"

"From not knowing, I can't rightly say."

"Here comes Punchy now," Emma ran and opened the front door. "Hi, honeybunch."

They remained in the doorway; hidden from view, they eyed each other covetously. Emma and Punchy had consummated their relationship during the aftermath of the Juneteenth brawl. In those days, sex outside of marriage constituted a sin. Vowing themselves to secrecy, they were discreet, nocturnal and clandestine, which added even more oomph to their youthful sinning.

"What made you late?" Emma cooed. "I was worried about you."

"Everything's okey-dokey. At the last minute, I decided to go back to the jewelry store."

"Oh, Punchy, you're so sweet."

They kissed.

James eased Lizzie to a stop in the Johnsons' driveway. His courtship with Mattie was proceeding in a merry way. He'd squired her to a rodeo. They'd had Sunday dinner at each other's homes. Mattie stood in the partially-opened doorway. When he saw her, blood raced through his veins; his entire being felt effervescent. Mattie's eyes sparkled. She felt a strange tremor within her. Her heartbeat titillated. They exchanged hushed honey helloes and joined their friends.

"Sorry to be late, folks. Big Sam made me work overtime again," James looked dapper in his new maroon beret.

"It's no big deal," St. Elmo gave James a pat on the back. "The carnival stays open late."

Emma nudged Punchy.

"Oh, right," Punchy brought a glittery engagement ring from his pocket and slipped it on Emma's finger. "This is it, everybody. Me and Emma are officially engaged."

# 3

The night air was as serene and soothing as a spiritual. A brightly-lit Ferris wheel twirled in the distance. Parked cars and buggies clogged both sides of the road. After a futile search for a parking space, James let his companions out at the entrance and parked Lizzie some distance away.

At the ticket booth counter, St. Elmo pushed six quarters toward a pair of coarse white hands with knotted blue veins. Cacophonous carnival cries resonated in the illuminated night.

"I got the ducats," St. Elmo waved the tickets as James came their way.

Weaving through the crowd, the couples made their way to the merry-go-round.

"I thought this was suppose to be a chocolate evening," Punchy observed the three European American couples standing in front of the fortune-teller's tent. "Ain't this suppose to be our night?"

"You know these white folks do anything they choose to," St. Elmo said. "We get one night out of the week to attend the carnival, a Thursday night to boot and they invade it. But just let one of us even peep through the fence on one of their nights and they want to lynch somebody."

"I'm telling everybody in advance," Mattie announced. "The merry-go-round ride is going to be my first and last ride tonight."

The couples got off the merry-go-round and huddled for a parley. After agreeing to rendezvous at the Ferris wheel, the gents went their way.

The ladies strolled to the fortune-teller's tent. Emma entered first and emerged several minutes later with a bemused expression on her face. Odilia went next. In due time, she came out with a smile on her face.

"Well, here goes nothing," Mattie entered the tent.

An orange-colored light bulb, suspended in midair, cast bogey-shaped shadows.

"Sit, pretty one," the middle-aged woman spoke with a sultry Mediterranean accent. Her wheat-colored fingers looked like they could squeeze the very truth from her crystal ball. "I have already foretold the future of your two friends."

When Mattie exited the fortune-teller's tent, Odilia asked her what she had been told.

"I can't believe it," Mattie answered. "She knew all about me. She even knew about James. She said there was a dark, handsome man in my life."

"She told me and Odilia the exact same thing, the heifer," Emma grumbled.

"Careful, Emma," Odilia whispered. "You don't want to

trifle with Gypsies. They know too many secrets. Mattie, did she mention anything to you about ships?"

"Yes, she said she saw me surrounded by a lot of ships."

"That's what she told us, too. Didn't she, Emma?"

"Un-huh. But you know what the old folks say," Emma scoffed. "*'Believe only half of what you see. None of what you hear.'*"

"Right this way, folks! Right this way! Just ten cents! Hit the coon and win a cigar!" the scraggly-voiced barker called. Behind him, at about three quarters of the distance between the pitcher's mound and home plate, a bull's eye had been painted on a square canvas. The center circle of the bull's eye was cut out. Within the empty space, a man with oil-black skin shifted his head back and forth, a devilish sneer on his squirrel-like face.

"Hit the coon and win a cigar!"

St. Elmo, Punchy and James stopped to watch.

A man with a sculptured goatee hurled the baseball dead into the center of the bull's eye. At the last moment the squirrel-like face ducked the ball and immediately reappeared, the devilish sneer still on his face.

"Come on, guys," Punchy wasn't impressed. "I feel like smoking a cigar." He led the way to the ticket booth.

Chance Mullins and his twin cousins, Ted and Jed Ray, walked several paces behind James and his friends. Chance wore a threadbare, tight-fitting yellow shirt that emphasized his massive chest and muscular biceps. The twins were thin and blond. Ted wore a faded blue shirt and red suspenders. Jed sported a white cowboy hat.

"How many throws do you want?" the portly ticket seller asked.

"Three, sir," Punchy reached into his pocket.

"Boy, didn't anybody ever learn you to keep out of a white man's way?" Chance bumped Punchy aside and took his place at the window.

"Ted, betcha a nickel I can hit that nigger before you do," Jed boasted.

James, Punchy and St. Elmo studied their opposite numbers: farmers, out for a little sport but dangerous because their favorite sport was baiting blacks. They quit the scene.

The couples left the Ferris wheel and made their way to the roller coaster. Mattie, true to her word, refused to participate.

"I'll stay with you, Mattie," James volunteered.

"Come on, everybody," Emma and the others departed.

"Mattie, why didn't you want to go on the roller coaster?" James asked.

"Because I'm afraid to. I've been afraid of rides ever since I was little," Mattie laughed at herself. "I only went on the merry-go-round to see if I was still afraid. I still am."

While their romance was proceeding in a merry way, there was an underlying tension. This tension was the residue from an unresolved issue between them: making love. The *issue* usually came up whenever they were alone.

"How you like my beret?"

"Turn your head around so I can see. I like it. You look like a real sport."

High above, amid the fearful but delighted shrieks of its occupants, the roller coaster plunged into the darkness.

There was a stand nearby. They walked over and James bought them Cokes.

"Mattie, the last time we talked, you said you would think about it," James alluded to the *issue*. "You decided anything yet?"

"Yes, I decided."

"You did?"

"Yes."

"And?"

Ted, Jed and Chance appeared.

"Boy, who'd you steal that cap from?" Chance demanded.

"Ain't no way a nigger could have a cap like that, unless he stole it," Ted sneered.

"Yeah," Jed grabbed at the beret.
"Mattie! James! What's the matter?" Emma called. She and the others ran their way. "What's going on?"
"What's it to you?" Ted snarled.
"They are friends of mine," Emma replied.
"Yeah, we are all friends," St. Elmo's voice crackled.
"What you white boys want?" Punchy uttered.
"Come on. Let's skedaddle. It ain't worth it," Jed urged.
The three kinsmen, visibly sulking, vanished.

The All-Colored Show occurred in a large, circular, white tent called the Jig Top. It was the carnival's most popular attraction. An equal number of whites and blacks filled the seats. A rope, extending across the middle of the tent, separated the races.

The couples sat near the front.

"Howdy! Howdy! Howdy! Welcome to our show," the master of ceremonies, a black man in blackface, told three corny jokes and introduced an ensemble of male and female dancers who zipped onto the stage and initiated a series of grinds, twists and twirls.

The band played a syrupy rendition of *Old Man River*. The curtain slowly rose, revealing a pastoral setting. There followed a farcical scene in which a male and female performer, aged with makeup, played a farm couple that initially declined their neighbors' request to join in their dancing. Thereafter, some good-natured teasing from their neighbors egged the couple on. They executed a few tenuous dance steps, then a few more and a few more.

"Look at them old-timers get to it," the chubby black man's deep voice made everyone around him laugh and giggle.

"Now, the finale," the master of ceremonies proclaimed. "The Cakewalk!"

Five pairs of dancers pranced onto the stage. The men, dressed in tuxedos and top hats, carried gold-tipped canes. The women wore bonnets and satiny dresses.

The audience howled and cheered.
The men twirled their canes.
The women, strutting their stuff, lifted the hems of their dresses—displaying raspberry petticoats with crocheted edges and fine, brown legs.

After the couples exited the Jig Top, they plotted their next move. Emma wanted to take another ride on the roller coaster. St. Elmo and Odilia decided to join them.
"Y'all know how I feel about rides," Mattie said. "Me and James will get the car and meet you at the front entrance."

Holding hands, Mattie and James followed the pathway.
"Ah, right. Hand over that cap you stole, nigger," Chance's voice demanded.
James and Mattie turned around.
Ted, Jed and Chance looked mean and serious.
"Hand over that cap, nigger."
"We going to make sure it gets back to its rightful owner."
"Yeah."
James decided that the best thing for them to do would be to the fight off the trio and run back to the carnival. But first, he wanted to try Mordecai's trick: "*If you catch a sucker, bump his head*," the one he'd committed to memory that day after the baseball practice.
"Y'all must be new in town," James said matter-of-factly, cool and confident. "If you was, you'd know better than to mess with me."
"What's that you saying?" Chance asked.
"If you lived around here, you'd know who I was."
"Who you think you are?" Ted snapped.
"There's nothing common about me, that's for sure. I'm Mr. Pettaway's number-two boy."
"So what?" Chance demanded.
"Yeah, we never heard of a Mr. Pettaway," Ted jeered.

"I knew y'all wasn't from round here," James laughed. "Everybody in town knows Mr. Pettaway. He runs his own business."

"Damn," Jed exclaimed. "His boss must be some big, important white man down here. Come on, let's skedaddle. It ain't worth it."

"Who you say is your boss?" Chance searched James' face.

"Mr. Aaron Pettaway. Where you say y'all come from?"

"We going to let you go this time, boy," Chance said. "I'm warning you, you better be careful from now on." As he and his kinsmen walked away, he called over his shoulder:

"Tell Mr. Pettaway hello for us."

## 4

James stopped Lizzie in the Johnsons' driveway and cut off the lights.

"James, wasn't you afraid?" Mattie asked.

"Naw. I figured we could fight them off and run back to the circus."

"I was scared to death," said Mattie. "I didn't know you were playing a trick. When you said: *'Y'all must be new in town. If you was, you'd know better than to mess with me,'* I almost died right there on the spot." Mattie laughed.

James stole a sideways glance at Mattie and sighed.

"Mattie, at the circus, you said you had decided," he brought up the *issue*.

"It's all right. I'll do it with you. On *one* condition, I'm only going to do it one time. I just want to see what it feels like. Is it a deal?"

"Yeah, great. It's a deal."

They kissed. Mattie disappeared into the house.

"Goll dang," James exclaimed. "I forgot to ask her when."

# 5

Oreville, seated at his desk, opened his writing pad to the pages he'd written the previous evening. "Dear father," he read out loud. "I hope this letter finds you and mother in good health. I am doing fine. Last week I organized the students into small study groups and I've assigned several of the most advanced ones to help the slower ones. I'll let you know how the experiment turns out.

"The students are so eager to learn. But they are constantly reminded of their lowly position. For instance, last month the seventh graders became excited when the principal announced that they would be getting new textbooks. When the books arrived, we discovered that not only had the white schools used them, they were hopelessly outdated as well. Never in my life have I seen such sadness and disappointment." Oreville made a correction and continued:

"The gubernatorial election is still months away, but the campaign, if it can be called that, has already become an ugly, mud-slinging brawl. Huey Long's 'Complete the Works' ticket leads the polls by a narrow margin. Neither the Republicans nor the Democrats discuss real issues like higher wages for workers and teachers, child labor laws, or legal protection for unions. Instead, they've made patriotism and white supremacy the issue.

Mr. Stier visited me here at the boarding house when he returned from his meeting with A. Philip Randolph. He said Louisiana is one of the poorest, most corrupt states in the Union and by making Negroes the scapegoat, Huey Long and his opponents don't have to address the real issues. Although our people are aware of what's going on, there's nothing they can really do about it at this juncture in time. But they have not lost hope and their spirit remains high. They have one thing that cannot be taken away from them, their deep abiding faith in

God. Religion is the source of their strength, the rock of their existence. That's why they are far more noble than their adversities."

The letter stopped there. Oreville tucked one hand under his armpit and cupped his face with the other. Sighing deeply, he recalled that he'd stopped at that point in his letter because he didn't know what to write about Mattie, who'd become a fixture in his correspondence to his father. He tried to convince himself that the rumor about Mattie and James was false, that his love would find a way to reach her heart. Still reflecting, he picked up his pencil.

"Mattie and I are somewhat distant right now," he wrote. "However, I believe if I am patient, matters will end up in my favor. She'll be worth the wait, I guarantee. She has such potential. As I've written before, sometimes I think I see more in her than she sees in herself.

"By the way," Oreville began a new paragraph. "Do you remember my writing to you about the game of verbal insults that some of our more earthy brothers down here indulge in? It's called the 'dozens.' Anyway, I did some research. The word 'dozen' is a carryover from slavery. They sold strong and healthy slaves individually. Weak and sick slaves were sold by the dozen. A slave who was a part of a dozen was often ridiculed by his fellow slaves."

He paused, reflected and continued writing: "Tell mother she didn't have to remind me that this year will be the first time I won't be home for Thanksgiving. Tell her not to worry. The church is going to hold a drawing to see which family will invite me to their home for Thanksgiving dinner."

# 6

Sanite DiDi rightly laid claim to a lineage that went back to the New Orleans Santeria Queens of the mid 1800's. She was ageless. Her raw-boned face had no eyebrows and no left ear. On

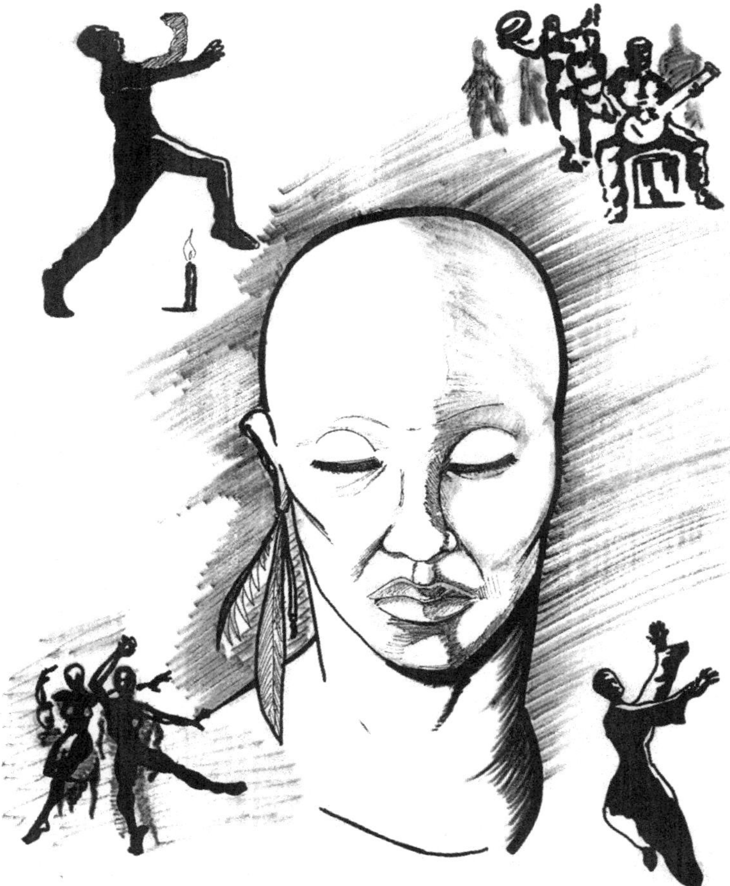

her right ear she wore an earring made from whitened bones and hummingbird wings.

Four flickering candles positioned in the center of the floor cast the room into semi-darkness. Orange-clad men, playing banjoes, drums and tambourines, created music. White-robed women with sublime sable faces slapped their thighs and stomped their feet. They chanted in rich, full-toned voices.

An ebony Adonis, his white shirt soaked with sweat, danced around the candles.

Eyes closed, Sanite DiDi inhaled the music.

Sugarbear experienced a distinctive oneness with his surroundings.

A nubile chanter, mounted by an evil spirit, jerked off her robe. Basking in unabashed nudity, she performed a dance that was supremely spiritual and intoxicatingly iniquitous.

Hard-faced and kind-faced African masks, herbs and animal bones dotted the walls of Sanite DiDi's spirit room. Jesus Christ, painted with pink lips and teary blue eyes, looked down from His cross at the altar. A life-sized statue of St. Andrew served as a silent sentinel.

"You who are with the faithful always," Sanite DiDi prayed to the Yoruba deity, Oshun. "I, your follower true, humbly beseech you to vanquish from this soul all that loves darkness and abhors light." She reached into the folds of her skirt and brought out a dime-sized, furry object that devoured the darkness.

"Your tobi," she pressed the good luck charm into Sugarbear's hand.

"Can I expect a visit from the spirit soon?"

"Who could know?" Sanite DiDi's eyes dilated. "Perchance the demon was only wounded and will return. Perchance your offering was accepted. Perchance not." Voice trembling, she surrendered to the spirit. "Who born of woman can divine His will? We who only serve and wait think pure thoughts. Let the inner vibrations flow. Feel the harmony of His divine oneness."

# 7

Mattie Johnson, Odilia Toy and Emma Pace walked leisurely across the bridge. In a heady mood, they were on their way downtown to shop for clothes to wear to Mordecai's birthday party that night.

"This is a fine kettle of fish," Odilia chatted. "Here I am, feeling like I want to stop this virgin business and me and Noah haven't even reached the kissing stage yet. He's too respectful. That's the trouble. He respects me so much that he won't take advantage of me like he should. Shucks, I'm tired of waiting. You don't become a real woman until you've been with a man."

"Wait a minute, I want to do something," Mattie said. Everything about her was blossoming. The movement of her body was graceful and winsome. She took a penny from her purse, tossed it into the grayish-brown river and silently prayed:

*Please, don't let what I promised to do with James tonight hurt.*

Emma, Odilia and Mattie took the alley that led to the rear and entered through the back door of the dress shop. Even though they'd shopped at the dress shop previously, they held their collective breath. Custom for blacks dictated they couldn't try on a dress before buying it. Once purchased, a dress could not be returned. So when they saw a dress they liked, they held it before a mirror and imagined themselves in it.

A yellow-brown dress caught Odilia's eye but Emma beat her to it. Odilia continued to browse but she kept a watchful eye on the yellow-brown dress. She held her breath and prayed that Emma wouldn't take the dress she wanted.

Emma compared the yellow-brown dress with a red one. She selected the red dress.

"Good. I'll take this one," Odilia grabbed the yellow-brown dress.

"No, wait," Emma protested. "I changed my mind. I want that one."

"Only because I said I wanted it."

"I just can't believe this, Odilia. I've been such a true, loyal friend to you. Mattie, haven't I been her true-blue friend?"

"My name is Bennett. I'm not in it," Mattie, standing before a mirror, held a seal-brown dress in front of her.

When they left the shop, Mattie, Emma and Odilia crossed the street.

"Here's a shoe store," Mattie said.

They stopped to look.

"I wonder how much they cost?" Odilia asked.

"Let's go find out," Emma led the way.

A "FOR COLORED" sign directed them towards the rear door.

"They look awful expensive," Odilia said as they entered.

"Maybe we better wait for somebody to come wait on us," Mattie cautioned.

"We're only looking," Emma picked up a fancy red shoe. "A pair of these would be swell. I wonder if they have my size?"

"I told you niggers before. Niggers ain't allowed to touch any shoes," the elderly white female clerk snatched the shoe from Emma. "You've spoiled it. Now you must buy the pair."

"I only picked it up. My hands ain't dirty," Emma exposed her palms. "See, they're clean."

"Don't you dare talk back. Niggers ain't allowed to touch any merchandise. Now you must buy the pair. It's pure and simple."

The manager appeared. He had a severe expression on his egg-shaped, sand-white face.

"She damaged a pair of shoes," the clerk fingered Emma.

"How much are they?" the manager asked.

"Nine ninety-nine," the clerk replied. "That includes the ten percent discount."

"But they are not even my size," Emma pleaded. "Even if they did fit, I can't afford expensive shoes like them. I don't make that kind of money."

"I'll fetch a policeman. Guard the rear door," the manager rushed out the front door.

The clerk blocked the path to the rear door.

Odilia took a handkerchief from her purse and covered her face.

"*Iway antca ewe ustjay ogo outway ethey otherway eway,*" she whispered.

"Yeah!" Mattie agreed. "Let's *ustjay ogo outway ethey otherway eway!*"

"What's that you gals saying?" the clerk demanded.

"We're saying it's time to git!" Emma said.

The trio scooted out the front door.

# 8

Googobs of people gathered at Mordecai's house to celebrate his birthday. The women wore bright-colored dresses and wide-brimmed hats. The men wore multicolored suits and flamboyant hats. They danced so hard the house positively rocked. Punchy and Emma served the food. Gabriel and Inez played records on the Victrola. St. Elmo and Odilia sat on the couch, looking like an old married couple. A slender young lady with rouged cheeks and red-coated fingernails danced with a nimble young man who held his coat swankily across his arm. His cherry-red suspenders dangled almost to the floor.

Three stylish dandies congregated near the punch bowl, preened peacock proud.

James, holding Mattie's right hand above her head, twirled her through graceful pirouettes as they glided about the dance floor. Grasping her hands, he rocked her back and forth to the rhythm. Sensing the distinctive allure of her body that seemed to be molded into her seal-brown dress, he stole sly glances. When the music stopped, he walked over to Gabriel, who discreetly handed him the key to Lizzie.

The lights went off.

Punchy and Emma brought in a three-layered cake with lighted candles. Amid a chorus of "ohs" and "ahs," Mordecai puffed out the candles.

Mattie and James slipped away.

# 9

James, arm encircling Mattie's naked waist, felt her beneath him. She was a perfume, not an earthly being. He inhaled her essence, which went to his head like costly champagne. Miraculously, he found his way. He heard himself moan. Her scent flushed his loins. James wanted to stop it. But he couldn't. He uttered a primordial cry. In one ephemeral second, he released all the love he knew.

"Goll dang!"

"What is it?"

"Nothing."

"I didn't know it would happen so quick."

"Don't put back on your clothes. It's not over yet."

That he'd spent himself so prematurely surprised and dismayed James. Although he'd never experienced anything similar, he felt certain that his zest would soon return.

They waited.

And waited.

And waited.

"James, it's getting cold. Can I put my clothes back on now?"

"Yes. You can put on your clothes."

## 10

When the communion ceremony ended, most of the churchgoers remained at the church to buy Sunday dinners and to await the results of the drawing.

Oreville Hunter and Reba Hightower walked up the aisle.

"Mr. Hunter, over twenty families submitted their names for the drawing. How does it make you feel to know that so many families want to have you in their home for Thanksgiving dinner?"

"How does it make me feel? I'm humbled by it."

"Yes, sometimes our people's capacity for generosity is truly amazing, especially when they have so little themselves."

Emma, Odilia and Mattie followed the trail that led away from the outhouse to the church.

"Emma, have you and Punchy set a date for your wedding yet?" Mattie asked.

"Not yet. Punchy wants to get married right away. But I'm enjoying my freedom too much right now," Emma answered. "Odilia, I see you brought Noah to church with you today."

"Child, that was none of my doing," Odilia said. "He took it upon himself to come."

"So, how are you two doing?" Mattie asked. "Has he asked you to be his girlfriend yet?"

"No, but last night we finally reached the kissing stage," Odilia smiled. "What about you and James? Are you back together yet?"

"I haven't talked to James in weeks," Mattie answered.

"You know what I always say," Emma said. "Men are like buses. If you miss one, there is always another one coming."

"I don't know about all that," Mattie said. "But I don't plan to sit around waiting for him."

"I'm behind you one hundred percent, Mattie," Odilia said. "I always felt that Oreville Hunter was a better match for you."

Oreville joined the line of churchgoers waiting to buy Sunday dinners.

Emma, Odilia and Mattie arrived.

"And how are you ladies?" Oreville asked.

Mattie, feeling somewhat vulnerable because of her break-up with James, was glad to see Oreville. She opened the conversation by mentioning that Bootsy was already bragging about how good their Thanksgiving program was going to be. Thereafter, whenever there was a lull in the conversation, she returned the conversation to Oreville.

Flattered and encouraged by Mattie's attention, Oreville dared to hope. After they received their dinners, Oreville asked Mattie if he could speak to her.

She nodded and they stepped aside.

"Mattie, can I walk you home after church?"

"I guess so. I'll have to ask my mother."

St. Elmo, Punchy and James sat in the rear of the auditorium.

"James, you sure missed it last night," Punchy commented.

"Yeah, we was all over at Mattie's house, playing whist," St. Elmo said. "We kept looking for you to show up. James, what's happening between you two?"

"I haven't talked to Mattie in weeks," James said. "She's the hardheaded type. I got me some better fish to fry."

"Attention. Attention, everyone," Reba Hightower, toting a brown paper bag, faced the congregation. "It's time for our drawing to see who gets to have our distinguished teacher, Mr. Oreville Hunter, in their home for Thanksgiving dinner. Minister Carridine will do the drawing." Reba presented the open mouth of the bag.

Minister Carridine pulled out a piece of folded paper.

"The winner is . . ." he unfolded the paper. "Mrs. Coreen Johnson."

"That's me! That's me!" Coreen waved her hand like an eager student certain of the answer.

Mattie and Oreville emerged from the church. They'd only walked a short distance when they heard James shout Mattie's name. He stood some twenty paces away.

"Well, up jumped the devil," Oreville said.

"I'd better go see what he wants," Mattie sighed. "So there won't be any trouble."

"Shall I wait for you?"

"No, don't."

Oreville stalked off.

Mattie went to James.

"What you want to talk about?"

"You changed your mind yet?"

"James, we made a deal."

"I wasn't at my best. I deserve another chance."

"I don't like how you treating me, James. I haven't seen you in all this time. You haven't said a thing about what happened between us. The last thing I remember, we were sitting in my living room talking. The next thing I knew, you headed out the door, saying we was through."

"Some things are too hard to swallow. I deserved a second chance."

"A deal is a deal. We agreed to only one time."

"I disagree with you."

"I disagree with you, too. So I guess that's that."

"If that's that. Then, this is this. We quits."

"No, I quit you first!"

"No, I quit *you* first!"

"I *quit* you first!"

"*I* quit you first!"

# 11

Coreen was taking Sugarbear's plate of food from the oven when he entered the kitchen.

"I was just beginning to worry about you," Coreen gave him a hug.

"The relief man was late. My, that smells good," Sugarbear went off to wash up. When he returned, Coreen put his plate on the table.

"I heard you singing and humming and whistling before you left for work," she said.

"Coreen, I've been waiting for the proper moment to tell you. The years of silence have been lifted. The spirit visited me. There's an abandoned sugarcane plantation in Lake Charles. I won't leave until after Thanksgiving."

"Oh, Sugarbear, Sugarbear," Coreen started crying.

"I won't be away long," Sugarbear stroked Coreen's hands. "I'll be back before the first of the year. I promise."

Everybody participated in the preparations for the Thanksgiving meal. Sugarbear chopped wood. Bootsy dusted and polished the living room furniture. Mattie and Lynn added an extension to the dining room table.

Coreen baked, boiled and broiled. She'd spoiled and pampered Sugarbear as so many women do to demonstrate their love for their man and his announcement had devastated her. She felt that her love was insufficient. That somehow, his leaving was her fault. That, in some way, she had failed. Coreen went into the workroom, brought out her bottle of gin and sipped for the third time that morning.

Sugarbear and Oreville sat at opposite ends of the crowded dining room table.

"Mistah Hunter, my name is Dudley Williams. I'm Coreen's baby brother," Dudley had a fleshy face and a double chin. He and his wife, Retha, sat at Sugarbear's left. "I'm well known around these parts for spreading the gospel. Nobody can conquer me when it comes to knowing the Bible."

"Amen," Retha uttered.

"Sugarbear, how about another piece of that turkey?" Dudley said.

"Most certainly, I'll be glad to cut you off a sliver."

"Mistah Hunter, do you accept the Bible as the word of God?" Dudley asked.

"I consider myself a good Christian, if that's what you're driving at."

"That's real nice to hear. Especially during these modern times with all the talk about scientifics," Dudley expelled the word "scientifics" from his mouth like it tasted nasty. "Mistah Hunter, do you consider yourself to be a knowledgeable man?"

"I try to be."

"I have a question for you, sir. Is the earth square or round?"

"I agree with those who say it's round."

"If the earth is round, where is it hiding its four corners? We all know that something square like a table has four corners. If the scientists with all their knowledge, can't circle a square, how in the world are you going to square a circle?"

"You've just made a profound statement, Mr. Williams. However, you are proposing that the earth is square when in fact it's round."

"The Bible says the earth is square. Read the first verse in the seventh chapter of the Book of Revelations, where it says: *'And after these things I saw four angels standing on the four corners of the earth, holding the four winds of the earth.'* If you believe the earth is round, you on the wrong side of the Good Book."

"Amen," Retha cosigned.

About a third of the guests remained. Mattie was trying to teach Oreville a dance. Oreville had energy to burn but he lacked rhythm and was slow to learn.

"Just think of these words while you dancing," Mattie demonstrated. " *'It started in Texas and then it went to France. Now it's the whole world's dance.'* See? And these words go with this next step: *'You scoot down front and then you wiggle* back. *Put your hand on your hip and let your backbone slip.'* That's all there is to it. It's easy."

"Sure, if you know how."

"Oreville, don't give up now," Mattie urged. "You're almost getting it. Let's start from the beginning. *'You sally to your left. Then you sally to your right.'*"

Coreen staggered into the living room. She spied Mattie and Oreville.

"Dancing with my daughter, are you?" she swayed. "I seen how you be looking at her. You want my Mattie, don't you? Don't deny it. I ain't no goddamn fool."

"Momma," Mattie pleaded. "Don't do this, please."

"You'll never have her to ruin," Coreen slobbered. "A woman should never be with a man that's too different from her."

Mattie and Oreville walked toward the orange-, pineapple- and banana-colored sunset. They stopped when they reached the highway.

"My mother's not that way all the time. It's only when she drinks."

"You don't have to explain anything, honest."

"Thanks."

"There's going to be a recital of spirituals at the auditorium. Would you like to go? You don't have to give me your answer now. Just say you'll think about it."

"No. I'll be glad to go with you."

"Swell. I'll give you the details at church on Sunday. I'll be seeing you."

"See you," Mattie said. "Thanks for being so understanding about my mother."

# 12

Thelma Jenkins studied her image in the mirror at Hazel's beauty parlor.

"That looks just fine, Hazel," she oozed with a sexuality that she took for granted. "Here you go." Thelma paid the beautician. "Keep the change. See y'all on down the road."

She crossed the street, went into Samson's barbecue joint and bought a rib sandwich. She sat near the window. Lizzie pulled up. Gabriel and Mordecai went in one direction. James came her way. The sight of him evoked a surprising, sudden shiver.

James spotted Thelma and joined her.

"Hey, Thelma. Long time no see. How you doing?"

"Just sneaking by. Here, by being careful. Where your brother and Mordecai go off to?"

"The barbershop to pick up Punchy and Noah. We're going out to some pasture. Gabriel's gonna give Noah some driving lessons."

"I saw you at the Say When last Saturday night."

"Oh, yeah. I didn't see you."

"Sometimes, it's not about who you see. But who sees you."

"Why didn't you say hello?"

"I was with my boyfriend at the time. He's the jealous kind. James, you still messing around with Mattie Johnson?"

"Naw, we quits."

"For real?"

"I haven't talked to her in weeks."

"See, instead of messing with her, you could have had me. You know about the dance at the auditorium tonight?"

"Yeah. Chick Webb and his band."

"I'll get away from my boyfriend if you promise to meet me there."

# 13

A copy of the famous photograph of Marcus Mosiah Garvey seated in an open convertible, wearing a fine military uniform with a single medal dignified the rear wall of the Black Star barbershop. The Black Star was one of the main stems of the political, social and cultural grapevine that connected and enlightened the community. Its proprietor, Cyril Kingsberry, was a tall, ivory-yellow-skinned, aristocratic-looking man. The community's most vocal nationalist, he was one of the faithful who heard Garvey speak in New Orleans before his deportation in 1927.

The topic of the day centered on a Harlem spiritual leader and a New York judge.

"Cyril, what do you think of that rumor about what happened to Judge Lewis, the man who sentenced Father Divine to a year in jail?" St. Elmo chatted.

"I'm waiting for the facts," Kingsberry clipped St. Elmo's hair. "I won't believe it until I read it in the *Chicago Defender*. We'll know soon enough. The paperboy will be here directly."

Mordecai and Gabriel entered and sat next to Punchy.

"What about Huey Long's 'Complete the Works' ticket winning the election in a landside?" St. Elmo asked.

"That was no election," Kingsberry sneered. "There's never going to be a real election until the black man gets to vote in it."

A paperboy dressed in brown knickers entered and gave Kingsberry a newspaper.

Kingsberry read the lead story quickly.

"The official word," he waved the newspaper. "Just four days after sentencing Father Divine to jail, Judge Smith is deader than a doorknob. That just goes to show you. You can't put God in jail and expect to be able to sit around and gossip about it."

# 14

As Lizzie tinkled through the sparkly countryside, the quintet chirped Fats Waller's version of *Lulu's Back In Town*. When they reached the pasture, James, Punchy and Mordecai got out. Gabriel and St. Elmo exchanged seats. St. Elmo put Lizzie in gear. She bounced off, jumping and bucking like a Texas bronco.

Mordecai, Punchy and James sat beneath a tree.

"Punchy, tell James what you told me about Mattie and the schoolteacher," Mordecai said. "James, Oreville Hunter has become a part of Mattie's family."

"Ah, man. I only said he had dinner over there, Sunday," Punchy protested.

"Another mule is kicking in your stall," Mordecai teased.

"Man, I don't care," James said. "Mordecai, how about coming with me to the dance tonight? Gabriel is just going over to Inez's house. I'll get him to let me use Lizzie."

"Chick Webb is my favorite drummer," Mordecai replied. "I'd love to hear him and his orchestra but I'm so broke I can't pay attention."

James offered to make Mordecai a loan.

"What's the deal?" Mordecai asked.

"I just want some company, that's all. You want to borrow the money or not?"

"Is fat meat greasy?"

# 15

Sodonia Pettaway entered the kitchen with a tin tub and sat it down on the floor. She went to the stove and tested the water in the kettle with her finger.

Aaron came in.

"Hi, dumpling. How was Bible class this evening?"

"Just fine, peaches."

"I heated up enough water for both of us," Sodonia emptied the kettle of water into the tub. "Aaron, them boys worry me. Especially James."

"You said you was going to speak to them," Aaron removed his shoes.

"I did. Before they left tonight. They promised to attend church tomorrow. It's so hard to get them to attend regular. All they ever think about is having a good time. Having a little fun every once in a while is one thing. But they're making it an occupation. It's time for them to settle down and start a family. I told you James and Mattie fell out, didn't I? She was just perfect for him."

"Whoo, wheee!" Aaron wiggled his feet in the water. "This water sure feels fine."

## 16

Chick Webb's final rendition, *Heebie Jeebies,* resounded in the background as the crowd flowed from the auditorium. James, Thelma and Mordecai, moving with the flow, walked toward the parking lot. It started raining. They dashed to Lizzie. James and Thelma hopped into the front. Mordecai tumbled into the rear seat.

Lizzie, with an effortless ease, surged off.

"Why don't nobody love me?" Mordecai emptied the gin bottle. "Women are nothing but gold diggers. Just as soon as they find out that you have feelings for them, they feel honor-bound to separate you from your money. Buy me this. Get me that. Take me here. There. Everywhere. There's no love for me in this town. That's why I'm leaving."

James slowed Lizzie in order to turn onto Mordecai's street.

"Keep going straight. I know where we can buy a nip," Mordecai directed James to a darkened house. The rain had gotten serious. Mordecai jumped out and returned in a few minutes. "I couldn't rouse anybody." He didn't sound displeased. "You and Thelma go on. I heard there's a new girl at Mary Jack the Bear's. Later." He ran into the darkness.

Lizzie's windshield wipers maintained a Sisyphean struggle against the rain.

"Thelma, why we going to your sister-in-law's house?"

"My brother is doing time on the parish farm. Stop right past that clump of trees. Stop!" Thelma leaped out, on the run.

James, dead on Thelma's heels, followed her to the darkened shanty. "Louise! Louise!" Thelma walloped on the door.

"Who is it?" a young woman's voice called from within.

"Open the damn door. It's raining down cats and dogs out here."

"I knew it was you," Louise Jenkins, holding a candle, opened the door. "There ain't another soul in the world who'd be banging on my door this time of night, excepting you."

"Louise, this is James."

"Hi, James. Thelma talks so much about you, it's like I already know you."

"Gal, quit gabbing. Come on, I want to ask you something. Sit tight a minute, honey," Thelma said. She and Louise disappeared into the darkness.

"Louise going to sleep with her kids," Thelma, holding a candle, led James into the bedroom. "Put your clothes on the chair, honey." She took off her dress.

James undressed and slipped under the covers.

A sudden burst of rain droned on the roof.

Thelma shed her undergarments and blew out the candle.

"Weee! It's chilly," she snuggled up to James. "Wait a minute."

"Where you going?"

"Nowhere."

"What you doing?"

"Shhhh."

"What were you doing?"

"I always say my prayers before I go to bed," Thelma slid under the covers. "You feel so nice and warm." She ran her fingers through the hair on the back of his head, surrendered her hot lips and thrilled his mouth with her tongue.

They fondled. Thelma got in the saddle and reared her head back.

"Oh, honey-honey!" she testified. "Oh, oh! Oh! Oh! You so

wonderful! Don't stop! Don't stop! Yes! Yes! Yes! Oh! James. Oh, honey-honey!"

James, experiencing her juicy substance, felt that exquisite sting. He hollered loud.

# 17

Aaron and Sodonia returned home from church. Sodonia held her breath as the wagon rounded the bend. She saw Lizzie.

"So they finally made it home," her anger boiled. "I'll kill them both."

Gabriel came out of the front door.

"Break your promise about attending church today, will you?" Sodonia was on the attack before her feet hit the ground. "Get your brother. And fetch my broom. I'm going to teach you both how to break your word to me."

James, looking weary and drowsy, appeared in the doorway.

"It's his fault," Gabriel explained. "I loaned him Lizzie. He was supposed to pick me up after the dance last night. He didn't show up until twelve o'clock today."

"Boy, where were you?"

James couldn't tell Sodonia the truth: in the aftermath of Thelma's fierce lovemaking, he'd fallen into a deep, delicious doze. He concocted a lie about how Lizzie ran out of gas and he couldn't find a gas station.

"I had to walk over ten miles to a friend of mine's house," he concluded. "When I woke up the next morning, I'd lost all my money."

"Boy, what's wrong with you?" Sodonia was furious. "You've been running around, acting like a chicken with its head cut off for the past month. Get my broom. I'm gonna whip you to within an inch of your life."

"Ah, Momma. I'm too old for whippings," James protested.

"Let me handle this, peaches," Aaron advised. "James, come with me while I unharness Kate. You right. You are too old for a whipping but you not too old for a good tongue-lashing."

James sat beneath the magnolia tree with his back pressed against the trunk. Cupping his cheeks with his hands, he stared straight ahead. Except for the slightest movement here and there, he maintained the exact position for almost thirty minutes.

Gabriel, carrying a glass of milk and a sandwich, appeared.

"Momma sent you this. What did Poppa have to say?"

"I got to start going with him to his Saturday evening Bible class."

## 18

Some twenty-odd laborers grouped about the company shed. Speaking through chattering teeth, they squeezed their chests, stomped their feet and blew hot breaths of air into their fists. One-third of them faced unemployment. There was an air of uneasiness as they waited for the foreman.

Big Sam stood alone, a scowl on his face. James approached.

"Hey, Big Sam. How you doing?"

"I'll do."

"Just between you, me and the deep blue sea, will my name be called, or not?"

"Wait and find out just like everybody else, which won't be long," Big Sam indicated the foreman's coupe that pulled into the yard.

The foreman, grasping the seat with a gloved hand, pushed his chunky frame from the car.

"All right. We got to let some of you go today. When I call your name, hop on the truck. If I don't call your name, that's it," the foreman had a thing for theatrics. Like an actor performing Shakespeare, he embellished each name with a resounding roll.

"Please, Lord, if you just help me out this one time," James prayed. "I won't ever bother you again in my whole life, please, sir."

The foreman cleared his throat and paused.

"Last, but not least," he pontificated. "James Pettaway!"

"Wow. Hot zigidy," James yelled. "This is the best day of my life."

## 19

Charlie Blue, a dreary-looking fellow with a sad face, drove the company truck down the highway. Big Sam snoozed. In the rear of the truck, which was uncovered, the men bunched together, pitting their bodies against the chilled wind.

"Big Sam," Charlie Blue urged. "Wake up, man."

"What is it?"

Parked civilian and deputy cars lined both sides of the road. A large crowd of white people, some standing on top of their cars, created a festive hum. Seated in his black and white sedan, a ruddy-complexioned deputy excitedly rapped into his microphone:

"The convict's been up there for more than an hour. They just brought in more dogs. Wow! This is better than a flick."

A roly-poly deputy, urgently waving his hand, motioned the company truck to stop.

"Where you boys going?" he demanded.

"To work a road, Captain," Big Sam answered.

"Park over there," the deputy walked away.

James, eager to discover the cause of the excitement, stood up.

A black man in tattered prison garb, eyes crazily popping, was clinging to a tree. A pack of Doberman pinschers, straining against their leashes, ringed the tree trunk. A bevy of deputies, brandishing their weapons, yelled vile threats.

Sheriff Westbrook Winchester, flanked by three deputies, warmed his hands over a blazing fire. In his late thirties, Winchester stood over six feet. Though he was overweight, his smooth vanilla-ice-cream-colored skin had a healthy glow.

"That photographer better get here pretty soon," he blew into his closed fist. "It's time to bring this damn shindig to a close."

The roly-poly deputy approached.

"Sheriff Winchester, I just cornered a truckload of niggers," he pointed.

"Sheriff Winchester," a deputy wearing a bandolier rushed up. "The photographer is here."

The photographer took pictures.

Groaning and sobbing, body writhing with fear, the convict eased out on the limb.

"Jump, nigger, jump!" the crowd chanted.

"We going to teach you to escape."

"Jump, nigger, jump!"

"We going to cut your dick off."

"Jump, nigger, jump!"

The convict slumped and swooned.

"Jump, nigger, jump!"

Finally, the convict jumped. Furry blurs with jagged teeth overwhelmed him.

James, horrified, watched the dogs rip the convict.

"Let's do something," he cried. "What kind of men are we to just watch and do nothing?"

"Who said that?" Winchester demanded.

Conditioned by slavery and segregation, the laborers, like Pavlov's dog, reacted instinctively: man by man, they turned their eyes toward James.

"Get down here, nigger."

James climbed down from the truck.

Winchester eyed him with a deliberate, cold, circular stare.

"I got this niggah, captain," Big Sam sprang forward and tagged James with a vicious right hook. The blow separated James from his senses and knocked him to the ground face down.

"What's your name, boy?" Winchester asked.

"Sam Rivers, sir. We just a crew of hard-working niggahs on our way to work a road, sir."

"All right. Get out of here."

"Thank you, captain. Two of you boys git down here and put this fool back on the truck."

After they'd traveled about a mile, Big Sam ordered Charlie Blue to leave the highway and take a trail that—barely visible from the road—wound its way through bushes and thickets.

"Where we going, Big Sam?" Charlie Blue asked.

"Stop," Big Sam hopped from the cab. "Hey, git down here." He called the muleskinner. "Go watch the road."

"Fine," the muleskinner hopped from the truck. "What am I watching for?"

"You can never tell about white folks. Sheriff Winchester might commence thinking about that fool and decide to come after him. Go on. Be careful not to let anybody see you."

James climbed down from the truck.

"You hit me, Big Sam," he raved. "You hit me."

"Easy, now. Easy," Big Sam advised.

Whirring siren sounds, becoming louder and louder, reached a crescendo and receded.

"James, you mean you never heard about Sheriff Winchester? Don't you know he done killed more niggahs than you can count on both hands? Didn't you see his eyes? He was going to kill you. My knocking you out saved your life."

"Thanks," James tested his jaw. "I don't know what happened. Something just came over me when I saw them dogs attacking that man like that."

The muleskinner returned.

"It was the sheriff and a carload of deputies," he reported.

"All right, boys. Us moving on. Everybody back on the truck," Big Sam called. "Not you, James. You fired. If I allow you to stick around, you subject to get us all killed someday."

"Big Sam, give me another chance," James pleaded.

"No, no. School is out," Big Sam hopped in the cab. "See over there? Go directly through them bushes 'til you hit the creek. Follow it for about an hour 'til you reach the highway."

James, a forlorn look on his face, watched the truck pull away.

## 20

Linda Edgewater's Cadillac swung into the Johnsons' driveway.

Coreen Johnson, holding two neatly-pressed dresses, came out.

"Hi, Miss Linda," she handed Linda the dresses. "We got a letter from Sugarbear. He'll be back soon. Things are so peaceful and pleasant when he's around. Everybody is so excited."

"Good. I'm so happy for you," Linda said. "By the way, I need someone to do some gardening. I lost my regular boy. Do you know of anyone looking for work?"

Coreen, as it turned out, did know of someone.

"What's his name?"

"James Pettaway. His mother and me are friends. I'll go by her house tomorrow and let her know you looking for somebody."

"Thanks," Linda backed down the driveway. "See you."

When Coreen entered the kitchen, Mattie was feasting on a peanut-butter sandwich with mayonnaise, cold leftover butter beans, crackling, sweet potato pie and a pickle.

"Didn't I hear you gagging earlier this morning?"

"It's only a stomach gripe," Mattie said.

"Well, howsoever. Remember, '*Deeds done in the night, always come to the light.*'"

The next morning when Mattie entered the kitchen, Coreen greeted her with a smug expression on her face.

"I heard you this morning. Sounds like your stomach gripe is getting worser."

"I'm all right," Mattie yawned.

Coreen asked about her period. Mattie admitted she was late.

"How late?"

"Over two months. But I've been late before."

"Gal, you pregnant. I can tell. You've been with a man, haven't you? And don't you lie to me, either."

"Yes, with James," Mattie blurted. "But only one time."

"Mattie, how could you? After all of my talking to you? After all of my warnings?" Coreen shook her head. "This really takes the cake. Somehow, I never expected something like this from you. I thought you had better sense. What happened? What were you thinking?"

"I don't know. I kept getting these feelings. I mean, I got curious. The feelings were so strong, I just gave in to them," Mattie started crying. "And he kept asking."

"Ain't any sense in crying now. What's done is done. I'll have to let Sodonia know," Coreen said in a comforting manner. "I was already going to her house today, anyway."

# 21

Sodonia Pettaway, still shaken by Coreen Johnson's recent visit, stirred cornbread batter in an earthenware bowl.

Gabriel entered.

"Hi, Momma," he bussed her cheek.

"I'm so glad you home! How was your trip?"

"Just great. I made it back in record time."

"Take a load off your feet and keep me some company whilst I finish cooking supper," Sodonia had no intention of telling Gabriel about Coreen's visit but she was secretly intrigued by the idea of being a grandmother. In a gush of emotions, she told Gabriel about Coreen's visit.

The front door slammed.

"That's James. Remember now. Don't mention a word to him about what I just told you," Sodonia whispered. "I want to wait and tell your father first."

When James entered, Coreen and Gabriel scrutinized him as if they sought to discover something different about him, like a halo or horns.

"I sure earned that dollar today," James went to the icebox and brought out a bottle of milk.

"You might be in line for something better than unloading potatoes. Mattie's mother was by here earlier today. A rich white woman she knows is looking for somebody to do some gardening."

"That job wasn't the only news Mattie's momma brought," Gabriel giggled. "Poppa."

"Poppa? What you talking about?"

"Gabriel, I told you that I wanted to tell your father first."

"Tell Daddy what? What you talking about, Momma?"

"Well, all right. Mattie's in a family way. She claims you the father."

Surprised and shocked, James lied: "I never touched her."

Gabriel cocked his head, frowning. James had given him the details of his tryst with Mattie on the night of Mordecai's birthday party.

"You sure, now?" Sodonia asked.

"It must be the schoolteacher. He practically lives at her house. Everybody knows that."

Sodonia, who had believed Coreen, felt a sense of acute disappointment. She reacted like so many mothers do under such circumstances: she experienced a staggering rush of motherliness.

*Oh, my poor, innocent baby. Wrongly accused by that shameless hussy,* her instincts cried. *Momma going to protect her baby. Yes, she is.* Driven by mother's passion, Sodonia lashed out at Mattie and Coreen in an uncharacteristic, shameful manner.

Aaron, unnoticed, came in.

"What all this ruckus about?" he demanded.

Sodonia recited Coreen's accusation and James' denial.

"I know exactly what to do," she concluded. "I'll speak to Reverend Carridine the first thing in the morning."

"Peaches. Let's talk to Coreen and Mattie first," Aaron suggested. "Maybe we can keep things private, between the two families."

"Everybody is bound to find out, anyway," Sodonia replied. "I'm going to speak to Reverend Carridine before that hussy and her mother can approach him with their lies."

## 22

Sodonia Pettaway joined Reverend C. C. Carridine in his chambers. She apprised him of Mattie's allegation and James' denial. She finished her account with a flow of indignant tears.

"Mrs. Pettaway, at this juncture it might be wise to bring both families together. I have a business meeting tomorrow evening. It should end about seven. We can meet after that. Bring Aaron. I'll make certain that Coreen is notified."

## 23

Bootsy guided Sugarbear's feet into the tub of warm water and washed his feet. Mattie trimmed his hair. Lynn entered with a plate of steaming food and placed it before him.

"So Coreen's at church, eh?" Sugarbear said.

"Yes," Bootsy said. "She wasn't gone five minutes before you walked in the house."

"Poppa, were you serious about not finding any buried treasure?" Lynn asked.

"Dead serious, I'm afraid. Not a single, solitary shekel. To tell the truth, the trip ended on a very disagreeable note. Daughters, take my advice. Never linger in the company of a fool. What happened was that . . ."

Coreen, surprised and jubilant, entered.

"Sugarbear, you're back. You're back."

"What's the matter, Coreen?"

"Mattie's pregnant. Now the boy claims he never touched her."

"The young Pettaway boy. Am I right?"

"Yes. I just left a meeting at the church with his parents and Reverend Carridine. We couldn't settle anything. We meeting with the Board of Elders next Monday evening."

"Coreen, I noticed that you removed my pistol from the table in the bedroom."

"No, Sugarbear. No," Coreen protested.

"I merely want to have a little man-to-man talk with the boy, that's all."

Left to his own devices, Sugarbear might have committed some rash act. There are few men who can prevail against the wails of four women hell-bent on preventing violence. Sugarbear was not one of them. He slowly gave in to the clamorous, though wise, pleading of his womenfolk.

## 24

That Saturday evening, when they were on their way to Bible class, Aaron confronted James: "I know what you told Sodonia. Gabriel said you told him you were with Mattie at least once. I want to hear the truth from you. Was you ever with Mattie?"

"Yes, sir. Gabriel said I should get married. But I don't know. I mean, I never thought about marrying so soon in life. What you think, Poppa?"

"First of all. Do you care for her?"

"I love her."

"That's good for starters. It's good you love her but getting married involves more than love. You can fall out of love, just like you fall in it. Marriage is different. Once you in it, that's it. There's no turning back. Especially when children are involved. It takes real dedication. When you were growing up, did you ever know a hungry day? Of course you didn't. I worked hard for you and your brother. A real man takes care of what he claims to be his own."

## 25

Reba Hightower, Thaddeus Stier, Bradford Sykes, Meldrick Merryweather and Reverend C.C. Carridine conferred in the chamber. They agreed on the first item on the agenda, that James and Mattie should marry. The next issue, the actual site of the marriage ceremony, proved to be ticklish. Only chaste brides were deemed worthy of a formal church wedding.

"Let them get married at the courthouse," Reba announced. "A formal church wedding is out of the question."

"Come, come," Meldrick said. "We're talking about one of our best families. Mattie's grandfather Cato helped found this church. It doesn't seem right for the church not to be involved."

"Let's not forget that her grandmother, Mattie Fae, was the church secretary before she retired," Bradford said.

"And she was the mother of the church," Thaddeus added.

The discussion continued and although it was not easily accomplished, they achieved a compromise. Reverend C.C. Carridine went to the door and beckoned the families.

Coreen and Sodonia barely acknowledged each other's existence. Sugarbear, seated next to Mattie, was breathing hard and looking mean. Aaron and James, standing beside each other, looked cool and collected.

"I'll get right down to the heart of the matter," Reverend Carridine began. "The board agrees that there should be a marriage. James, are you prepared to accept your obligation?"

James and Aaron exchanged a fleeting glance.

"Yes, sir. Poppa said. I mean, I'll do the right thing," James said. "I'll marry her."

No one noticed the pained expression on Mattie's face.

"Very well," Reverend Carridine said. "The actual site of the ceremony proved to be a very thorny issue. I can assure you all that we . . ."

"Reverend Carridine, what about me?" Mattie said passionately. "No one asked me if I wanted to get married. And I don't. I wouldn't marry James Pettaway for nothing in the world." She ran from the room.

## 26

When Coreen and Sugarbear returned home from the meeting at the church, Mattie was seated on the couch, staring into space.

"Mattie, what's wrong with you?" Coreen sounded disgusted.

"Why did you run off like that?" Sugarbear asked, amazed.

"What you think is going to happen when the baby gits here?" Coreen demanded. "It's definitely going to git here. You can't bring a child into the world without a father. A child needs his father's name."

"What about the family honor?" Sugarbear hollered.

Aaron Pettaway knocked on the front door.

Sugarbear invited him in.

"Mr. Johnson, I'd like to speak to your daughter, if I may."

"There she is," Sugarbear nodded in Mattie's direction.

"Excuse me, Mattie. I don't mean to hurt your feelings but the teacher's name has been bandied about. Is he anyway involved in this?"

"No, sir. We are only friends. He ate dinner with us twice. One time, I went to a recital with him. Mother made me take Bootsy with us."

"Help me understand, then. If my son's the father, why won't you marry him?"

"I don't know. I mean, I know. It just don't feel right. I don't want James to feel obligated. Like I'm being forced on him."

Overwhelmed with feelings, Mattie started crying. "I'll never marry someone who doesn't love me."

"James loves you. He told me so himself."

## 27

Mattie and James entered the jewelry store.

"Y'all want something?" the clerk spoke with a nasal twang.

"Yes, sir. We want to see some wedding rings," James answered.

The clerk ushered them to the counter.

"Don't worry about the cost. I got some money saved up," James whispered. "Besides, Mrs. Edgewater liked the way I worked so much, she's going to get her husband to hire me at his bag factory. Why did you tell my father I don't love you?"

"Because of the way you treated me."

"I'm sorry. I know I acted stupid but I never stopped loving you. What about you? Do you still love me?"

"Yes, I still love you. But until the wedding, I'm going to continue to dislike you for the horrible way you've treated me," Mattie pinched James' stomach.

"Ouch."

"That's for being so mean to me."

## 28

Under the compromise reached by the Board of Elders, Minister Carridine married Mattie and James at the church on a Saturday afternoon. Only the immediate family members attended.

Minister Carridine presided over the ceremony with an imperial air.

"Best man. The ring, please."

Gabriel passed the ring to James, who slipped it onto Mattie's finger.

Solemnly and sincerely, Mattie and James exchanged vows.

"I now pronounce you man and wife."
They kissed. Two was one.

## 29

A group of guests carrying colorfully-wrapped gifts entered the Knights' mansion.

"Welcome to the wedding reception," Inez Chambers ushered the guests inside. Emma Pace and Odilia Toy took their gifts. Curtis and Beatrice Jollivette manned the coatroom. Lynn, Shelby Staggs and Bootsy, standing at a table stacked with pyramids of food, served the guests. Dudley and Retha Williams served drinks from behind the bar.

A photographer took pictures of the bride and groom.

Bradford and Nancy Sykes, Thaddeus Stier and his wife, Essex and Betty Dawson, Meldrick Merryweather and Reba Hightower observed the proceedings with interest.

Sugarbear, Coreen, Aaron and Sodonia joked with each other like long-lost friends.

Mordecai, Punchy, St. Elmo, Gabriel and the groom crooned *Ain't Misbehavin'*.

Mattie Pettaway, bridal bouquet in her hand, stood at the top of the stairs. She looked down upon the eager faces of her single female guests.

"Here it is," she tossed the bouquet.

Which prompted a mad scramble. Lynn, simply by overpowering everyone else, prevailed. She held the bouquet high above her head like a trophy.

# *When Matters of Pride and Principle Collide*

Spring, 1942.

That Sunday, Reverend C.C. Carridine christened Lynn and Shelby Staggs' baby boy, their first child after nine years of marriage. Deacon Merryweather offered a prayer. Reba Hightower praised Lynn, who was now the choir director. She also asked for a moment of silence for Coreen who had died from a stroke several months ago.

Afterwards, there was a gathering at the home of the Staggs. Mattie Pettaway and her two sons rode with Lynn and Shelby. When they arrived at the house, Lynn gave Shelby the baby and took off her shoes. Next, she put on Billie Holiday's recording of *The Very Thought Of You*. She went into the kitchen and started warming up and preparing the food.

"You need any help?" Mattie joined Lynn. "Junior boy, you and John go sit down in the living room."

"Yes, mother," the brothers said politely. Junior boy wore a brown suit; John, a blue one. They were ten and eight respectively. Tall and trim, they looked ridiculously like their father. For the remainder of the afternoon they kept to themselves and spoke only when spoken to.

"Glad y'all could make it," Shelby greeted two of his co-workers and their wives.

Shelby's mother, sister and aunt arrived.

"Let me hold him, son," said Shelby's mother, a short, friendly woman of sixty.

It seemed that everyone wanted to hold the little guy. They passed him around, patting his head and touching his cheeks, like he was a mojo.

Lynn played Billie Holiday's *The Man I Love*. She and Mattie went into the dining room and started setting up the table.

Dudley and Retha Williams eased in.

"Hi, Uncle Dudley," Lynn said.

"Hi, auntie," Mattie gave Retha a hug. "Junior boy. John. Come say hello to your aunt and uncle."

They came over and stood slightly behind Mattie. Holding onto her skirt, they kept their heads down. John started sucking his thumb.

"Can't you two speak?" Mattie asked.

Junior boy and John responded by holding tighter to Mattie's skirt.

"What's the matter, the cat got your tongue?" Dudley made a face.

"Did you hear me? I told you to say hello."

"Hello, Uncle Dudley."

"Hello, Aunt Retha."

"I don't know what's wrong with y'all. Go back and sit down."

Dudley and Retha, who had not been on the scene since Coreen's funeral, played twenty questions with Mattie.

"Where's Bootsy? I noticed that she wasn't at the church," Dudley said.

"We haven't seen her in a while," Mattie replied. "I'll tell you about it later."

Retha wanted to know about Sugarbear. Mattie said he'd recently sent her a photograph of himself from Mexico.

"What about your brother-in-law?" Dudley asked. "I hear the army drafted him."

"Yes, he's going in next month."

"You heard anything from Curtis and Beatrice?" Retha inquired.

"I got a letter from Beatrice about a month ago. Curtis is working for the Ford Motor Company. She said she's expecting another baby in the fall."

"Where's James today?" Dudley asked.

Oscar and Odilia St. Elmo, Emma and Bertrand Haskins bounced in. Both couples had been married for ten years. St. Elmo and Punchy carried the presents.

"Cut off the lights and call the law!" Emma greeted everyone.

"Lynn, congratulations," Odilia said. "I'm so happy for you and Shelby."

"Why, thank you, Odilia."

"Where's James?" Emma inquired. "I didn't see him at the church."

Mattie decided not to tell the whole truth. James had stayed out all night. He arrived at home as she and her sons were leaving for church.

"James stayed home. He said he wasn't feeling too good," she added.

Gabriel Pettaway and his girlfriend, Cybil Jones, appeared. Getting drafted had cast Gabriel into a suspended state of disorientation; indeed, he viewed his situation from afar, like it was happening to an old schoolmate that he was not particularly fond of.

"I brought my cards," Cybil Jones announced. Thirty-six, she had gray eyes and long brown hair. Her purple dress emphasized her paper-sack-brown, velvety shoulders. "Let's get a whist game started. I want to sharpen up for the Knights' whist tournament."

Meanwhile, Billie Holiday crooned *All of Me.*

## 2

Mattie Pettaway prepared breakfast.

"Morning," James entered and sat down at the table.

"Morning," Mattie placed a plate of food before him.

"What time you suppose to see that white lady?"

"Ten o'clock," Mattie put a sandwich in James' lunch box.

"I'm still not sold on you working. Taking care of the house and the boys is enough for you to do. So, Dudley and Retha are coming over for supper tonight, huh?"

"Yes. James, you are wrong as two left shoes," Mattie gave James his lunch box. "Staying out all night like you did."

"Come on. Don't start that again."

"Yesterday at the christening everybody kept asking about you. I felt like a fool."

"I told you last night that I couldn't catch a ride."

"You've been getting back home before. Why all of a sudden you can't? Like I said, I haven't lost my hearing. I know Thelma Jenkins is back in town."

"Here we go again. You ever seen me with her? No. Like I said, if you can't prove anything, then you ought not to say anything. Until you catch me with her and tap me on the shoulder, you don't have a case. To prove just how wrong you are, I'll make you a promise. If you ever catch me with Thelma and tap me on the shoulder, I'll take off my belt and let you whip me right there, on the spot."

"James, don't play with me."

"Come on, babe," James took Mattie in his arms. "You know it's you and me, from the same oak tree."

"I'm serious, James."

"I am, too. You're my woman. I'm your man."

## 3

James hurried down the road. Grass, wet with dew, sparkled

like a garden of green emeralds. Hyperactive birds answered each other in pert, twittery voices. Just as James reached the highway, Forrest Edgewater arrived in his late-model Buick sedan.

"Morning, Mr. Forrest," James hopped in.

"Morning, James."

They rode in silence but you could sense that they shared a genuine affinity.

"How is Mattie?"

"She's feeling much better now. Thank you, sir."

"Tell her Mrs. Edgewater said if she gets sick again, she'll take her to our doctor. By the way, I'm giving some raises next month and your name tops the list. I'm proud of you, James. You are my best worker. You take good care of your family. You attend church regularly and there's that colored lodge you belong to. You're different from other niggers, James. I not only trust you to manage my factory but you're one of the few people I'd trust with my wife."

Forrest turned onto the road that led to the bag factory.

James got out at the rear entrance and entered the semi-dark building. He flicked on a row of lights and went to his cubicle. He put away his lunch box, retrieved his toolbox and went to the main floor. He turned on the sleek electric machines and walked down the aisle. Head tilted like a demanding symphony conductor, he listened carefully to the unique melody of each machine. Hearing the number four machine tweet a discordant chord, he retrieved a wrench from his toolbox and adjusted the chord to a steady hum.

The women, pastel-pink faces framed in white bandannas, assumed their positions, three to a machine. Rolls of paper, turning slowly, unfurled like toilet paper.

James returned to his cubicle and poured himself a cup of coffee.

"Morning, James," Douglas Bixby, the gardener, ambled in.

He had smooth ebony skin and a bullet-shaped head. "How's it going?"

"I'm fine. How about you?"

"I can't kick. I mean, I could kick but how high would it be? Know what I mean?" Bixby laughed at himself. "Where you want me to start mowing?"

"I'll show you. Just let me finish my coffee first."

"James. Do you think the majors are going to play baseball this season?"

"Most certainly. War or no war. And the Yankees are going to win the World Series again, too."

After James finished his coffee, he and Douglas Bixby went outside.

"I'm sorry I won't be at the Knights' whist tournament Saturday night."

"You really going to miss something. Every year it gets bigger and better. You can start over there," James pointed.

"See you," Bixby went off.

Sonny Patterson, a gangly man with bronze-green eyes and thick, buff-colored hair, sat in the cab of his six-wheeler. He jerked his head back and forth, looking into the side mirrors as he tried to back his trailer to the platform. There was just enough space between two parked trucks. He took a bad angle and had to try again. Seeing James, he waved his slender white hand.

"James, I'm having hard luck backing this thing in. See what you can do."

"Sure thing," James got behind the wheel and backed the truck to the platform.

James and Sonny had started working as truck drivers on the same day and they'd become work buddies. In fact, James showed Sonny some of the delicacies about driving that Gabriel had taught him. But his feelings about Sonny changed when Sonny revealed that he was the type of white person who liked to murder-mouth blacks to other blacks. Due to Southern racial etiquette, James could not openly express his true feelings but inwardly, he had started resenting Sonny.

After discovering that Sonny earned four dollars and eighty-six cents more a week than he did, he became so resentful he couldn't stand to be in Sonny's company. To get away from him, James had taken a job inside the factory, even though it meant a reduction in pay. He took advantage of the opportunity and over the years, his wages steadily increased. But he never discussed salaries with any of his coworkers.

## 4

"Gee! Gee! Haw!" Aaron Pettaway barked commands to his horse, Francis.

Junior boy and John watched appreciatively as their grandfather plowed their father's garden. Barefooted and barechested, they wore light-colored short pants.

"Junior boy! John!" Mattie called from the back porch. "If you want to meet your father, you'd best run along."

The brothers dashed toward their father.

"Howdy, sons," James called.

"Daddy, let's race home," Junior boy urged.

"Ah right, if you want to get beat again."

"You going to give us a head start to the big tree?" John asked.

"I sure am not."

"Ah, Daddy," the brothers pleaded.

"All right, then. Go on."

James started running when his sons reached the big tree. He caught up with John and zipped by him. Junior boy maintained a good lead until he reached the top of the hill. His legs wobbled and he couldn't catch his breath.

"I got you. You little rascal. I got you," James took his role as a father seriously. He had his own philosophy about the proper way to raise his sons to be strong men. He never cut them any slack. Any victory would be earned. He swooped past Junior boy. He beat him by a good ten yards and performed a victory dance.

Junior boy and John stopped at the well for a drink.

"Wow, Junior boy," John said. "I thought you had him beat for sure. What happened to you?"

"I don't exactly know. All of a sudden it was like I was running in molasses. My feet were moving but not my body. The next thing I knew, Daddy was hurrahing in the front yard. I'll beat him the next time, you just watch."

James and Aaron heaved the plow onto the wagon.

"The boys said you and Mattie had a big argument last night. Shouting and cussing. I just don't understand it, son. Your mother and me were married over thirty years. Until the day she died, we never exchanged a single word in anger."

"It was different with y'all. Momma wasn't always telling you what to do."

"Son, you know how much I loved Sodonia. But let's be honest about it. She spent most of her waking hours telling me what to do. Or trying to. No, son. That kind of carrying on is wrong, especially in the sight of the boys. When you wrong, it's my fatherly duty to chastise you. While I'm at it, there's another subject I must mention. Son, you don't seem to realize that the earth is large but the circle is small. Purely by chance, I heard some gossip about you and some gal name Thelma, who's back from Detroit."

"See? That's what burns me up. People talk when they should be listening. It's true that I was in her company a few times but that's all finished and done with. You know what she did? She grabbed a knife and tried to . . ."

Junior boy, clutching a jar of iced tea and John, carrying a glass, ran their way.

"Poppa, I'll finish telling you about it some other time," James whispered.

"Momma sent you some tea."

"Here's a glass, Grandfather."

"Thank you, boys," Aaron replenished himself and climbed in the wagon. "See y'all at church, Sunday." He tugged the reins and Francis trotted off.

Mattie put a pan of stuffed bell peppers in the oven.

"Hi, baby," James entered and gave Mattie a kiss. "I'm going to change my clothes. The boys and me are going to do some work in the garden."

"Don't you want to know what happened with the job? I got it."

"How much is she paying?"

"Two dollars a week. Just to take care of her three kids while she at work. She's got lots of books I can borrow, too."

"You can borrow books from the library. Go back and tell her your husband won't let you work for less than three-fifty a week."

"But I already promised to take the job."

"I'm getting a raise next month. It's not like you have to work. Find somebody else for her. There's plenty women who'll work for them kind of wages. But as for me, I got too much pride to let my wife work for two dollars a week."

Junior boy and John shot marbles.

James approached.

"Daddy, you want to shoot some?" John asked.

"I don't have time to beat you all today. Listen, you two. Your Uncle Dudley and Retha are coming over for supper tonight. If Dudley starts telling stories about haunts, don't be getting scared like you did before. Act like men. Haunts ain't nothing but superstition. When you dead, you done. Ah right, let's go get them gardening tools."

# 5

That night, James refilled his glass with ice tea. Junior boy and John attacked their food. Mattie spooned a stuffed bell pepper from the platter and put it on the plate held by Retha. Retha passed the plate to her husband.

"Thank you, wife," Dudley said. "Mattie, yesterday at the christening you mentioned that Sugarbear sent you a picture of himself from Mexico. Us wouldn't mind seeing it, if you don't mind."

"Junior boy, go get the album for me."

"I'll get it," John ran off. He returned with the album and handed it to Mattie.

Mattie opened the album and showed the photograph: Sugarbear sat at a table surrounded by a group of clay-colored peasants with smiling faces. His left hand rested on the table. His right hand, clasping a knife, was poised to cut a piece of cheese. Beneath his sombrero, which was tilted forward slightly, his eyes stared fiercely into the beyond.

"That's him, all right," Retha chuckled. "In his letter, did he mention anything about coming home?"

"No. After mother's funeral, he said he'd never come back to this town again."

"Mattie, I was thinking about our conversation yesterday," Dudley said. "How did Bootsy find out that Sugarbear wasn't her real daddy?"

"About a week after mother's funeral, we were going through her papers and Bootsy saw her birth certificate."

"Now, I agree, it must have been hard for Bootsy," Dudley pouted. "But for her to change so quickly. To just up and quit church and start drinking and running with that bad crowd, I'll never understand that. Your mother and me were raised in an orphanage. But we didn't turn out like that. Does anybody want that last bell pepper?"

The moon exposed the tops of the trees, the outhouse silhouette and the spectral-shaped shrubbery that sloped into the gully.

James went into the backyard and dumped some coals on the ground. Then he added several sticks of wood and put a match to it. When the fire started to flame, he threw some damp rags on it. This immediately created a towering, sweeping, flatulent cloud of smoke whose purpose was to keep away the mosquitoes.

"Oh-wee! That smells awful," Mattie declared as she and Retha came out of the backdoor. "James, could I speak to you for a minute?"

"Sure," James followed Mattie inside.

"I took ten dollars from under the mattress and loaned it to Retha. They're doing kind of bad right now. Is that all right by you?"

"Sure," James hugged Mattie. "Hey, that was some meal you cooked."

"Thanks, honey. I guess you better get back to the company."

"Ain't you coming back outside?"

"No. I'm going to lay down for a minute."

"You feeling sick again?"

"Oh, no. I'm just a little tired, that's all."

James returned to the back porch. The smoke lingered like a foul-breathed mother-in-law. James fired up a cigarette. Dudley cut himself a plug of tobacco. Retha took a pinch of snuff. Junior boy and John kept Dudley—against whom they had previously schemed—under surveillance.

Night creatures chirped, croaked and hooted.

"I'm going to tell you boys a true story about Shyloe," Dudley spat an ugly brown glob. "It's real scary. Maybe y'all better run inside and hide under the bed."

Dudley proceeded to tell the old tale about the man who bets he can spend the night in a haunted house. During the course of the night, he is visited by a series of bloodcurdling, demonic creatures. Each creature is more ferocious than the previous one. As each one departs, it asks the same question:

"Are you going now, or are you going to wait until Shyloe comes?"

Finally, overcome by fear, the man decides to leave before the host arrives. When Dudley finished his story, the brothers eyed him dubiously. Visibly disappointed that he hadn't succeeded in frightening them, he spat another ugly brown glob.

"We'll be seeing you, James."
"Tell Mattie goodnight for us," called Retha.
A profound silence enveloped the night. The couple, following Dudley's flashlight, walked in the middle of the road. The moon played hide-and-seek with moving clouds, periodically disappearing and reappearing. The time between the intervals was really of a short duration but to Dudley, who was quite superstitious, they seemed unreasonably long.
"Whooooo . . . Whooooo . . . Whooooo," the utterances murmured behind them.
"Wife, that don't sound like no owl."
"It sure don't."
"Whooooo . . . Whooooo . . . Whooooo," the utterances murmured, closer.
"Don't look back," Retha commenced to trot.
Dudley couldn't resist. Looking back, he glimpsed the appearance of two white forms floating across the air.
"Oh, my God! It's haunts for true," he cried, totally terrified.
Shrieking and begging Jesus for mercy, Retha and Dudley sprinted into the darkness—much to the delight of Junior boy and John, who removed their sheets and congratulated each other with playful slaps on the back.

# 6

A group of Knights exchanged colorful bursts of conversation as they set up the card tables in the ballroom for the whist tournament.

"Things must be going pretty good at the bottling company," Punchy signified.

"Why you say that?" St. Elmo asked.

"You been thinking about buying a car, haven't you? Emma said Odilia told her you been looking around."

"I just started looking but I've been saving for years."

"Seen anything you like so far?"

"Yeah, a '37 Pontiac but it looks new," St. Elmo answered. "Gabriel is coming with me next Saturday to look it over. If it checks out, I'm buying it."

"Noah," Bradford Sykes walked up. "What time do you want me to make the presentations to the winners?"

"Around eleven o'clock, give or take a few minutes."

"Our board meeting should be over by then. If it's not, send someone for me."

# 7

That same evening, Lucinda, Gabriel Pettaway's mustard-colored Dodge, eased on down the road.

Gabriel sat beside the driver, Cybil Jones.

"There's a steep curve coming up," he cautioned.

"Relax, sugar," Cybil responded. She wore a voguish orange dress and white gloves. "I've got everything covered."

Emma Haskins and Odilia St. Elmo sat in the rear seat. Like Cybil, they'd dressed up for the Knights' whist tournament.

"Gabriel," Emma tapped his shoulder. "You never did say exactly when the lodge is giving you your going-away party."

"Saturday after next."

"I sure hope the army don't start drafting married men," Odilia declared.

"They already are. And married men with kids, too," Cybil said.

"Y'all might laugh but I wish the services would accept women, too," Emma announced. "I'd volunteer. Just to show that us women can be as patriotic as the men."

# 8

The whist tournament, the Knights' most popular fund-raiser, owed its success to the fact that it gave the ladies the opportunity to jump sharp and be seen at their very best. That evening, they created a striking scene of peppertone gold, lobster red, blue violet, mustard gold, burnt orange, hare brown and sweltering green.

Gabriel guided Cybil to the bar where James served drinks to Odilia and Emma.

"Where's Mattie, James? Don't you *allow* her to be out after dark anymore?" Odilia asked, kidding on the square.

"Don't blame me. The boys are taking part in the Juneteenth program at church and she took them to the rehearsal."

St. Elmo appeared.

"Gabriel, do me a favor," he said. "Go upstairs and tell Brother Sykes I'll need him down here in about fifteen minutes to make the presentations to the winners."

When the board completed its agenda, Essex Dawson and Bradford Sykes remained behind with Thaddeus Stier to discuss his trip to Chicago, where he had participated in a Policy Conference called by Asa Philip Randolph.[*]

Thaddeus, voice vibrant with passion, revealed the subtext of the conference: "The liberals are only interested in symbolism and tokenism. They are so afraid of anything that smacks of real change, it's pathetic. The communists are against any move they think will detract from the war effort. You know how they are: rule or ruin. So we were not surprised by their criticisms of our all-Negro stance. But as we made it clear in our position paper, we are an oppressed people and oppressed people must rely upon themselves if they are to achieve their freedom. No one would claim . . ."

---

[*]On June 25, 1941, reacting to a threat by A. Philip Randolph to organize a march on Washington, President Franklin Roosevelt signed Executive Order 8002, which integrated the war industries, and established a Fair Employment Practice Committee.

The secret rap resounded on the door.
"It's unlocked," Bradford called.
Gabriel entered and delivered St. Elmo's message.
"Tell him I'll be right there," Bradford closed the door behind Gabriel.
"Thaddeus," Essex said. "You probably haven't heard about it but the army drafted Gabriel Pettaway."
"That's the type of blatant hypocrisy we're up against," Thaddeus uttered. "They make us fight for their freedom but refuse to give us ours."

# 9

St. Elmo steered his newly-purchased Pontiac down the road. Gabriel sat next to St. Elmo. James, Mordecai and Punchy sat in the rear.

"Mordecai, my going-away party next Saturday night at the lodge is for members only," Gabriel said. "But we're having an after party. You'll be there, right?"

"If you come by and pick me up. Where you having the party?"

"At that new place, the Club Delisa," Gabriel answered.

"Good choice," Mordecai said. "It's one of them Harlem-style clubs with dancing waiters. James, you and Thelma Jenkins must have closed up the joint the other week. When I left, it was after twelve and you two were still going strong."

"Man, I ain't seen Thelma since then," James replied. "When I took her home, she grabbed a knife and tried to kill herself. I mean she really flipped her wig. I had to stay with her the whole night, trying to calm her down."

"That's one of the oldest female tricks in the game," Mordecai sneered. "You should have let her keep the knife. She wasn't about to kill herself."

"James, what was she upset about?" Punchy asked.

"She wants me to go to Detroit with her. I love my wife and

kids. I'm not going to leave them. I didn't know Thelma was this crazy. If I ever see her again, I'm crossing to the other side of the street. Say, Mordecai, how about doing *Shine?*"

"Yeah," St. Elmo urged. "You haven't done that one in a long time."

"Don't mind if I do," Mordecai said. "It was one helluva day when the news reached that Atlantic seaport town.

That the great Titanic was going down.

Shine was in the boiler room down below. Until the water came up to his waist.

Then he scooted up to the main deck in the utmost haste.

He said: 'Captain, oh captain, this ship is going down.'

Captain say: 'Shine, Shine, turn yourself around. This ship's got ninety-nine pumps to keep the water down!'

Shine say: 'Captain, them pumps is all burnt out inside.'

Shine jumped on the rail and poised to dive.

The captain's redheaded daughter came on the deck. Her drawers were below her knees and her dress was pulled above her neck.

She said: 'Shine, Shine, save poor me. I'll give you all your eyes can see.'

Shine say: 'I'm sure your stuff is good, while it last. But I'm swimming now to save my own black ass.'

Shine dove in the ocean and he swam on and on.

A great big shark came his way.

The shark said: 'Shine, Shine, you better swim fast. 'Cause I'm gonna sink my teeth into your ass.'

Shine said: 'You might be king of the ocean, you might be king of the sea. But you'll be just another dead fish if you mess with me.'

Shine swam on and on and on."

# 10

James went to the window and scanned the darkness.

Automobile headlights approached.

"On time she came," James, thinking that it was St. Elmo, opened the front door. Disappointed, he watched Mattie and his sons get out of the car.

"I figured you'd be at Gabriel's going-away party by now," Mattie said.

"St. Elmo is running late."

"Daddy, I did good at the Juneteenth rehearsal."

"I did, too. Didn't I, mother?"

"Yes, John, both of you did very well. Go get ready for bed."

Junior boy and John ran off.

A car horn honked.

"That must be St. Elmo and the fellows. See you, baby," James gave Mattie a quick kiss and went out.

Mattie's pajamas-clad sons raced in.

"Let me see."

They showed their freshly-brushed teeth.

There was a knock on the door.

"I wonder who it is," Mattie opened the door.

Emma, Cybil and Odilia, fashionably dressed, entered. Odilia carried a red dress.

"The roosters are away and now the chicks are free to play," Emma said. "Cybil's driving Gabriel's car. We're going to do some sho-nuff, sho-nuff partying tonight. Care to join us, Mrs. Pettaway?"

"No, thanks."

"Mattie, you *never* go anywhere anymore," Odilia lectured. "You're turning into a regular old stick-in-the mud."

"Come with us," Cybil urged. "We gonna shake our money-makers tonight."

"We're going to a nightclub," Emma said. "The whole town talking about the blues singer that's appearing there, Muddy Waters."

"Come on, Mattie," Odilia declared. "The words of the blues might be sad but the music makes you feel good."

"I don't have anything to wear."

"You always said how much you love this," Odilia showed the red dress.

"I can't leave the boys by themselves."

"Of course you can't," Emma agreed. "Mr. Pettaway will keep them for you. I've already asked him."

# 11

Dark shades covered the ballroom windows. Spiraling wisps of smoke formed a silvery haze. Some fifty neatly-dressed Knights, seated at white-coated tables, ate heartily. There was an air of gaiety, of camaraderie and tradition. You could feel the proud male vibrations.

The Knights' involvement in the military began in the 1880's. Silas Morningstar, one of the founders, served in the Tenth Cavalry. Silas, tiny black eyes glittering with interest, sat at a front row table with the veterans of the First World War—Bradford Sykes, Essex Dawson and Thaddeus Stier.

Gabriel, seated with St. Elmo, Punchy and James, was the first Knight to be drafted into the Second World War. A waiter served Gabriel his third helping of ice cream and apple cobbler.

"When this is over, you guys coming with me to pick up Mordecai, or do you want me to drop you off at the Club Delisa first?" St. Elmo asked.

"Maybe you should drop us off first," James said. "So we can get a good table."

Essex Dawson went onto the stage.

"Brothers! Brothers!" he waved his arms. "It's time for our after-supper entertainment. So without any further to-do! Righteous Ray Rudledge and the Three Snapping Purses: Mamie, Mindy and Mary Lou!"

The house lights gradually dimmed. Orange stage lights, glowing seductively, slowly blossomed. Righteous Ray Rudledge stepped out. Dark-suited and chubby, he could have easily been mistaken for a preacher, professor or a poet. He sat at the piano and played lewd boogie-woogie.

Like moving shadows, the Three Snapping Purses danced onto the stage. Mamie wore a full-length white gown that emphasized her Coke-bottle shape. Mindy, wide mouth painted naughty purple, twirled a fox fur. Mary Lou, adorned in flamingo pink, played coy peek-a-boos with two white feathered fans.

The Knights expelled a tremendous, lustful roar.

Mamie, Mindy and Mary Lou commenced to roll, bump and grind. Then they stripped naked and tossed their G-strings to hot, eager hands. Thighs spread, they squatted enticingly. Whispering hot obscenities, they let mischievous fingers tuck rolled-up currency into their snapping purses.

## 12

There was no moon at all. A brilliant falling star lost its track in the darkness of the sky. The headlights exposed an intersection with four-way stop signs. St. Elmo slowed to a stop. He glimpsed headlights to his right. As he entered the intersection, the other car ran the stop sign, sideswiped his car and went into the ditch.

St. Elmo parked and ran to the car. The headlights were on and the motor was running. A white female, slumped forward, rested her head on the steering wheel. Seeing a gas station in the distance, St. Elmo ran to it.

"What you want, boy?" the attendant, a raw-boned white fellow, eyed St. Elmo.

"Mister, there's been an accident. Could you call an ambulance?"

"What sort of accident?"

"At the intersection, sir. A white lady ran the stop sign and almost hit my car. She ran her car in a ditch. She might be hurt. But it wasn't my fault."

"Boy, go back and wait. I'll call for an ambulance."

Whirring sirens heralded their arrival. Two cars carrying two pairs of white deputies squealed to a stop. The first pair hurried to the car in the ditch.

The other pair, brandishing flashlights, accosted St. Elmo.

"Where you coming from, nigger?" asked the granite-faced deputy.

"From my lodge, sir. We was giving a going-away party for one of our members who's going into the army."

The granite-faced deputy thrust his light in St. Elmo's eyes.

"Nigger, you drunk, ain't you?" he demanded.

"No, sir," St. Elmo replied. "I had one drink earlier in the evening but I'm not drunk. I'm not lying, sir."

"Hell, the nigger ain't been born who knows the difference between a lie and the truth," the other deputy said. "Stand up straight, nigger. Say your ABC's."

St. Elmo swallowed deeply and recited the alphabet.

"Ah right, nigger. Say them backwards."

A pearl-colored ambulance, siren blistering, red lights flashing, arrived. The driver and his prissy blond assistant hopped out.

"This way," the deputy with a cleft chin beckoned.

"What's the story?" the driver asked.

"It looks like you got sent on a wild goose chase."

The ambulance driver stuck his head inside the window. The car reeked of alcohol and vomit. The driver was sprawled across the seat.

"She's drunker than a skunk and out like a light," the towheaded deputy laughed.

A car approached, spotlight glaring.

St. Elmo raised his hand, shielding his eyes. He heard car doors slam, treading feet and muffled voices.

Silence.

"Talk, nigger!" Sheriff Westbrook Winchester's voice shattered the silence.

"Sir?"

"Talk, nigger!"

"Well, sir, I stopped at the intersection," St. Elmo felt himself trembling. "I had the right of way but the white lady ran the stop sign and . . ."

"Repeat that, nigger."

"Yes, sir. I stopped at the intersection. I had the right of way but the white lady . . ."

"Niggers don't have any rights where white people are concerned," using the side of his pistol, Winchester cracked St. Elmo's jaw.

## 13

Cozy and funky, the Club Delisa, as befitting a temple for the blues, exuded an aura of eroticism and mysticism. Lower-class African Americans formed the core of the true believers. That night, having received by word of mouth that a new messiah, Muddy Waters, plied in their midst, they arrived *early* to witness the appearance of a chosen one.

Muddy Waters didn't disappoint. He opened with *Hoochie Coochie Man*. Guitar in his lap, nimble fingers evoking voodoo chords, he and his band did magic. An elegant waiter boogied up to their table and served drinks to James, Punchy and Gabriel. On the dance floor, high-fashioned couples swayed with the winsome blues air flowing from the bandstand. *Muddy's voice was pure and divine.* A waiter, twirling a silvery tray, performed libidinal dance steps. The table of peasants partied hard; their loudness complemented their countrified attire. At the angular bar, sure-handed bartenders in racy hats served straight spirit shots to the multitude. A flashy group of chappies and chippies partied like Roman lords and ladies. Belly shaking like jelly, a tubby sergeant tossed and turned his skinny-legged partner about the dance floor.

"Ah right, y'all," Muddy Waters announced. "We're going to play a tune written by a great piano player and a very good friend of mine, Avery Parrish, *After Hours*."

The sound of the haunting, adagio, gutbucket blues prompted a frantic scramble to the dance floor.

Thelma Jenkins, wearing a tiger-colored dress, sat down next to James.

"Why you ain't been to see me, honey? I miss you something awful. Just sitting next to you makes me wet. Come on. Dance with me."

"I don't feel like dancing."

"James, don't make me get down on my knees and beg. Only one dance. I won't bother you anymore. Honest, sweetie. For old times' sake."


Odilia, Cybil, Emma and Mattie swept into the Club Delisa. Propelled by some irresistible galvanism, they went straight to the dance floor. Emma saw James and Thelma dancing together. She nudged Mattie and bobbed her head in their direction.

Mattie, a devilish smile on her face, strolled over.

"Hi, James," she tapped his shoulder. "Are you having a nice time?"

James and Thelma jumped away from each other.

"Mattie, what you see is a lie."

"I know the truth when I see it. Your belt, please."

"But Mattie, it's not how it looks."

"*'If you ever catch me with Thelma and tap me on the shoulder, I'll take off my belt and let you whip me right there, on the spot,*'" Mattie mimicked James. "Always talking about pride. Are you going to keep your word, or not?"

James pulled his belt off and handed it to Mattie.

"Now take off your coat. I want to get your butt real good. Bend over," Mattie began lashing James. Suddenly, she stopped. "Oh, my God!" She collapsed on the floor.

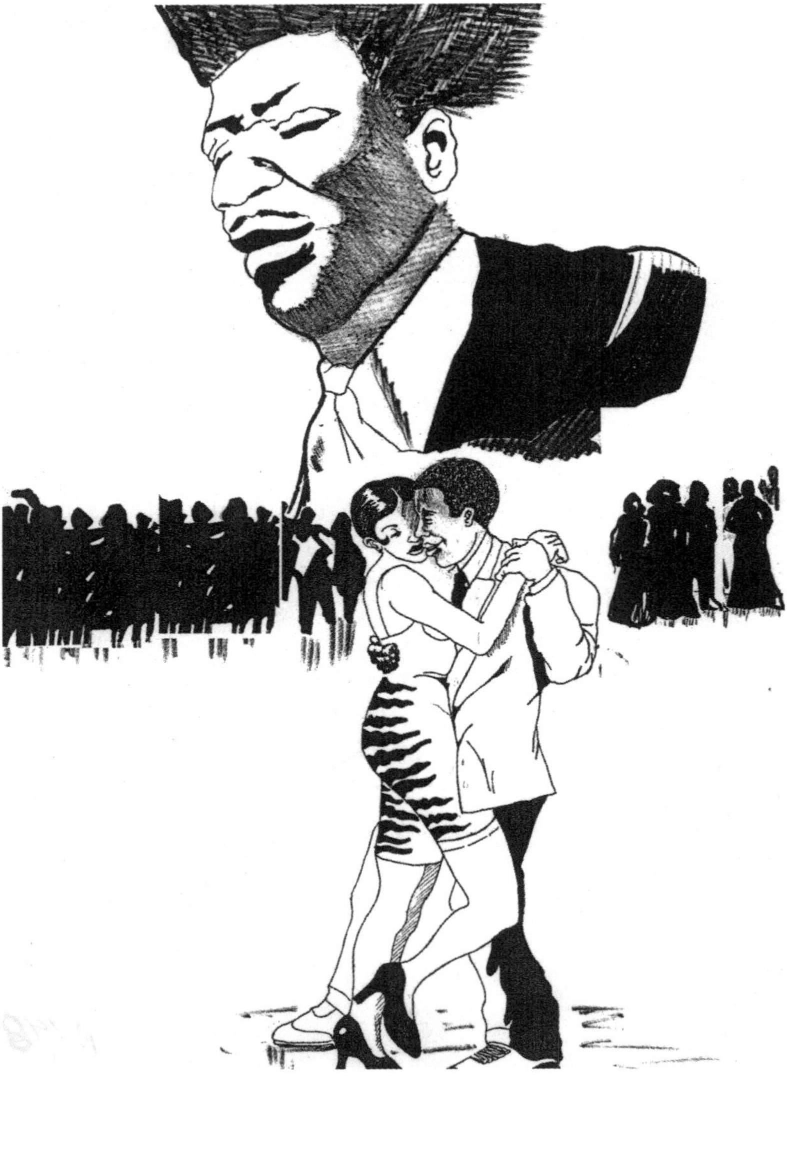

## 14

Dr. Malcolm Dobson beckoned Linda Edgewater into his office.
"Malcolm, exactly what is Mattie's problem?" Linda Edgewater asked.
"I'm only a general practitioner. But if I had to hazard a guess, I'd say it falls in the general category of female trouble. There seems to be an inflammation . . . ."
Mattie came out of the examination room.
"Here you are, Mattie. We were just discussing your condition. The doctor says it's female trouble."
"On the other hand, it could be a simple infection. I'm going to try a treatment but I can't guarantee the results. If it is female trouble, you'll have to consult a specialist. Unfortunately, the only good ones are in New Orleans."

## 15

St. Elmo sat on the side of his hospital bed. Dr. Edgar Hill, using a scalpel, removed the bandage from his face.
"Just a few more seconds, there. How does the jaw feel?"
"It's still a little sore."
"Here, this prescription should be of some help. Take one every four hours, or when you feel any pain. Is there someone coming for you?"
"Yes, sir, James Pettaway and my wife."
"Excellent. Come to my office next week for a checkup," Dr. Hill moved on.
St. Elmo put his personal items in his overnight bag. Then he tore out a page from a *Life* magazine and put it in his pocket.

## 16

James, Odilia and St. Elmo stared at the Pontiac. Windows smashed. "Nigger" etched into the doors. Tires slashed.

"Oh, my God," Odilia sobbed.

St. Elmo lifted the hood. Dirt covered the engine. The battery was gone.

"This is a real killer," St. Elmo slammed down the hood. "For simply trying to perform a good deed, I got pistol-whipped and fined twenty-five dollars for resisting arrest. Now my car is ravaged. You know what it is? These white people down here refuse to treat us like human beings. God blessed us with a divine spirit just like he did to every other human being he created. I'm through with the South.

"See this?" he showed the page he'd torn from the magazine at the hospital.

"This article is about a shipyard in Oakland, California, that needs workers, black or white and they are willing to train you. Odilia, I'll leave first. Then, after I save up enough money, I'll send for you. There's too much fear here. A black man's life is always under a threat in the South. They never stop putting our humanity to a test. I'm sick and tired of living in fear all the time."

## 17

James came out of the rear door of the factory.

"James, I've been looking for you," Sonny Patterson called. "My carburetor's acting up again."

"O.K. I'll get my toolbox."

Sonny followed James into his cubicle.

"What do you think about the five-dollar raise we got today?" Sonny asked. "I thought sure as hell Edgewater would start paying me forty dollars a week, at least. But I guess I can live on the $38.50 for a while. How much was your raise?"

"I didn't go get my check yet," James collected his toolbox. "You ready to go?"

After James adjusted Sonny's carburetor, he put his toolbox

away. He glided down the aisle. As he approached the office, a smile took over his face.
*Hot zigidy dog! If Sonny got a raise to $38.50 a week, my raise must be over forty dollars! Wait 'til I tell Mattie. I can buy her that watch she liked. The boys could stand some new shoes. On the other hand, maybe I won't touch the extra money. Maybe I'll put it with the money we're saving for our house.*

Verna Steele rapped a snappy cadence on the typewriter.
"Good afternoon, Miz Steele," James entered the office.
"Hello, James," she had a chalk-white face, watery gray eyes and thin, cottony curls edging her ears. "I know why you're here." She gave James his check.
"Thanks, Miz Steele."
James went to his cubicle and placed his check face down on his table. Using both hands, he fingered the top edge, lifted it and took a peek.
"What?" he pressed down the check abruptly; his mind rejected what his eyes saw. He peeped again. The amount remained unchanged. *This can't be my check. Thirty-two dollars and sixty-four cents can't be right. Sonny said he's making $38.50.*
He subtracted the amount of his check from Sonny's: four dollars and eighty-six cents! *Four dollars and eighty-six cents . . . Damn! That's the same difference we had when we first started working here! But that can't be right. He's only a truck driver. There's no way he could still be making more money than me. I'll go speak to Mr. Edgewater and straighten this out.*

James knocked and entered.
Forrest's desk displayed family pictures.
"How is it going, James?"
"O.K., I guess. Mr. Forrest, I came to ask about my check," James handed Forrest the check. "I was wondering if there's a mistake."

Forrest read the check and returned it to James.

"No, there's no mistake."

"Oh . . ."

"Is there something else?"

"What it is, Mr. Forrest, Sonny said he makes $38.50 a week."

"That's true."

"Mr. Forrest, I don't think that's fair. Sonny started out making four dollars and eighty-six cents a week more than me for doing the same job. Here it is, ten years later. He's still a truck driver. I manage your factory. Yet he makes more than me."

"I can't pay a Negro as much money as a white man. It's a matter of principles."

"I realize it's not my place to say, sir. But sometimes in the name of fairness, you should forget about principles and do what's right."

"You are right. It's not your place to say. Now go. I have work to do."

James returned to his cubicle and laid his head on his desk.

*All these years, I been thinking I was special. I loved Mr. Forrest. I thought he felt the same way about me. I would have done anything in the world for him. Oh, God! It's not fair.*

Forrest stood in the doorway.

"James, you can work a half day on Saturdays," he said. "I'll pay you double time. That way, you can more than make up for any difference."

# 18

James and Aaron chopped weeds from a row of tomatoes.

"You know what it is, Poppa? White people down here don't want us to be human beings. A Negro who's trying to be a good Christian, trying to live right, doesn't mean a thing to them. They'll still misuse you. Another reason I was thinking about going is that I don't want to raise my sons in the South. They can never be men down here."

"Your boss did offer to let you work on Saturdays, didn't he?"

"It's still not fair. I manage his factory. Why must I work overtime to make as much money as a truck driver? It makes me mad just thinking about it. A man's got to have his pride."

"What's your plan for Mattie and the boys if you go to California with St. Elmo?"

"I'll save my money and send for them. What do you think, Poppa?"

"Let me pray on it."

## 19

James swept the floor of his cubicle. He'd already filled the trashcan with old work clothes, shoes and other artifacts accumulated over the years.

"Good. I caught you before you left," Douglas Bixby entered. "I'll miss you, James. You've been a real straight shooter with me from the day we met. Say, you're not throwing away your clipboard, are you?"

"Un-huh. Take it, if you want."

"Thanks, James. Old man Edgewater sure is something, ain't he? Rather than pay you what you're worth, he'd rather hire two white men to take your place."

James knocked on Forrest's door and entered.

"I'm here to pick up my check, sir."

"I've included a bonus," Forrest handed James a check. "To show my appreciation for you staying on a month to train the new men. Linda said you and a friend are leaving for California on Monday."

"Yes, sir. See you, Mr. Edgewater."

"See you, James."

Forrest watched Lucinda ease onto the gravel road. Both, in their own way—James, behind the wheel; Forrest, at his window—experienced an acute sense of sorrow. Unable to stifle their emotions, they cried.

# Summer Love

### Summer, 1943.

THE RAYS OF THE EARLY MORNING SUN slipped through the window. Junior boy, in the lower bunk, slept soundly; above him, John, knees making a tee-pee with the covers, snored in iambic pentameter. Outside, gray sparrows with brown-tipped wings, immersed in busy work, chirped and chattered.

Junior boy rolled over and checked the clock: seven-thirty! He sprang from his bed, put on his swimming suit, dressed, went into the kitchen and wolfed down his breakfast. He grabbed his cap, tipped out the front door and hopped on his bicycle.

He was almost out of the front yard when Mattie called from the porch:

"Boy, you come back here," she adjusted the belt of her bathrobe. "When are you going to read this letter from your father?"

"Can't I read it later?"

"No. You're not putting it off another day," Mattie led Junior boy into the living room. "So busy with your new friends. Here. Read it out loud. You know how much I like to hear you read. Take off your cap in the house."

"*'August 18, 1943. Oakland, California. Dear wife. How*

*are you and the boys? This letter leaves me in good health and doing fine. Except for the fact that I am still sleeping in the bath tub.'* How come Daddy sleeps in a bath tub?"

"Because there's a housing shortage out there."

" *'I heard that one of the other roomers is moving in with his girlfriend, so I might have me a nice eight-hour bed before long. You all are really going to like the weather out here. It seems like it never rains. The sun shines every day. By the way, next week I am going back to the housing office.'* What's a housing office, Momma?"

"A place where you find out about renting a place to live."

" *'Tell Junior boy and John I said hello and to be good boys. Also tell them that there are lots of parks out here for them to play in. Well, that is all for now. Your loving husband, James. P.S. Odilia is working as a riveter in the shipyard. Me, her and Noah are working on the same shift.'* Can I go now?"

"Yes. But you be back home before I get back from work."

"Yes, ma'am."

"No tree climbing. You hear? I don't want you coming home hurt again. Remember, no swimming. And keep away from them white boys. You hear me?"

"Yes, ma'am."

"Give me a kiss."

## 2

Junior boy hopped from his bicycle, pocketed several rocks from his stash and continued on his way. His new friends, Myles and Myrtle Covington lived in South Bend, Indiana. They were visiting their aunt, Beryl Baker, for the summer. Myles was Junior boy's age, eleven. Myrtle was fourteen. Their father was a pilot in the 99th Pursuit Squadron and they had pictures to prove it.

Myles, who loved football, deified Notre Dame. All summer,

he entertained Junior boy with stories about Knute Rockne, the Four Horsemen and the Seven Mules.
Junior boy admired Myles.
He loved Myrtle.
Gripping the handlebars, pumping with all his might, he rapidly descended into the gully, whizzing past underbrush, down, down, until he swished across the trembling bridge into bright sunlight. The road inclined steeply and he had to push his bicycle. After he passed the giant pine tree that he and Myles had dubbed "Big Bertha," it was downhill until he reached the elementary school for white children. He feared this part of his journey because a group of white adolescents, led by Fat Freddy, hung out on the playground. He scanned the deserted playground, relaxed and coasted, the whispering wind nibbling at his ears.

About fifty yards before he reached Beryl Baker's house, Junior boy parked his bicycle, stashed his rocks and followed the footpath. The backdoor was unlocked. He entered, locked the door behind him, tipped into Myrtle's bedroom, undressed and slid under the covers. Snuggling up to Myrtle, he fitted himself into the contours of her nude, honey-colored body. He toyed with her sleep-scented, autumn-colored hair. The warmth of her breasts and thighs aroused him.
Myrtle stroked his head.
He tongued her almond-colored nipples the way she'd taught him to do.

An hour later, Junior boy retrieved his bicycle and pedaled back to Beryl Baker's house. He gave the swing on the veranda a gentle push and knocked on the door.
Beryl Baker appeared.
"Good morning, Junior boy. Come on in," Beryl's gray hair was coiled beneath her orange bandanna. "Myles is still asleep."

"That's O.K., Mrs. Baker. I'll work on my model airplane."

"Have fun. I'm going to catch a few more winks."

Junior boy was working on a British Spitfire; Myles, a German Stuka. They had spread their blueprints on the floor behind the piano. Using a razor blade, he started cutting the ribs for the right wing.

Myles Covington stood in the doorway.

"Pettaway, I'm getting ready to have some cereal," short and wiry with long arms, he had reddish-brown hair and wide-awake brown eyes. "Care to join me?"

"If you insist."

"Who's insisting? You joker."

"You turkey," Junior boy stuck out his leg and tried to trip Myles.

Myles maintained his balance. On their way to the kitchen, they took turns trying to trip each other.

After breakfast, Myles and Junior boy worked on their models. Then they went outside and played commandoes. They went from gunplay, to hand-to-hand combat, to a wrestling match. Junior boy was tall and determined; Myles, short and quick.

"Time out! Time out," Myles, dramatically gasping for air, halted their play. "My sinuses are acting up again."

"You all right, Covington?"

"I tricked you!" Myles tackled Junior boy and they tumbled to the ground.

"Boys, it's time for your lunch," Beryl Baker called.

Myrtle joined them. When they finished lunch, Myles, in deference to his sinus condition and Beryl, in deference to her age, retired for their naps.

Junior boy and Myrtle went to the veranda. Myrtle wore Junior boy's cap. She carried a novel with a false cover. Acting like she was the queen of the hill, she sat in the swing and opened *The Sport of the Gods,* the controversial novel by

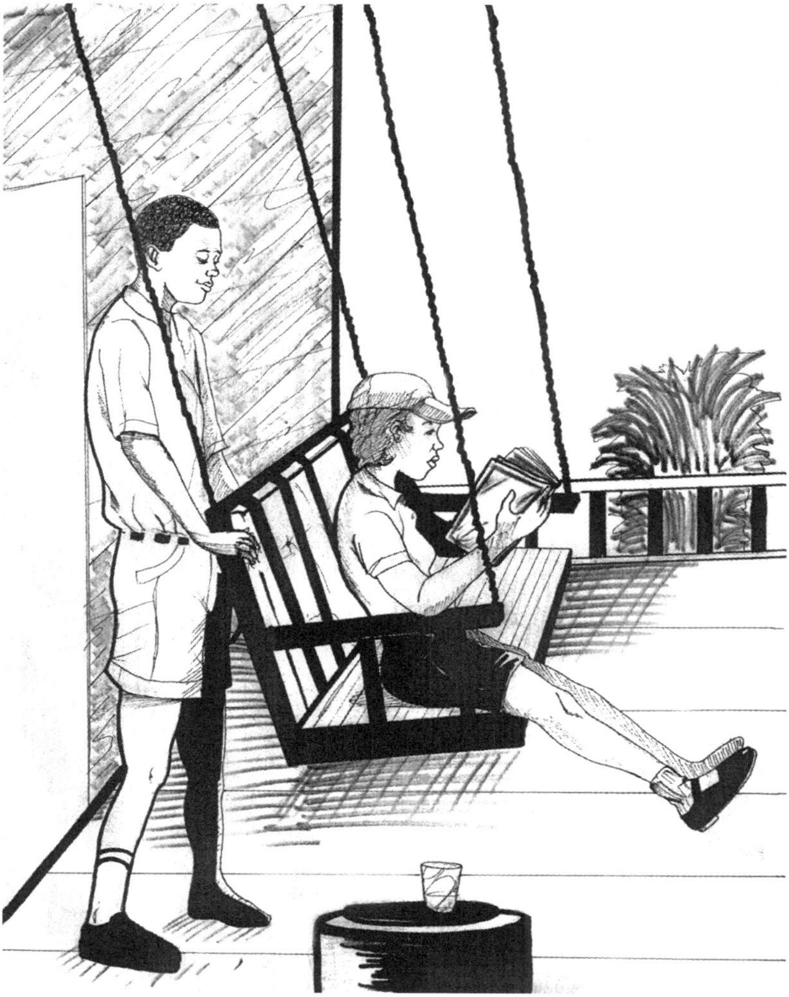

Paul Laurence Dunbar. She had underlined in red her favorite passages.

Junior boy pushed the swing gently.

"I shall start at the Banner Club scene, where Hattie first meets Joe," Myrtle had committed herself to the theater. Voice throaty, she began reading.

The way her lips moved fascinated Junior boy.

"Myrtle, it's time for your piano lesson," Beryl Baker called from within.

"Oh, pooh! Just when I was getting to the good part," Myrtle closed her book and went inside.

Myles came out of the front door.

"You got on your swimming suit?" Junior boy asked.

"Need you ask?"

They hopped on Junior boy's bicycle and started off.

"Myles," Beryl Baker came out on the porch. "Don't forget what I said. No swimming and don't get into trouble with those white boys. No climbing trees now. Remember what happened the last time. That goes for you, too, Junior boy."

"Yes, auntie."

"Yes, Mrs. Baker."

"Wait a minute," Junior boy said as they approached his stash of rocks. "You want some?" He hopped off the bicycle.

"It's not the time for Fat Freddy and his gang of ruffians. They usually swim later in the afternoon."

"Suit yourself. I'm not taking any chances."

They arrived at a fork in the road, parked the bicycle and took the trail that led to the inlet. They climbed over a weathered gate and sauntered across the meadow. A majestic black bull, resting in the shade of a tree, observed a herd of cows. Moving aside foliage with their hands, they made their way through the shrubs and bushes. Even before they reached the inlet, they could hear ringing laughter and jolly squeals. Dropping to the ground like commandoes, they wiggled forward and peered through a tiny opening: cream-colored arms, legs and alabaster butts splashed in the water.

"I'll divide my rocks with you; I've got eight. Let's ambush them for once."

"I've counted nine of them. Fat Freddy would just lead a counter attack and we'd be forced to make another strategic withdrawal," Myles said. "Wait a minute, wait a minute. They've left their clothes under that tree. See? I've got an idea. Let's steal them."

"Their duds?"

"Yeah. Then we'll tie them together and hang them on top of Big Bertha."

"What a great idea," Junior boy said. "The only thing wrong with it is that I didn't think of it myself."

"Here's the plan, Pettaway. Wait until I sneak around to the other side. When I give you the signal, begin your attack. While they're busy with you, I'll snatch their clothes. After you run out of ammo, make a strategic withdrawal. We'll rendezvous at Big Bertha."

## 3

Myles, standing beneath Big Bertha, tied the pilfered clothes together.

"It worked," Junior boy ran up. "It worked. I got Fat Freddy in the breadbasket. You should have seen him. All bent over, holding his belly like it was a pumpkin."

"Beautiful," Myles tied the string of clothes to his waist.

The first limb was about ten feet from the ground. They'd learned to scale the trunk like mountain climbers. Moving cautiously, they began the climb. About halfway, they carefully avoided the broken limb from which they'd recently fallen.

They reached a new height.

Suddenly, the limb cracked beneath them. The limb righted itself, swayed and cracked again, causing them to fall to the limb below them. They crawled to the trunk and hugged it with devotion, not daring to look up or down.

Their eyes met. It was classic: one was afraid; the other was glad of it.

"What do you think, Pettaway?"

"I figure we climbed high enough, for today."

"Me, too."

Myles tied the string of clothes to a limb. They made their slow descent.

They arrived at the fork in the road.

"See you, Pettaway." Myles hopped off the bicycle.

"Later, Covington."

"We're going to complete our mission on Monday, right?"

"We're going to climb Big Bertha for sure."

"All the way to the very top?"

"All the way to the very top."

"See you on Monday?"

"See you on Monday," Junior boy rode off.

# 4

Mattie worked as a maid in a downtown boutique that specialized in exclusive women's apparel. That Saturday afternoon at closing time she locked the door behind the last customer and started vacuuming. When she finished, she went into the dressing room. She put on a pair of beige riding pants, slipped on a pair of elegant cordovan boots and studied her reflection in the mirror.

*Not bad, for an old lady.*

She had purchased the pants and boots at a reduced price after a valued customer demanded a refund after wearing them in a horseshow.

## 5

Cybil Jones sat in a booth at the Do Drop In Cafe. She worked as a ticket seller at the colored window of the movie house. She wore a brown uniform and an orange fez with black trimmings.

"Mattie. Over here," she waved.

"What's up, Cybil?"

"Not a whole bunch."

"Where's Emma?"

"In the ladies' room. I still can't believe she volunteered for the Waves."

"It didn't surprise me. Remember the way she talked about joining, even before the navy drafted Punchy? You got any mail from Gabriel lately?"

"No. It's not like I'm missing very much. The censors don't let anything through. They even cut out the dates. The way Uncle Sam gouges letters is far too cold. All I know is that Gabriel is somewhere in Italy. Here she comes now."

Emma lent her white uniform an understated elegance.

"Emma!" Mattie gave her a hug. "How long is your furlough?"

"Two weeks."

"Emma, take this seat, I must return to the theater soon," Cybil gave Emma the inside seat. "You two are really going to enjoy the feature, *The Duke Is Tops*. Ralph Cooper and Lena Horne play the lovers. It's funny and there's a lot of good singing and dancing."

"Emma," Mattie said. "When's the last time you heard from your husband?"

"Oh, Punchy's doing real good. I got a letter from him a few days ago. His ship is somewhere in the Pacific. He couldn't say where. '*A slip of the lip can sink a ship.*'" Emma put her purse in the space next to Mattie. "Have you heard that Reverend Carridine is in the hospital? He had a stroke."

"I'm sorry to hear that," Mattie replied.

"Emma, check out Mattie," Cybil said. "All she needs now is one of those riding caps and a horsewhip and she could be mistaken for Miss Lady Vanduckinghamm."

The waitress appeared.

"What would you ladies like?" she asked.

Mattie ordered the liver dinner.

"A chicken sandwich for me," Emma said.

"Hmmm, everything looks so good," Cybil studied the menu. "I'll have the chitterlings dinner, please."

The waitress went off.

"Emma, is that all you going to eat, a sandwich?" Cybil asked.

"You know what they say: 'A *moment on the lips. A lifetime on the hips.*'"

## 6

Emma and Mattie exited The Do Drop In and walked toward the theatre.

"Mattie, tell me something. In one of your letters, you mentioned that you were going to see a specialist in New Orleans about your condition. Did you ever go?"

"Yeah, I went. He said I should have an operation."

"So, when are you having it?" Emma asked.

"Never, I hope. I'm trying some new medicine. So far, I feel just fine."

A white patrol car came their way. Sheriff Westbrook Winchester, flanked by two deputies, sat in the rear of the car. When he sighted Emma and Mattie, his body became rigid.

"Turn around," he ordered the driver. "Slow down. Stop ahead of them two nigger wenches." Winchester jumped out and ran to Mattie and Emma. "What in the Sam Hill you niggers think you doing?"

Emma and Mattie froze with fear.

"Gal, what kind of uniform is that?"

"The Women Accepted for Volunteer Emergency Service, sir. I'm a Wave."

"I don't give a good goddamn what you are. You can't walk the streets dressed in a uniform like that. You'll confuse people. And you, you can't wear a fancy riding outfit like that. Only well-to-do white ladies dress like that. Turn your black asses around and git off this street. If I ever see you again, you better be wearing clothes that's fit for nigger wenches. Now git! Go on! Git!"

# 7

That Monday morning, Junior boy, riding his bicycle with no hands, glided toward the Baker house. He parked his bicycle, stashed his rocks and took the footpath. When he reached the backdoor, he tried the knob. The door was locked. Deciding that it was too early to wake up Beryl, he went on the veranda and lay down in the swing.

High above, a V-shaped flock of geese flowed in harmony across the horizon.

Beryl Baker, carrying gardening tools, discovered her sleeping guest.

"Junior boy, why are you sleeping out here?" she nudged him.

"I got here a little early. I didn't want to wake anyone up. Is Myles still asleep?"

"I'm sorry, honey. Myles and Myrtle are gone. Their mother and father arrived unexpectedly on Saturday and picked them up."

Junior boy couldn't think of anything to say.

"Myles left his model plane. He said he wanted you to have it. Myrtle was so sad she didn't have the chance to say goodbye to you. She asked me to be sure to tell you that she has your cap. She said you would understand."

# 8

Junior boy tied the pilfered clothes around his waist and continued climbing. He approached the limb from which he and Myles had fallen. Fear flitted through his heart. He hesitated. *Maybe I should turn back? What if another limb breaks?* He reminded himself that Myles was gone and it was up to him to complete the mission. He made his way around the limb. When he reached the top branch, he viewed the magnificent expanse. He tied the string of clothes to the trunk. Feeling Big Bertha's gentle sway, he longed for Myrtle.

# California Bound

**Autumn, 1943.**

C.C. CARRIDINE SAT IN A ROCKING CHAIR on his front porch. He was surrounded by a group of parishioners who had dropped by to pay their respects and cheer him up.

"Reverend Carridine, your being up and about like this sure fooled a lot of people," Mattie smiled. "Thank God."

"I guess He has more work for me, because when He calls, you must go. Mattie, it was so nice of you to come over with your two fine sons to say goodbye. In case some of you folks are unaware of it, Mattie and her sons are taking the train next Wednesday to join her husband and their father in Oakland, California. So many of our young people have left us already. I realize they've moved on in search of a better life. But if this continues, I fear that someday there won't be anyone left in the South to carry on after my generation is gone."

## 2

Animated clusters of African American in-migrants, surrounded by their friends and relatives, jammed the colored waiting room of the train station. Bound for Detroit, Chicago and Oakland, they carried wooden and leather suitcases and boxes of all sizes.

They also carried brown paper bags that bulged with baked sweet potatoes, biscuits and fried chicken.

One cluster, centered around Mattie Pettaway and her sons, was especially lively: Cybil Jones, Shelby, Lynn and their son, Aaron Pettaway, Dudley and Retha, Meldrick Merryweather and Mordecai Leaks.

"Miz Mattie Fae Pettaway," Mordecai smiled. "Go on with your bad self."

"Mordecai, I'm so glad you came."

"You know what occurred to me?" Mordecai said. "Life can be so mischievous at times. I was the first one to talk about leaving town. Now, I'm the only one still here."

"All aboard for St. Louis, Missouri," a voice cried. "All aboard for St. Louis!"

## 3

"St. Louis the next stop. St. Louis. St. Louis!" the conductor called.

"Momma, is St. Louis across the Mason-Dixon line?" John asked.

"Yes, John," Mattie returned to her Bible.

"Junior boy, trade seats with me. I want to look out the window, so I can see the Mason-Dixon line when we cross it."

"There's nothing to see. It's only an imaginary line. You probably don't even know what it means."

"I do, too. In the bad old days when our people were in bondage, if they crossed it, it meant freedom."

"It's still an imaginary line."

"It ain't!"

"It is!"

"It ain't!"

"It is!"

Mattie, who had taught her sons about the Mason-Dixon line, remembered Oreville Hunter. During the summer after she married James, he resigned his teaching position and returned to Chicago. Years later, she heard he was a successful lawyer. During the early years of her marriage, whenever things with James went sour, she thought of Oreville and wondered what her life would have been like if she had married him. However, she hadn't thought of Oreville in years. She never regretted her decision to marry James. He was a good provider. They loved each other.

She felt sad and excited at the same time—sad because of the friends and family she'd left behind; excited at the prospect of starting a new life with James and her sons in a place where there was no fear; excited at the prospect of getting a job as a riveter in the shipyard, like Odilia.

## 4

The train pulled into the St. Louis station.

As soon as she and her sons were off the train, Mattie dropped to her knees.

"What are you doing, Momma?" Junior boy asked.

"Thanking the Lord for delivering us from the South."

"I want to thank Him, too."

"Me, too."

They gave thanks.

# The Private and the Captain

# The Last Antebellum Autumn

## Louisiana, 1860.

"THIS MORNING, IT IS MY CHRISTIAN DUTY to warn you of the awful misery that awaits every one of you if you are condemned to hell—an existence far more painful than your lot as slaves here on earth," the minister said. A portly man of fifty, he had silvery hair and a crinkled, white face. He paused and looked slowly over the rows of tan, brown and black faces. "Serve God if you would save your souls in heaven and on earth. Obey your master as dutifully as you serve God."

Caesar Pettaway sat with his wife Nydia and their three sons. In his early twenties, he had smooth, black skin and a handsome, round face. His massive shoulders and powerful arms bulged beneath his shirt. He lowered his head and sighed. Whenever he attended church, he experienced a feeling of melancholy. He hated slavery more than he loved the Lord. He wondered how it would feel to be free.

Nydia, who was a year younger than Caesar, held their youngest son in her lap. Totally absorbed, her brown eyes sparkled.

"Your master, Purcell Pettaway, is God's earthly overseer! Be dutiful and honest with him. Do not be sullen, or lazy. Do not seek to run away. Be faithful. And take better care of his animals. Purcell Pettaway is, by God's will, your earthly keeper. It is God's will that you should serve him faithfully. God will weigh your sins on the Day of Judgment. If you have not been faithful slaves here on earth, He will cast your souls into the fiery flames of hell where you will burn throughout eternity! Amen."

Nydia, who lived to sing each Sunday, led the congregation in a moving rendition of *There Is a Holy City*.

# 2

The morning sun created a white haze in the distant sky. Falling leaves, changing to brownish gold and dull orange manifested Mother Nature's perpetual cycle of life, death and renewal. The Pettaway family emerged from the church. They took the sandy trail that curled through the slave quarters where slaves swept out their shacks, chopped firewood and tended small plots of vegetables.

Caesar carried his youngest son piggyback. His two other sons hopped and skipped ahead. Nydia walked beside him. Caesar and Nydia had been born on the Pettaway plantation. Caesar never knew his father and cherished only a vague but warm memory of his mother. Purcell Pettaway sold her when he was seven and deposited him with Nydia's family. On Caesar's tenth birthday, Purcell Pettaway sold him to his current master, Bosley Legouis. Bosley assigned him to a four-year apprenticeship with a journeyman carpenter. Caesar never forgot his surrogate family. After completing his apprenticeship, he asked Bosley Legouis' permission to visit Nydia's family. To his delight, Bosley not only gave his permission but he also convinced Purcell Pettaway to allow the visits.

Time passed.

Nydia and Caesar fell in love. Both were deeply religious. Although marriages between slaves carried no legal status, they didn't care to live in sin. Caesar went to Bosley Legouis who

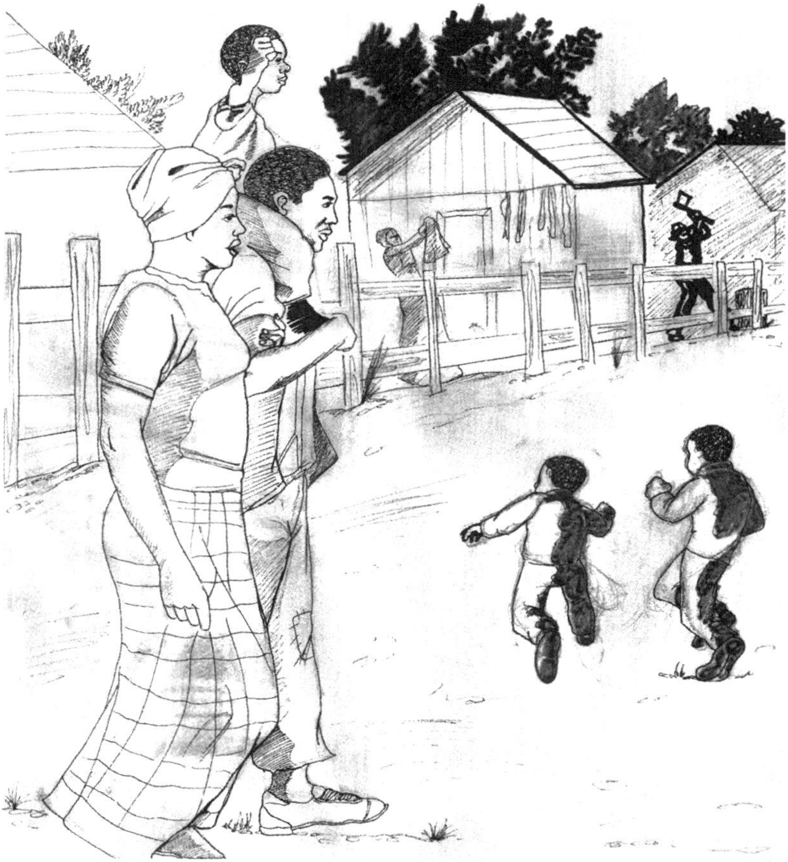

promptly gave his permission. Later, Bosley broached the matter with Purcell Pettaway.

Purcell, a third-generation slave owner, didn't consider slaves human. At first he refused: "By God, man! Marriage between two beasts is an abomination. It mocks the sacred institution of holy matrimony."

"But Purcell, it is widely known that a married slave is more contented, more productive and less likely to create mischief," Bosley replied. When he proposed a joint ownership of any issues produced by the marriage, Purcell Pettaway consented.

Slave laws dictated that Caesar and Nydia live separately. They could only spend every other weekend together. They'd been married almost six years and Caesar never missed a visit.

"After I buy mine, I'll buy freedom for the whole family," Caesar took his son from his shoulder, held him and looked into his eyes. "What you think of that, son? One day, I'm gonna buy you your freedom!" He tossed his son high in the air and caught him. "Nydia, you mighty quiet about my good news."

"Husband, say it again. How master Legouis is going to give you freedom."

"When I was brought to him, he was washing the blood from his hands that he got from the cock fighting in a shiny white pan. He said I am to pay him money each month and in twenty years, I am free from bondage."

"Husband, take care. You always say how your master hates we niggahs so."

"Yes, it's truly a riddle, Nydia. I can't reason it out myself. Master Legouis just said that come Wednesday next, I mark my contract."

# 3

A colorfully-costumed slave coachman applied the whip as the carriage whisked across Purcell Pettaway's plantation. Bosley Legouis, a short, stocky man of forty-seven with reddish-white cheeks, dozed in the rear seat. The oldest son of wealthy French

American Creoles, he managed his family's import business. He owned fifty slaves. He was more the broker than a master. Except for the thirteen slaves employed in his personal service, he hired out the others to different contractors.

They had been traveling three hours when the coachman slowed the carriage and pulled off to the side of the road to make way for a column of shabbily-dressed female slaves who carried hoes on their shoulders like ragtag soldiers.

## 4

The carriage stopped in front of the whitewashed Pettaway mansion. A gap-toothed mulatto female escorted Bosley inside and waddled off. Shabby rugs. Frayed curtains. No piano or musical instruments. Bosley, who traveled in the upper echelons of Manhattan and Paris society, viewed his surroundings with a snobbish indifference.

"Legouis, what a pleasure to see you," Purcell Pettaway was a wiry, silvery-haired man of sixty-seven. "You are right on time to see Justin instruct his first slave."

"Thanks for inviting me to witness your grandson's *rite de passage.*"

"Come, I have ordered my two finest horses. How is the wife? Is she still in New Orleans with her family?"

"Yes, Madame's constitution remains delicate, it grieves me to say."

Justin Pettaway, snug-fitting gray military uniform accentuating his trim frame, led his horse from the stable.

Purcell and Bosley appeared.

"*Mon ami,*" Bosley shook Justin's hand. "How good it is to see you. Purcell said you graduated at the top of your class at the academy. Congratulations."

"Yes, sir. Thank you," Justin blushed.

A weathered male mulatto with large, doe-like eyes emerged from the stable with two saddled horses.

# 5

Tiers of ancient trees surrounded the valley.

Purcell, Justin and Bosley dismounted when they reached the main shed. The odor of burnt human flesh poisoned the air. Inside the shed, an unconscious slave was draped over a barrel with a newly-branded "P" on his naked rump.

The overseer stirred the fire in the forge.

"What have we here?" Purcell approached the slave with the newly-branded mark.

"He just passed out, sir," the overseer answered. "I sent a nigger to the well for a bucket of water."

"Let's take a walk to the well, shall we?" Purcell suggested. "I feel a mite thirsty."

They passed a pilloried female slave whose head hung like a wilted flower.

"You are still resolved as to your plans, eh, Legouis?" Purcell scoffed. "Justin, he is setting another one of his niggers free."

"I'm not setting Caesar free. I'm simply allowing him to buy himself from me over a period of twenty years. The average slave rarely lives beyond thirty-five. Even if he does manage to live long enough to fulfill his contract, where is the loss to me? In twenty years he will have paid me over thirty times the money I originally invested in him. Purcell, as you well know, I think our slavery system is too inflexible. It needs refining. We have punishments but no rewards. Slaves have no incentive to be productive. But you take my nigger, Caesar. Now that he is buying his freedom, he'll work ten times as hard and my investment in him is secure. My models are the Romans. Their slave empire lasted a thousand years. I'm convinced that with a few adjustments, ours can perpetuate itself into infinity.

"We must be clever. Our slave labor force, as it is presently constructed, cannot compete with paid labor. It is because of the

North's superior industrial production capabilities that I'm opposed to the South's headlong plunge into war with them."

A series of paths ended at a pole that rose phallically from the bloodied earth.

"Remember, Justin," Purcell Pettaway put on a pair of kidskin gloves. "When instructing a nigger in proper behavior, the idea is to cut without wounding severely. Niggers are expensive animals. Pop the whip loud. That is of the utmost importance. A nigger will still remember the sound long after the cut has healed."

A group of young slaves sat in a semi-circle around the pole, their hair knotted with tiny webs of cotton and strings.

"What have we here?" Bosley studied the adolescents.

"We rounded them up so they can watch," Purcell yawned.

"Perhaps I should have a look," Bosley said. "Let's go over, shall we?"

The young slaves stood up as Purcell and Bosley approached them. Purcell ordered them to undress. Bosley stopped in front of a female. He inspected her teeth and breasts, turned her around and tested her buttocks.

Two drivers, acting on the overseer's orders, tied a male slave to the pole.

Justin practiced with a bullwhip.

Bosley observed a group of poorly-dressed, adult male slaves. Their arms were tied behind their backs.

"Any unusual offenders today, Purcell?"

"Just the usual. Runaways. Except for that one," Purcell indicated the slave tied to the pole. "He damn near hacked another nigger to death with an axe. Hell, there is nothing wrong with niggers fighting one another. In fact, I encourage it. It makes them even lustier. But we cannot have them killing and maiming each other."

# 6

Red velvet room saturated with sultry-scented incense.

White curtains.

Walls with portraits of big-bosomed female nudes with curvaceous white thighs.

Bosley Legouis, buck naked, sat in an elevated, king-size chair lined with fur. On the silky white bed below him, three nude teenage female slaves fondled and kissed each other for his pleasure.

Caesar Pettaway saw but did not study his surroundings.

"Do you understand our agreement?"

"Yes, master."

Bosley, yawning and stretching, went to the cabinet.

"Mark your 'X' here," he beckoned Caesar. "Both copies." Bosley handed Caesar a quill and returned to his chair.

A bare-chested, effeminate male slave who couldn't have been more than fourteen entered with a basin filled with scented water and a towel. Slipping to his knees, he cleaned Bosley's genitalia.

"One copy is for you. Leave the other," Bosley spread his thighs, allowing the bare-chested slave easier access. "Now go." He turned his attention to the bed.

# Captain Cailloux

## A Partial Listing of the Characters*

Brigadier General William F. Dwight,
*Union Army, commander of the Louisiana
Native Guard's First and Third Regiments*

Officers of the First Regiment
Colonel Chauncy J. Basset, *regiment commander*
Major Francis E. Dumas, *battalion commander*
Captain Andre Cailloux, *commander of Company B*
Captain P. B. S. Pinchback, *commander of Company C*
Captain Lionel Gardere, *commander of the field hospital*

The Fourth Platoon, Company B, First Regiment
Second Lieutenant Warren Underdue
First Sergeant Jasper Browning
Corporal London Rapier, *leader of the Third Squad*

The Third Squad
PFC. Caesar Pettaway
Pvt. Alpheus Hunter
Pvt. William Purvis

*The assault on Port Hudson is based on a real incident.

## Port Hudson, Louisiana, 1863.

THE UNION ARMY'S FIRST LOUISIANA Native Guard, a regiment composed of African American volunteers, bivouacked on a meadow about a mile from the Confederate-held Port Hudson. The sounds of marching men and virile voices barking out cadences mingled with the rays of the morning sun.

Captain Andre Cailloux eyed the mirror hanging from the tree as he shaved his handsome face. He often boasted that he was the blackest man in New Orleans. In his early thirties, he was a highly respected man of wealth and attainment. Everything about Andre—from his suaveness to the precise manner with which he articulated each of his words, savoring them as if they were succulent grapes—denoted a man of culture and refinement. Yet for all of this, there was something in his fierce black eyes and his haughtiness that let you know he was a man of action who courted and thrived on danger.

"*Mon Dieu!* After all the months of training how could General Dwight simply dismiss our lads from the Third two days before the battle?" Andre turned his head toward his tent mate, Captain Pickney Benton Stewart Pinchback. "He claims he no longer has faith in them. What's your thinking, Pickney?"

"I think the general's actions were arbitrary and uncalled for," P.B.S. Pinchback, a handsome, camel-colored man of twenty-six, trimmed his beard. "I'm sure Major Dumas will be able to convince him to rescind his dismissals."

Andre sat at the table, studying the chessboard. Pinchback, seated on his cot, polished his sword.

"What's the time, Pickney?"

"Don't worry. There's still plenty of time before our briefing with the general."

Captain Lionel Gardere stuck his head inside the tent.

"Ah! Here you are, lads," he said. As a youth, he dreamed of becoming an opera singer. However, the persistent pressure from his Afro-Creole parents disabused him of the idea. Like his father, he became a physician. The only remnant from his dream was the way his bass voice modulated when he spoke, as if he were singing an aria. "I come bearing a message from Major Dumas. All officers are to report immediately to Battalion Headquarters."

"Lionel, do you know why he wants us?" Andre asked.

"You know how meticulous the major is. He wants to give you a briefing before your briefing with General Dwight. Well, I'm off to see how the construction of the field hospital is going. See you, lads."

## 2

The grand white mansion that Brigadier General William F. Dwight commandeered for his headquarters overlooked the meadow on which the First and Third Louisiana Native Guards prepared for battle. He'd converted the drawing room into his office. Seated behind a mahogany table, he finished composing a dispatch. Ruddy-complexioned. Grayish-blond mane. Bushy eyebrows. He smacked his thin lips and signed his name with an expansive flourish.

"Sir," a red-bearded adjutant entered. "The *New York Times* reporter is here."

"Let him wait. Have this delivered to General Weitzel. Send in Bassett."

"Yes, sir," the adjutant took the dispatch and withdrew.

"Good morning, sir," Lieutenant Colonel Chauncy J. Bassett entered. He had close-cropped hair and deep whiskey eyes. "It looks like the good weather is holding. There's not a cloud in the sky."

"I wanted to speak to you before my briefing this morning.

Regarding the morale of your regiment, are your troops ready for battle?"

"They have wonderful voices. The way they sing you'd think they were going to a camp meeting. As to their being ready for battle, I must confess, I have grave reservations. This entire experiment with colored troops is a colossal mistake. I consider it my duty to urge you to make a contingency plan in case they should turn and run at the first sound of gunfire."

"What about those colored officers, in regards to their fitness to lead?"

"They seem fit enough. Physically. They march and maneuver the troops well. But I fear that when they face the enemy's artillery for the first time, they'll abandon the field quicker than their men."

"That will be all, Colonel."

"Very well, sir," Chauncy went out.

*Hmmm*, Dwight reflected. *To accord the duty of leading the assault to the Third Regiment with its newly-appointed white officers is problematical. To accord it to those colored officers is also problematical. What a devilish dilemma.*

# 3

"Gentlemen, your attention, please," Major Francis E. Dumas addressed his officers. "I have some grave news." He was a spirited, honey-colored man of thirty-five with curly brown hair and dreamy brown eyes. Along with Andre and some of their rich friends, he financed, recruited and trained the ex-slaves and freemen who now formed his battalion. "I regret to have to inform you that my effort to get our fellow officers from the Third reinstated has failed."

The officers reacted with dismay and anger.

"On what basis did General Dwight make his decision?" Andre asked.

"He said it was simply a military decision," said Dumas. He

was the only African American officer in the regiment with combat experience. He'd fought in several scrimmages in Mississippi. "From that point of view the dismissals are not unusual. He refused to deal with the racial and political implications. I've considered contacting our political friends in New Orleans but the battle will be over before we could get a message to them."

"Major," Pinchback raised his hand like a schoolboy. "There is a rumor that General Dwight dismissed our lads from the Third so he could have white officers lead the attack tomorrow."

"General Dwight wouldn't dare deny us the honor," Second Lieutenant Warren Underdue exclaimed. He was the twenty-one-year-old son of a well-to-do merchant. His uniform still bore the creases where it had been folded. "What justification could he have for such a dastardly decision? The First deserves the honor of leading the attack."

"Well spoken, lad," Andre's voice resonated with passion. "I say quite candidly that if those are Dwight's plans he's going to have a fight on his hands. I'll not yield on this. I believe that now is the time, chosen by God, for the salvation of our people."

# 4

When they arrived at General Dwight's headquarters, Major Dumas and his officers dismounted, hitched their horses and entered the mansion. The hallways and rooms buzzed with pre-battle excitement; messengers dashed hither and thither; majors, colonels and generals came and went.

General Dwight held his briefing in the ballroom. He had the air of a man who is quite pleased to be in his natural habitat. Speaking softly, he explained the importance of their mission. Port Hudson was the last remaining Confederate fortification on the Mississippi River. With its deadly batteries, it prevented the safe passage of Union supply ships and gunboats. His voice rose when he pointed out that in accomplishing their mission, they would be cutting the Confederacy in two.

"Our mission has an added significance. It is being coordinated with General Grant's attack on Vicksburg," General Dwight said in a forthright manner. "Gentlemen, we *will* perform well. Now to the battle plan."

Using his metal-tipped pointer, he directed his officers' attention to the map on the wall. "As you can see, Port Hudson is well fortified. Two batteries of field artillery. And a sixty-two-pound Columbiad in the center of the line, here. The overall plan is to form a semicircle, employing three columns. General Godfrey Weitzel will command the right column. General T.W. Sherman, the left. The Third and the First will form the center column. All three columns will attack at ten o'clock. General Weitzel's artillery will begin the bombardment at six."

The briefing progressed smoothly until Dwight pronounced his decision to accord the duty of leading the attack to the Third Regiment.

"Sir," Dumas jumped to his feet. "We have been with our men since they were construction engineers. We have witnessed their remarkable transformation into a unit of finely disciplined fighting men. If you deny them the privilege of leading the first attack, they will lose faith. Not only in us but in themselves, as well."

"Yes, the First must lead the battle," a chorus of angry voices demanded. "There can be no other way."

"Gentlemen. Gentlemen," Dwight said. "I am impressed by your fervor. However, after much consideration, the decision has been made."

"Consideration? Consideration?" Pinchback sputtered. "What consideration?"

"Colonel Bassett, do you agree with this?" asked Dumas.

"I am in full accord with General Dwight's decision," Colonel Bassett replied.

"You mean you're not protesting this?" Pinchback said.

"Of course not," Andre spat out his words as if he'd bitten into a wormy apple.

"What are you implying, Captain?" Colonel Bassett demanded.

"Let us be frank," said Andre. "The political and social contradictions inherent in the colored man's presence in the army are no secret."

"What utter nonsense," General Dwight said.

"Come, come, General. We are all aware of the rumors regarding the colored man's effectiveness as a soldier. Rumors that valor and bravery are innately foreign to us. Rumors that colored officers cannot lead colored troops into battle. How ridiculous. What of the great blackamoor, Hannibal? Bonaparte, after studying his battles, declared him to be the master of Genghis Khan and Alexander the Great. He is . . ."

"We know you received military training in Paris, Captain," Chauncy muttered. "But this is not the time or place to digress."

"Very well, I'll come to the point. I offer you and the general a challenge. I challenge you to test those rumors about our valor on the battlefield. There it will be determined, once and for all, who is brave. Who can lead. On the battlefield, the First will demonstrate that two-o'clock-in-the-morning courage that the great Hannibal said was so essential and yet so rare."

5

Bubbly white clouds exposed patches of the blue infinity. The reflection from the sun made the Mississippi River shine like a brilliant mirror. Shrill sounds of fifes and the rat-te-tat/did-de bunk, rat-te-tat/did-de bunk rattle of drums riddled the air.

The Fourth Platoon, rifles angled symmetrically, drilled to the metronomic barks of First Sergeant Jasper Browning, who—under the scrutiny of Lieutenant Warren Underdue—maneuvered it back and forth across the field. As a slave, Browning had been an engineer on a riverboat. Everything about him was big, especially his head, chest and feet. Sometimes at the front of the platoon, sometimes in the rear, sometimes marching in place, he orchestrated an artful array of flanks, rears and columns.

"Platoon, halt!" Sergeant Browning ordered. Chin tucked over his neck, he stood tall and rigid. "Lieutenant Underdue, your troops, sir."

"Well done," Underdue executed a perfect salute. Stomach held in, chest pushed out, he inspected the ranks. "Dress that line, soldier!" He upbraided a hapless private. Like many second lieutenants, he tried to hide his inexperience by a showy display of arrogance. He completed his inspection and ordered Sergeant Browning to take the platoon to mess.

Browning marched the platoon double-time. He was well liked by his men, who considered him hard but fair. When they reached the mess area, he lined up the squads according to their performance rating.

"Third Squad leader, take your men first," he directed.

"Squad, at ease," Corporal London Rapier ordered. A tall, solid man of twenty-seven, his snaky eyes detracted from his otherwise handsome face. "Private Pettaway, lead the way."

"Come on, boys," Caesar Pettaway said. In his facial expression and his manner, there was hardly a trace of his former self. He had the look of a man who's been relieved of a heavy burden. His face glowed with the delight of someone who is happy with himself; indeed, he had a new sense of himself, made evident by the way he walked and talked.

"Not so skimpy with the rations today," said Caesar. "Fill that spoon, cook. Fill that spoon."

"Move that line, soldier," the cook ordered.

"I ain't budging until I gits me a fair spoonful of them beans."

"Soldier, I serves you just like I do everybody else."

"But my two good eyes don't say so."

"Ah right, just this time," the cook served Caesar another spoonful of beans. "But remember, tomorrow is another day."

Caesar and his fellow squad members ate festively, enjoying a camaraderie that was more like clansmen than soldiers.

"You figure we finally gone git a chance to shoot some rebels, Alpheus?" Caesar wiped his mouth with the back of his hand.

"'Tis most certain," Alpheus Hunter, the best student in their reading and writing class, wore thick, round spectacles. He carried his Bible with him everywhere. "Why you think we been doing all that drilling and shooting practice for? Why you think they had us march all the way up here?"

"We done drilled and marched before," Caesar chomped a biscuit. "Before long, we'll be off to build another bridge. Or work on another road."

"Oh, no. We gonna scuffle with them rebels," Alpheus Hunter had been enslaved on a plantation where he attended religious meetings in the middle of the night. He still had owlish ways. "Mark my word."

"Alpheus, I just wanna know one cotton-picking thing," William Purvis loved to tell tall tales. He claimed that he'd participated in an all-night poker session in which all of the players won. "Why you so sure we gonna do some scuffling?"

"I drempt it last night," Alpheus answered.

"Hmph! I'm gonna tell you something," Purvis laughed. "Start filling up one of your hands with your dreams. Then start filling the other hand with bull hockey. See which one gets filled first."

The ex-slaves were intelligent but uninformed. Many ideas and topics simply lay outside their purview. They'd heard rumors of Denmark Vesey and Nat Turner but they had no conception of the systematic nature of slavery. They were unaware of the abolitionist movement, or any of their renowned anti-slavery contemporaries: Sojourner Truth, William Wells Brown, William Lloyd Garrison, Harriet Beecher Stowe, Charles B. Ray, Harriet Tubman and Frederick Douglas. They had no sense of the world or their place in it. Nor did they realize that there were millions of other black men and women still enslaved in America. Uninformed though they were, they shared a binding trait: each in his own way never allowed slavery to corrupt his psyche. They didn't understand the system abstractly but they sensed its insidious nature and they could not adjust to it. Their disdain for slavery was instinctive, individualistic and personal.

# 6

Gliding in unison, six drummers, four fife players and six flag bearers marched behind the First Regiment color bearer, Corporal Anselmo Placiancois. Placiancois, tall and slender, marched with the elegance of a Masai warrior.

Captain Andre Cailloux, striding his bobtailed chestnut horse with the attitude of an Arabian prince, rode up to the Fourth Platoon.

"Platoon! Attention!" Underdue demanded.
"Platoon at ease!" Andre ordered. "Soldiers!"
The platoon hooted and yelled and whooped.
"Soldiers!"
The platoon hooted and yelled and whooped.
"Soldiers!"
The platoon hooted and whooped.

Captain Cailloux's success with his men stemmed from the fact that he knew all good soldiers share two qualities: discipline and self-respect. He was firm and demanding; however, he avoided brutal or summary punishments. He treated them not as ex-slaves but as soldiers. In turn, they felt a love for him that bordered on deification.

"Soldiers of the Fourth Platoon, I bring you joyful tidings.

The First has been accorded the prized duty of mounting the first attack tomorrow. Company A and our company have been given the honor of leading the first charge."

The men cheered and hooted.

"Tomorrow will be the first time that colored troops will fight in such large numbers in this great war. The entire nation will be watching to see if we will flinch under fire. We will not flinch. We will put to rest those malicious rumors about our fitness as soldiers, about our courage and our manhood. Tomorrow we shall engage the rebels on the battlefield and there we will defeat them."

"Death before dishonor!" the platoon chanted. "Death before dishonor!"

# 7

Silvery moonbeams brightened the Mississippi. Smoke rose from the campfires. Melodies from harmonizing soldiers disappeared into the darkness like nightingales.

Alpheus Hunter, William Purvis and Caesar Pettaway, seated around the fire, cleaned their rifles. They looked forward to life.

Caesar pictured himself, Nydia and their three sons and daughter on a farm.

Alpheus wanted to preach and spread the Gospel.

"What about you, Purvis?" Alpheus asked. "What you gonna do after the war?"

"Find my momma."

Corporal London Rapier sat some distance away. Snaky eyes smoldering, he stared into the fire. Rapier was Haitian; that is, his forbearers had been a part of the parcel of Haitian slaves who, in the early 1800's, were brought to New Orleans by a Bonapartist master fleeing Toussaint L'Ouveture's revolution. His grandmother had entered into a *marriage de la main gauche* with a rich planter. It was due to her machinations that he and his mother were set free.

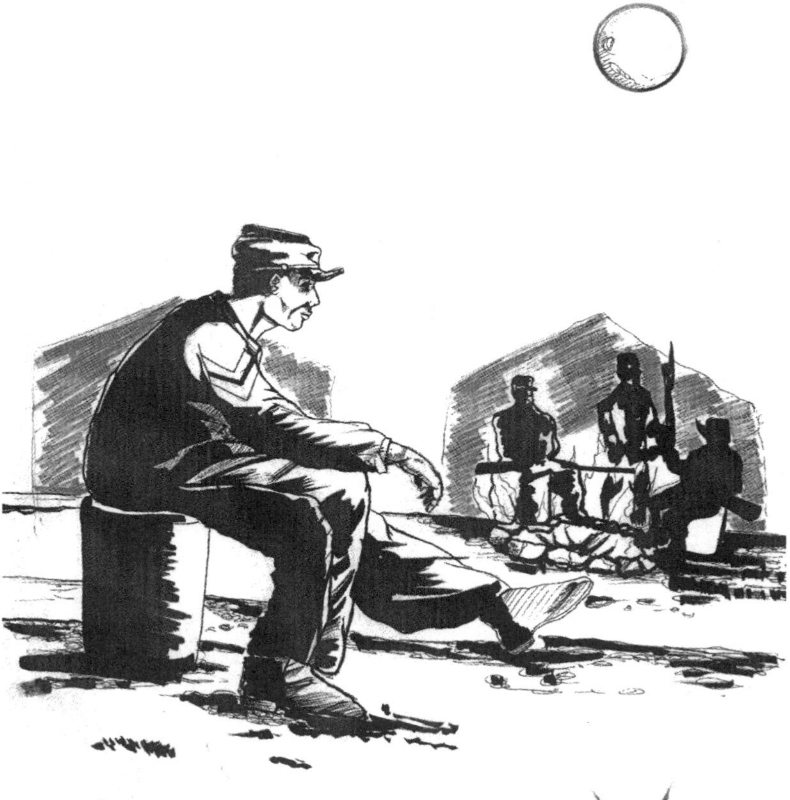

Other than the fact that he was a free man in New Orleans before the war, he revealed very little about himself to his men. However, since there was nothing in their past that could have prepared them for the likes of Rapier, it was just as well. The knowledge that he'd been a professional criminal with several murders correctly attributed to him would only confuse them.

At an early age, London discovered that the life of a poor, free black man in a slave society presented too many cruel and ironic contradictions. Aggressive and self-centered by nature, he rejected the bare, bleak, mean space allotted to his caste and turned to crime. He committed his first kill at seventeen in a knife fight—a boyhood pal with whom he'd quarreled over the spoils from a heist. After countless graphic demonstrations of ruthlessness, resourcefulness and loyalty, he became a highly respected member of the New Orleans criminal hierarchy.

*Tomorrow all wrongs will be righted. I will have my manhood,* London mused. Tomorrow he would shed blood again. This time the blood would sanctify his spirit.

A Gothic fog materialized. The harmonizing gradually faded.

One by one, Caesar, Purvis, Alpheus and Rapier entered their tents.

The moon dropped behind the trees.

Silence reigned.

# 8

Bombardment rumbled in the distance.

Andre, seated on his cot, made corrections on a writing pad.

"You're pacing again, Pickney," he said, not looking up.

"I'll clear the table in case Major Dumas needs it for our briefing this morning. Andre, you never stated your opinion about the battle strategy."

"Line up troops in three columns in broad daylight and attack a well-fortified enemy. What kind of strategy is that? Our generals have obviously never studied Hannibal. Where are the feints? The movements? The deceptions?"

"Even though you've read your poem to me, I still marvel at your imageries. It's so, so poignant. My God, what a presence of mind: composing a poem to your fiancé on the morning of the battle."

"But *mon ami,* how else would I occupy my mind except with thoughts of Marinelle d'Angelo?"

Major Dumas and several of his officers entered.

"Gentlemen, we've been ordered to capture the Columbiad," Dumas pulled a map from his pouch.

"Over here, sir," Pinchback offered. "I've cleared the table for you."

Dumas spread the map.

"What have we here, Major?" Andre asked.

"A six-hundred-yard no-man's land. We must cross it to reach our objective."

"With artillery support we could slice through here," Andre commented.

"Our artillery support will be minimal, I'm afraid," Dumas replied. "General Weitzel will only release one battery to us."

"My God, man, how can we be expected to complete our mission with only a single artillery battery at our disposal?"

"We can still do it, Andre," Pinchback wanted to fight, no matter what. "Even with limited artillery support, we can slice them. Just like you said."

"Hunngh," Andre grunted. "What of reserves?"

"There are none," Dumas answered. "We must provide for ourselves."

"The battle must be postponed," Andre announced. "We are without proper artillery support, without reserves. I'll go speak to Dwight myself. This is nonsense."

"Stay, Andre," Dumas cautioned. "It's been decided. We must fight on this day."

"The major is right, Andre," Pinchback said.

"So be it," Andre shrugged his shoulders. "I have no quarrel with fate."

## 9

A bugler with stark eyes and puffed cheeks called assembly. Anselmo Placiancois, feet accentuating the martial rhythm laid down by the six drummers, led the fife players and the flag bearers toward the staging area. A column of troopers marched behind them, intuitively in step with each other.

Lieutenant Underdue and Sergeant Browning ordered the ranks of the Fourth Platoon. Caesar Pettaway stood in the third rank in front of William Purvis and Corporal London Rapier. He absorbed himself in the various episodes that unfolded before him.

Captain Cailloux's horse pranced as he stopped in front of the Fourth Platoon.

"First Sergeant Browning, what are you about on this fine morning?" he asked.

"I'm volunteering along side the lieutenant, sir," Sergeant Browning grinned. "Just to make sure that him and the boy don't come to no mishaps."

An artillery shell whizzed overhead and exploded in the distance.

It was ten o'clock.

"First Regiment color bearer," Major Francis Dumas rode up to Anselmo Placiancois. "You will defend your flag. But you will not yield it."

"Yes, sir," Anselmo, chin uplifted, chest unfurled, replied. "If I do not return this color to you, I will be seated at the feet of our dear Lord in Heaven."

Dumas rode off.

The bugler sounded charge on the double. Anselmo Placiancois, holding the regimental flag high, trotted ahead.

"Death before dishonor!" yelling and shouting, bayonets reflecting the sun, the troopers rushed forward. "Death before dishonor!"

Caesar Pettaway emerged from the forest. In the distance, Port Hudson loomed like an Egyptian sphinx, its solid ramparts firmly astride the cliff. A puff of smoke rose from behind the parapet and the Columbiad thundered. Caesar dashed around a palisade. Cannonballs whizzed overhead. He jumped over a felled tree but he failed to see a tree stump until it was too late and he tumbled over it and fell onto the parched earth. Quickly righting himself, he felt a burst of exhilaration when he caught a glimpse of Underdue, Browning and Anselmo Placiancois, who, holding his flag high, zigzagged and jumped through the brushwood. He felt a momentary but intense calm when he spied his two clansmen, Purvis and Corporal Rapier, up ahead, running deftly. An enemy shell exploded behind him. Two soldiers tumbled and fell into a gully. A figure screamed as it stumbled and lunged itself into a sharpened wooden stake. Another artillery shell exploded. The distorted bodies of the drummers and the fife players twisted to the ground. Within seconds, a canister fell. The flag bearers vanished like ice cubes in hot water. An exploding shell disemboweled Lieutenant Underdue and tore out Alpheus Hunter's heart, sending their bodies hurling into the air.

Regiment flag held high, Anselmo Placiancois led the charge around a huge rectangular ditch. A line of Confederate sharpshooters rose from a concealed pit and emitted a deadly hail of bullets that thinned the first rank.

"This way!" Placiancois uttered his last words. A hail of bullets propelled his body back into a ditch. Rebel sharpshooters killed the first two troopers who attempted to reclaim the fallen Regiment flag but the third trooper, a corporal, grabbed the flag and darted behind a slope.

Grapeshot rattled the earth.

Caesar saw Corporal Rapier and Purvis firing at the rebels. He hit the dirt and crawled over to them.

"'Tis about time you got here, Pettaway," Rapier reloaded his rifle. "You missing all of the fun."

"Yeah, Rapier done already killed three rebels. I got one," Purvis said.

Caesar noticed Purvis' bloody thigh.

"Purvis, you been shot."

"It ain't nothing except a li'l itch," Purvis replied.

The bugler ordered retreat. The platoon withdrew to the rear to regroup.

## 10

"General Weitzel is a scurrilous son-of-a-bitch!" Colonel Bassett called. Accompanied by his retinue, which included the *New York Times* reporter, he galloped down the hill. "That's the first thing you can tell your readers."

The reporter could have been mistaken for a comedian by the way he held onto the horse's reins with one hand and juggled his stovepipe hat with the other.

"Why do you say that, sir?" he asked.

"When I accompanied General Dwight to his headquarters to find out why he hadn't attacked, he and his two aides were eating their goddamn lunch. Weitzel insisted on finishing his tea. General Dwight had to give the son-of-a-bitch a direct order before he'd move his goddamn lard-ass!"

## 11

"May God be with you," Major Dumas called.

"I won't let you lads down," Andre rode off.

Dumas rejoined his officers. Momentarily, a mounted messenger delivered the latest battlefield report. Dumas and his officers were discussing the messenger's report when Pinchback rode up and dismounted.

"Major, Colonel Bassett was not at his headquarters," he saluted. "However, I learned what happened to our artillery support. The battery came under heavy fire from the Columbiad and they had to withdraw."

"General Sherman didn't begin his assault until after eleven," Dumas exploded. "It's one o'clock and General Weitzel still hasn't taken to the field. Now there is no artillery support. This is a hell of a way to conduct a campaign."

"Yes, it is, sir."

"I'm sorry. You're only the messenger," Dumas said. "I'm upset by the latest report. The rebels won't let us remove our dead and wounded from the field."

"That's unheard of," Pinchback exclaimed. "It's a traditional courtesy that armies routinely extend to each other."

"Their refusal applies only to us," Dumas made no attempt to hide his disgust. "They've allowed the white troops to remove their dead and wounded."

Pinchback started to ask why the rebels singled out the African American troops for the breach of courtesy but he knew the answer, which only strengthened his resolve to volunteer to lead the next charge.

"Major, may I speak to you privately?" he asked. "Sir, I'd like to . . ."

Colonel Bassett and his retinue rode up.

"Dumas, how have your troops responded under fire?"

"Bravely, sir. They've made four charges. Each one more heroic than the last."

"And your losses?"

"Over twenty-five percent, I'm afraid."

"High," Chauncy said.

"But acceptable for a first assault," Dumas replied.

"General Dwight sends you this message: he will consider your mission a failure if you do not capture the Columbiad."

"Assure the general that our mission will be accomplished. Captain Cailloux has volunteered to lead the fifth charge."

"I'll deliver your message personally," Chauncy trotted off.

"You were about to say something, Pinchback?" Dumas asked.

"It was nothing. Nothing at all."

## 12

The sun dominated the sky.

"Follow me! *Suivez moi*! Follow me! *Suivez moi*!" Andre's sword glistened in the sun. "*Suivez moi*! Follow me! *Suivez moi*!" He led a phalanx of troops around the huge rectangular ditch. When he reached the crest of the slope, the hidden rebel sharpshooters sprang up from their pit and emitted a blaze of fire.

Andre twirled and stumbled to the ground.

Caesar, reacting instinctively, rushed toward Andre. A shell exploded. Pain streaked across his forehead. He felt himself falling. Bullets whispered above him. He opened his eyes and witnessed the specter of darkness closing in on him. Unexpectedly, he felt calm and peaceful. His mind fused with the darkness.

Andre felt the pain in his arm as he crawled up the slope. When he reached the top, he observed the rebel sharpshooters.

*I didn't know you were concealed behind your ditch, my friends, so I stumbled into your trap.* Andre's eyes followed the path that led to the parapet and the Columbiad. *Next time, I will deploy some troops to distract you. Then, I will lead my men around your flank and the Columbiad will be ours.*

The bugler sounded retreat. Andre and his men withdrew under the roving Confederate artillery fire.

## 13

The crowded field hospital vibrated with sounds of pain.

Captain Lionel Gardere and an aide appraised a stomach with exposed entrails.

"They got him here too late."

"I'm afraid so, sir."

"I'll give him this to relieve his pain," Lionel applied a dosage of morphine.

"Doctor, come," another aide appeared. "It's another one of those patients."

Lionel went off with the second aide.

William Purvis, seated on the side of the cot, tied his shoes.

"He insists on returning to the battle," the aide said.

"I say to you, sir, 'tis only a li'l itch," Purvis explained.

"Soldier, do you realize that if you leave now, your wound will start bleeding again?" Gardere asked. "You could lose your leg."

"Sir, 'tis only a li'l itch," Purvis insisted. "I gotta go see about my friends."

"Go then," Gardere said.

Purvis rushed off.

Colonel Bassett and his retinue entered.

"What's the casualty estimate, Captain Gardere?"

"Judging from our wounded, I'd say it's quite high."

"How have our troops performed?"

"Bravely, from what I gathered. There's talk of one gallant charge after another."

"That confirms the other reports."

"Despite such losses, their zest for battle continues to be extraordinary. Even before we can finish attending to their wounds properly, several of them have insisted on returning to battle."

"It's time to end this carnage. These gallant soldiers and their officers have more than proven their mettle. I'll request General Dwight's permission to withdraw," Colonel Bassett led his retinue from the tent.

An out-of-breath corporal rushed in.

"Dr. Gardere, Captain Cailloux has been wounded!"

## 14

Andre, seated on his cot, munched an apple as Gardere dressed his wound.

"Lionel, I've a bottle of champagne. Care to join me?"

"No, I must return to the hospital," Gardere took a sling from his medicine bag.

"What is this, eh?"

"There'll be no more fighting for you," Gardere helped Andre into the sling. "If your wound starts hemorrhaging, you'll lose your arm." He went out.

Andre took off the sling and slipped it under his pillow. Using his good hand, he reached under his cot and pulled out a mahogany-colored leather case.

Captain Pinchback rushed in.

"I heard you were wounded. Are you all right?"

"But of course, *mon ami*. My arm is a little stiff, that's all. Lionel just left, I'll be all right. Sit down," Andre opened the leather case. It held two silvery goblets and a bottle of champagne. "You arrived just in time."

"Here, let me open that bottle for you. What happened out there, Andre?"

"The men fought bravely. Remember this morning when we discussed tactics? Was it only this morning? I spoke rubbish. Battle plans don't win battles. Battles are won by the will of the soldiers. In some cases, by the will of a single soldier."

"How'd you get injured?"

"Rifle fire. We ran into a trap but I've devised a trick for the next charge."

"Now is the time for fresh troops. Let me lead my company in the next charge. My men are eager to fight. You could show me on the map what you saw and . . ."

"Show you? How can I show you what's not there? That map is useless. Now, be a good lad. Pour the champagne. Let's drink to the capture of the prize."

## 15

Major Dumas and his officers ceased their conversation as a courier rode up. The courier dismounted and handed Dumas a dispatch. Dumas read quickly.

"General Dwight sends word," he announced. "The day is over for us. We've been ordered to withdraw. Well done, men. Now we must give our lads at the front the news." Dumas and his officers mounted their horses and rode into the forest. Pinchback, riding swiftly, came their way.

"Captain, are you coming from the front?" Dumas asked.

"Yes, sir. Andre is leading the sixth charge."

"We must stop him," Major Dumas and his officers galloped off. "We've been ordered to withdraw."

## 16

Sergeant Browning led his troopers through a maze of artillery fire. As Andre had instructed, when they reached the rectangular ditch, he and his men made a wide arc around it.

Andre, wielding his sword, directed his men to the other side of the ditch and deployed them behind a slope.

A thin line of blood had coagulated along the edge of Caesar Pettaway's grazed forehead. He opened his eyes, glanced at the sky and closed them again. Thirsty and parched, he assimilated the sounds of exploding shells and whistling bullets.

Browning and his troops, concealed behind a slope, readied themselves.

"Y'all remember, now," Browning whispered. "We gonna rush them for about ten yards. Then we're gonna scoot right back here."

At Browning's order, the troops ran down the slope.

The rebels popped up from the pit and fired. Browning ordered his men back. He lost three troopers, including William Purvis, whose dead eyes registered acute surprise.

Caesar saw Andre. He fingered his eyes and shook his head vigorously like you do when you want to regain your senses.

*It's truly a vision. I just saw the captain fall dead on the ground.*

Andre peeked over the edge of the slope. The rebel riflemen were totally distracted by Browning's maneuver.

*And now to the prize,* Andre took a deep breath. "*Suivez moi!* Follow me! This way to victory!" Andre climbed to the crest of the slope where an exploding shell greeted him and blotted out his last words.

Caesar looked in disbelief as Andre's metal-studded body spun to the ground. He'd failed to aid his captain before. He would not fail him this time. He ran toward Andre. The sharpshooters opened fire. Sharp stings peppered his legs and side. Stumbling, he fell down beside his fallen commander.

# 17

Captain Pinchback walked aimlessly about the tent. He knew he must pack Andre's belongings but he was unable to muster the energy to do so.

Sergeant Browning, followed by Corporal Rapier, entered.

"It's us, Captain," Sergeant Browning said. "Sir, all the officers from our platoon are dead. You the only one we could trust to come to."

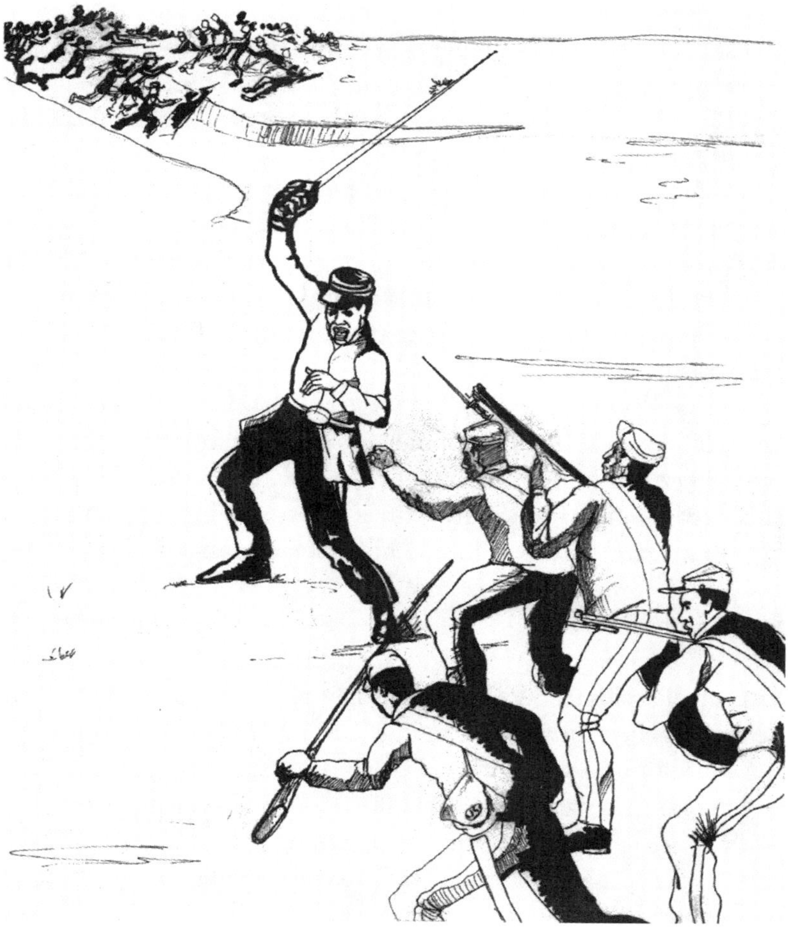

"You being our captain's best friend," Rapier added.
"How can I be of service to you?"
"You see, sir," Browning wiped his brow. "The men are mighty upset. They don't like the captain's body being left out there on the field."
"We are most anxious to do something about it," Rapier said.
"Sir," Browning's voice cracked with emotion. "The moon will be full tonight. We want to take a few of the boys and go get the captain. We'd like your permission."
"Permission granted, Sergeant. In fact, I'll lead the expedition."

# 18

The moon appeared to be suspended in the sky. Rebel riflemen fired blindly in the night. Pinchback, Browning, Rapier and three other troopers snaked their way to the area where Andre had fallen. Minutes flew by. They were almost ready to give up but upon hearing Caesar's feverish moans, they discovered him lying beside Andre.

# 19

Hundreds of mourners representing all classes and races clogged the streets, eager to pay their respects to the fallen hero. It was the largest funeral ever held in New Orleans. Inside the overflowing cathedral, Corporal Caesar Pettaway, holding onto his crutches, sat with Nydia and their three sons and daughter. Sergeant Rapier, Sergeant Browning and Captain Pinchback sat behind the Pettaways.

A black veil covered Marinelle d'Angelo's face.

General Dwight, voice cracking with emotion, eulogized Andre:

"Captain Cailloux was an inspiration to his men. His courage inspired their courage. He was the rarest of men. A gallant leader of gallant men. The brave who led the brave," Dwight pulled a paper from his pocket and held it up. "This is a *New York Times* article, dated June 1863, about the valiant effort of the First Louisiana Native Guard at Port Hudson. Quote: *'No body of troops, Western, Eastern, or rebel have fought better in the war,'* end of quote. I say to you, whatever future historians may write about the great battle at Port Hudson, whatever controversies may ensue, there can be no doubt about two things: the valiant effort displayed by the First Louisiana Native Guard and the bravery of Captain Cailloux, who demonstrated that two-o'clock-in-the-morning courage that the great Hannibal said was so essential and yet so rare."

# Splendor amid the Pines

### Tuskegee, Alabama, 1906.

CAESAR AND NYDIA PETTAWAY HAD three daughters, ten sons, over sixty grandchildren, almost four hundred great-grand children and another generation of swiftly multiplying great-great-grand children. Pettaways flourished and thrived in Louisiana and spilled over into Arkansas, Kansas and Texas. The majority were farmers and carpenters. However, there was a smattering of semi-skilled and skilled workers, teachers, musicians and preachers. There were many high-achieving, remarkable women in the clan; however, the Pettaways were patriarchal. Dominated by hardworking, lusty, spirited males who boasted that they loved their families and feared only God.

The Pettaways had their share of rascals, doxies and ne'er-do-wells in the skeleton closet. They also had more than a few family feuds that went beyond beyond. And a family legend of a poignant love story about two second cousins:

Sodonia and Aaron.

Born on the same day, they had developed a splendid affinity ever since being placed in the same crib at a family gathering. Over the years, whenever their families congregated they only played with each other, laughing and talking, communicating on a pre-conscious level.

Aaron and Sodonia drifted apart when Aaron entered his teens. He announced his disdain for girls and started hanging out with his older brother, Lincoln. When Aaron developed an interest in girls, Sodonia appeared. They took long walks together and spent time with each other whenever it was possible.

Some malicious tongues gossiped about the amount of time they spent together. A few family members expressed their concern when they noticed that somehow Sodonia managed to get into a squabble with any girl who showed any interest in Aaron. However, most family members considered their relationship harmless and insisted that they would eventually outgrow each other and part.

About one hundred members of the Pettaway clan gathered in a meadow with a stream from which fish were jumping. They had arrived from Arkansas, Texas and Louisiana to attend the Negro Farmers Conference at Tuskegee Institute, hosted by its founder, Booker T. Washington.

It was also Caesar's birthday.

That morning, that is, on Caesar's birthday and the day before the conference opened, Sodonia Pettaway walked across the campground. Seventeen and willowy, she had an exotic face, glittery dark eyes and classic Negroid lips. Her loose fitting white dress concealed her well-formed breasts and fine legs. Balancing a bowl of eggs in her hands, she walked with the poise of a Watusi maiden.

Just as Sodonia reached the campsite, Debra Pettaway came out of the tent.

"Good morning, Auntie," Sodonia said.

"Good morning, Sodonia. How are you?"

"Just fine, thanks. Momma sent you these," Sodonia handed Debra the bowl.

"Tell her I said thanks."

Across the way, Debra's son, Lincoln, chopped wood.

"Is Aaron around?" Sodonia asked.

"No, as a matter of fact. He's gone hunting with his father." Sodonia excused herself and joined Lincoln.

"You early but you late," Lincoln said. Other than the fact that he had an idiosyncratic disposition and liked to play around too much, he was fairly likable. "Aaron's gone hunting with my father."

"I know."

"When did y'all git here?"

"About a week ago. With nothing to do but fight flies while Daddy and them set up the camp. How long have Aaron and your father been gone?"

"Since daybreak."

"See you," Sodonia turned to go. "By the way, there's gonna be a barn fire, fireworks and a band down by the lake. Tell Aaron I said to meet me there around dusk."

Lincoln gathered an armful of wood and returned to the campsite.

A rider on a black and white spotted horse galloped up.

"Morning, folks," he said. "I'm attempting to locate a Mr. Rapier Pettaway."

"He ain't here," Lincoln said.

"I'm his wife. Can I help you?" Debra asked.

"No, I'd just like to speak to him . . ."

Rapier Pettaway and his son Aaron approached the campsite. Rapier, a solemn expression on his face, carried his rifle. Aaron, handsome face gleaming with pride, carried three rabbits and four ducks.

"Rapier, he's here to speak with you," Debra indicated the stranger.

"Take this, son," Aaron handed Lincoln his rifle. "Help your mother and your brother clean the game."

Lincoln went off with Aaron and Debra.

"You want to speak to me, sir?" Rapier asked.

"Yes. My name is Bilial Sojourner," he dismounted. "I met your cousin Jasper at the institute a few days ago. He told me about your carpenter shop. Would you mind telling me what happened?"

"Ain't much to tell. The Klan showed up in the middle of the night and burnt it to the ground. I lost everything. My wood. All my tools."

"It's a common practice nowadays in the South. It's called whitecapping. The whites plan to drive all Negroes out of business."

"Well, I'm sick and tired of it. They done some petty things in the past but this is the first time they done something this awful. They sure some lucky scamps. If I'd caught them at it, they'd be dead and buried by now. It's a purely evil man who wants to stop another man from earning an honest living."

"Mr. Pettaway, I'm an agent for a man who's looking for good carpenters," Bilial Sojourner said. Speaking with the intensity of a true believer, he spoke glowingly about his employer, Edwin P. McCabe.

# 2

Around dusk.

Sodonia wore silver earrings. Her proud bosoms prodded her white blouse.

An aggregation of musicians tuned their instruments.

A stocky man in a white cowboy hat put a torch to the huge pile of wood:

"Ah-whump!" the barn fire resounded.

The musicians, creating a multi-rhythmic, staccato sound, played Scott Joplin's *Pine Apple Rag*.

Scores of dancers formed a conga line around the barn fire and stomped thunder with their feet.

Aaron, a red and white polka-dot scarf tied around his neck, arrived.

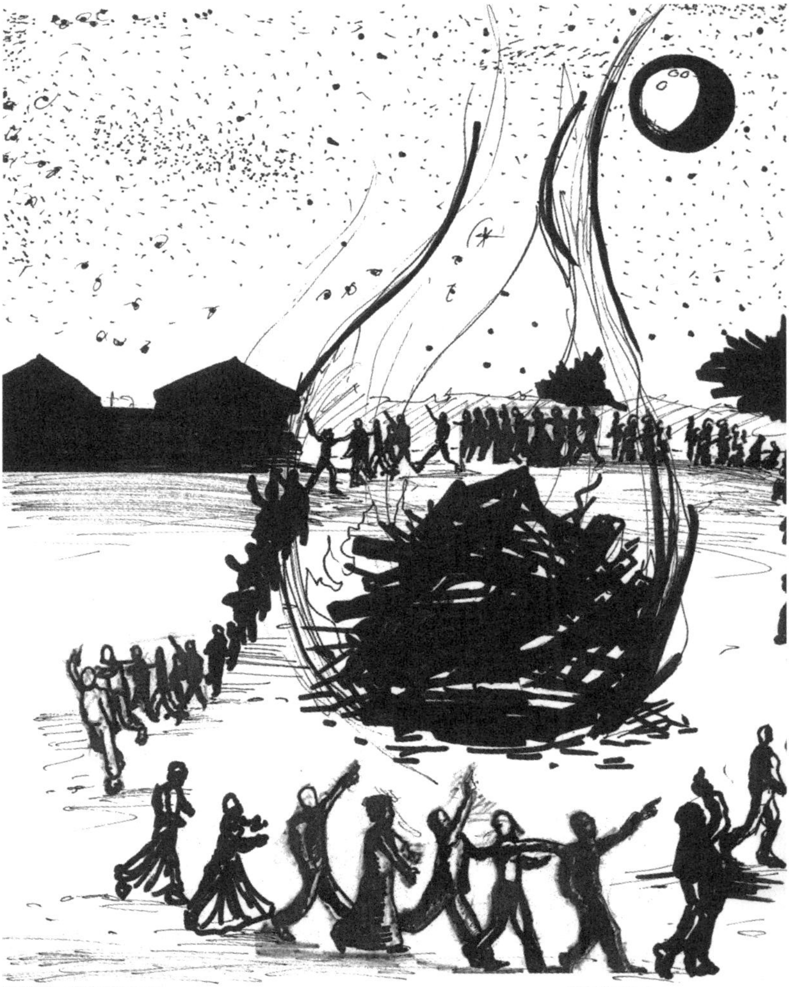

"Hey, girl," he smiled, revealing his even, white teeth.

"It's about time you got here," the light from the barn fire ricocheted off Sodonia's earrings. She took Aaron's hand.

The dancers, still stomping thunder, pointed their index fingers toward the sky.

Sodonia and Aaron joined the conga line. Faces glistening, willowy bodies flowing with the tom-tom beat, they celebrated life.

The music stopped.

"Whoooo-wheee, Sodonia. That was all right."

"For true. But it sure makes a body weak in the knees."

"And thirsty, too."

"Yeah, let's git some lemonade."

Sodonia and Aaron walked to the refreshment stand. Lincoln and Ransom Green stood nearby, lollygagging.

Ransom Green styled a straw hat. His mother died at his birth. Caesar and Nydia took him in. Ransom turned out to be more Pettaway than many Pettaways.

"Sodonia, let's bust a jig on the next go round," he said in a playful manner.

"I'm tired of dancing right now," Sodonia flashed a suggestive smile. "Try me a li'l later. I'll be more than glad to accommodate you."

"How you doing, Aaron?" Ransom asked. Aaron and Ransom chatted pleasantly, which was a drag for Sodonia. Whenever the opportunity presented itself, she tried to make Aaron jealous.

Aaron bought two lemonades and gave one to Sodonia.

"Aaron, I'll meet you here later, all right?" Lincoln said. "You're welcome to come, too, Sodonia."

"For what?"

"To shoot some craps."

"I don't know whether to be insulted or what, Lincoln. Let me pull your coattail. I didn't travel all these many miles just to gamble in a hot tent full of tobacco smoke and a bunch of bourbon soppers. Aaron, come on." They went off.

"Sodonia, I sure hope you change your mind about coming by Grandpa's tent," Lincoln called. "I want to win back them six bits you beat me outta the last time we shot dice." He put on a laughing exhibition.

Aaron and Sodonia joined the crowd and listened to the musicians make mahogany melodies.

"You feel like some more dancing?" Aaron sipped his lemonade.

"Not unless you want to."

"Naw. I done kicked up enough dust for the time being, I reckon."

A colorful burst of fireworks sprinkled the sky.

"Aaron, why you not jealous of me?"

"Ain't any reason to."

"Aaron, sometimes you such a dunce. That's not the way jealousy is," Sodonia said seriously. "Jealousy has reasons with minds of their own." Her mood shifted to a brighter mode. "Have you missed me?"

"Yes."

"A lot?"

"Yeah, a lot."

"A *whole* lot?"

"A *whole* lot."

Rapier Pettaway and Bilial Sojourner crossed their view.

"Who's that with your father?"

"Some dude that's been hanging around all day."

"Let's go see Big Poppa. Come on."

"His tent the other way."

"I know. I must stop by our tent first and git his present. Come on."

## 3

The moon looked lonesome shining through the trees. A lantern hanging above the entrance of Caesar's tent projected a flickering light. The light distorted the faces of the dozen or so men and women who milled about; some stood, others sat on their haunches; some waited to greet Caesar; others, having already paid him homage, simply remained to share some fellowship and exchange opinions.

"Yes-sir-rhee! The good Lord's done sent man a signal. A mark of His displeasure," a throaty voice disclosed the biblical significance of the earthquake in San Francisco. "It's all in the Scripture. There, for all to see."

In the distance, a chorus of frogs croaked a refrain.

"The *Pittsburgh Courier* said that over the last sixteen years, they've lynched over two thousand of us."

From afar, a wolf howled; the frogs ceased their refrain.

"The only solution is the federal government. They ought to do something."

"Ah, the government ain't going to do squat for colored folks. Look at how President Roosevelt dismissed that battalion of colored soldiers in Brownsville, Texas, without a fair hearing. Between the lily-white Republicans and the gold Democrats there ain't much to choose from."

## 4

Illuminated by kerosene lanterns, Caesar's tent bubbled with laughter and rocked with vibrant vibrations. Caesar wore white overalls. Eyes sparkling, he sat on his cot amid his presents. He'd retained his wit. His bright, fiery eyes emitted a certain vitality.

A man with a handlebar mustache strummed a mandolin.

Well-wishers came and went.

Maia Pettaway, Caesar's youngest child, stood nearby. In her early thirties, she was tall and statuesque. Her oval face could easily have been the model for a terra-cotta Benin sculpture. She loved her father. After Nydia's death, she'd voluntarily assumed the responsibility for taking care of him.

Sodonia and Aaron popped in.

"Big Poppa, this is for you," Sodonia held up her colorfully-wrapped present.

At the sound of Sodonia's voice, Caesar's body became lively, like he'd just heard some bouncy music.

"Child, I been expecting you," he let Sodonia kiss his cheek. "Who is this boy?"

"It's Rapier's youngest son, Poppa," Maia said.

"Pshaw. I was jest joshing. I know Aaron. Howze tricks, young fellah?"

"Everything's fine, Big Poppa."

"Here, Big Poppa," Sodonia gave Caesar his present.

Caesar took out a gold-trimmed navy captain's cap and put it on.

"It fits, too," he smiled. "What you bring, young fellah?"

Caesar's question caught Aaron by surprise.

"Huh? Oh! I- I- I-," he stammered.

"The scarf you wearing look mighty new."

"It is. I bought it just before we left home."

"Your scarf," Sodonia whispered.

"What?"

"He wants your scarf."

"Yeah, yeah. Why don't you take it, Big Poppa?" Aaron tied the scarf around Caesar's neck. "I was just warming it up for you."

"Look, everybody," Caesar called. "Look at what these children brought me." He did an impromptu dance step.

The mandolin player played a melody.

The celebrants stomped and clapped a rhythm.

"Poppa. Take it easy," Maia cautioned.

As was his habit, Caesar ignored Maia.

"Ain't every man who reaches 71 can do this," he danced.

# 5

Booker T. Washington, seated behind his desk, awaited the arrival of his secretary. He absentmindedly re-read the letter from his daughter, Portia, who was studying the piano in Germany. Booker was born a slave, the product of a white father and a black mother. A spry, dust-colored man of fifty with piercing gray eyes and heavy-set jaws, he had created himself through hard work, compromise and temperance. He had a fervent belief that of all the men of his generation, he was the only one who knew the best way to advance the cause of his people. He was also a sagacious and sometimes malicious man who had, through his successful, behind-the-scene machinations, earned himself the *nom de guerre*, the Fox.

Up since five that morning, he'd already read the Bible, chopped some wood for exercise and breakfasted. He had also given his two sons their instructions for the day and made an appearance at Porter Hall, where the conference registration was going well. He put aside the letter, took his gold-plated watch from his vest pocket, studied its face and returned it to his pocket.

*When Emmett arrives with his report, we must devise further strategies.*

Though he was at the height of his power, he had his share of detractors. *Yes. We must deal with those jackanapes.* He referred to the members of the Niagara Movement, who had scheduled a conference at Harpers Ferry. He'd planted a spy. That was how, two weeks before the conference opened, he had a list with the names of the major participants. For the third time, he read the names on the list:

"Monroe Trotter, Ida Barnett Wells, Jane Addams, Reverend Francis J. Grimke, Florence Kelly, W. E. B. Dubois . . ."

"Good morning, Booker," Emmett J. Scott, well dressed and handsome, entered. "Grist for the mill." He waved his report.

"One second," Booker drew the curtains, plunging the room into semi-darkness.

## 6

The conferees assembled on an open field, facing a platform on which there was a row of empty chairs and an American flag. They were in an anticipatory, receptive mood. During the next four days they would be attending workshops and seminars on a variety of subjects: the evils of the mortgage system, the one-room cabin, buying on credit, how to build schoolhouses and prolong the school term, crop rotation, marketing and distribution seeding and fertilization, the proper way to care and feed chickens, pigs and cows, how to improve their moral and religious convictions.

The Fisk Jubilee Singers, wearing purple robes with starchy white collars, marched down the aisle and sat in the front row.

Sodonia Pettaway, seated in the middle, wore a blue denim skirt and a white blouse with buttons in the back. She looked around, trying to spot Aaron.

The crowd gasped and caught its breath.

Booker, followed by Emmett, three conservatively-dressed white men, three conservatively-dressed black men and a black woman in a gray suit with a white carnation walked down the aisle onto the platform and took their seats.

"Good morning, all. My name is Emmett Scott. I'd like to introduce Minister W. R. Pettifore, who will officially open today's conference with an invocation. Minister Pettifore is the founder of the Birmingham Alabama Penny Savings and Loan Company. He is also the president of the Negro Bankers' Association."

Minister Pettifore delivered a melodious invocation.

Emmett introduced the Fisk Jubilee Singers, who electrified the audience with soulful renditions of *Keep Me from Sinking Down, O, Brothers, Don't Stay Away* and *Go Down Moses.*

Annette Hopkins, the president of the National Association of Colored Women, delivered a provocative address entitled "Lifting As We Climb," in which she urged everyone to regard it as their duty to uplift their race and its less fortunate members.

Sodonia looked slowly over the crowd. For an instant, she thought she saw Aaron. She knew that couldn't be. To be sure, she looked again.

Aaron was sitting with Lincoln and Ransom Green!

*Am I wrong about our agreeing to sit together?* Flipping the pages of her memory, she recalled the exact words of their last conversation. Yes, they had definitely agreed to sit together. *Something's outta kilter!* Then it all became clear to her. Something happened last night after she and Aaron parted. Putting two and two together, she came up with three: *Aaron is fooling around with some gal!*

"The matters to be considered at this conference are those that our people have in their own power to control," Booker spoke softly, like he was addressing a group of friends around a cozy fireside. "We must work out our own destiny through the slow process of natural growth, rather than by any easy, sudden or superficial method. We must work out our destiny through thrift, hard work and our moral virtues . . ."

Sodonia, unable to contain her anger, sprang from her seat and rushed to the row in which Aaron was sitting.

"Aaron," she beckoned with her finger.

Somewhat embarrassed, Aaron joined Sodonia in the aisle.

"Treating me like I'm your fool. Having me saving a seat for you like a dunce."

"Keep your voice down."

"What you say?" Sodonia hollered. "I don't give a hoot if everybody in the entire world hears me."

"Let's get away from here," Aaron led the way.

". . . We must shoulder much of the blame for our present status. The primary responsibility for our advancement resides in us! For, it is not in the province of human nature that the man who is virtuous and cultivates the best farm or business shall very long be denied the proper respect by the members of his entire community."

# 7

Aaron sat on the library steps. Sodonia, pouting and panting, remained standing. Aaron, choosing his words carefully, told Sodonia that he hadn't sat with her because he had something important to tell her but he'd wanted to wait until they were alone.

"We are by ourselves now. So tell me."

"Doggone, Sodonia. I didn't want it to be like this."

"I wanna know, now."

"Remember the man we saw with my father last night? He's an agent for some guy name Edwin McCabe. McCabe has started a colored town in Mound Bayou, Oklahoma. He's looking for carpenters. Daddy signed a contract. We're moving to Mound Bayou."

Sodonia's entire body slumped. She cried, whimpering and shaking.

"Don't cry, Sodonia, please."

"I'll be all right. Just walk with me a bit."

They made their way across the campus. Aaron stopped Sodonia and wiped away her tears with his fingers. Rolling his eyes playfully, he noisily sucked on his fingers like they were lollipops.

"You so silly," Sodonia laughed.

They left the campus and walked into the forest. Sodonia, making a sudden movement, stood close to Aaron. Their eyes shyly embraced.

"Aaron, I'm sorry."
"What's to be sorry about?"
"That I never let you."
"Let me what?"
"You know."
"No, what?"
"What I won't let you even *think* about us doing together."
"Oh."
"I changed my mind."
"Oh."
"Do you want me?"
"Gosh darn, Sodonia."
"Do you want me or not?"
"Gosh, yes."
They embraced. Their hot tongues mingled.
"Come on," Sodonia took Aaron's hand.
"Where?"
"We'll know when we see it."
They followed a trail of daffodils, snowballs and lilacs.
Finally, they saw it:
A grassy mound beautified by a shaft of sunlight shining through the pines.
A woodpecker rapped incessantly.
Sodonia took off her skirt and shed her panties.
Aaron got naked.
"Undo these for me," Sodonia indicated the buttons on the back of her blouse.

He'd seen her naked once when they were eleven. They'd climbed a tree and her dress got caught on a limb. She didn't have on any panties. She hung on the limb for several moments, revealing her smooth, slender body. That long ago image in no way prepared him for the sight of the brilliant black form that revealed itself when she removed her blouse.

They indulged in long, eager kisses, mouth drinking from mouth. Swallowing each other's breath. Hot hands explored hot bodies. They united. He gasped. A shudder shook her frame. Evolving into each other, they vanished into oneness.

# 8

Rapier Pettaway and his family moved to Mound Bayou. Except for Aaron, who, on the eve of their departure, eloped with Sodonia.

Marvin H. McMillian, Jr., born in 1968, grew up in Oakland, California. Marvin expressed an interest in art at an early age. He remembers drawing on his brother's and sister's homework assignments until his mother reprimanded him and gave him brown paper bags to draw on.

He attended the Arts High School and Oakland's California College of Arts & Crafts. Marvin also studied at the Academy of Arts in San Francisco. He has given numerous lectures on art and offered encouragement to the children in the community.

His style is fresh. He has a complete mastery of color, harmony and design. His art displays great detail and emotion. He gets many of his ideas from his environment.

Marvin lives in Oakland, California.

Contact: http://www.m2-Designs.net

Charlie Louis Russell, Jr., was born in Monroe, Louisiana, on March 10, 1932. His father, Charlie, Sr., moved to Oakland, California, in 1942 and became a shipyard worker. The family was reunited a year later when he, his younger brother William and their mother, Katie, moved to Oakland. Charlie graduated from Oakland Technical High and then attended Santa Rosa Junior College, where he developed an interest in writing. He also served in Korea with the U.S. Army.

He earned a B.S. in English from the University of San Francisco in 1959. In 1966, he received a Masters in Social Work from New York University. From 1963 to 1970, he was a member of The Harlem Writers Guild, chaired by John Oliver Killens. In the early '70s, Charlie was writer in residence at Barbara Ann Teer's National Black Theatre in Harlem. In 1986, he earned his M.F.A. from the University of California at San Diego.

His publications include *A Birthday Present for Katheryn Kenyatta*, a novella published by McGraw-Hill, 1967; "Quietus," a short story published in *Langston Hughes' Best Negro Short Stories*; and *Five on the Black Hand Side*, a play published by Samuel French.

Charlie also wrote the film script for *Five* and received the 1972 N.A.A.C.P. Image Award for best film script. *Ebony Magazine* recognized *Five* as one of the ten best African American films of all time.

He lives in Oakland, California. He has two children, Katheryn and Joshua. In his travels he has visited the Caribbean, Asia and West Africa.

Contact: www.theworthyones.com